# WESTERN MOVIES

## Classic Wild West Films

Collected & Introduced by
Peter Haining

*with contributions from*

Max Brand
Zane Grey
Ernest Haycox
O. Henry
Dorothy M. Johnson
Louis L'Amour
Elmore Leonard
Larry McMurtry
Arthur Miller
Clarence E. Mulford
Jack Schaefer
Owen Wister

This first world edition published in Great Britain 1997 by
SEVERN HOUSE PUBLISHERS LTD of
9–15 High Street, Sutton, Surrey SM1 1DF.
This title first published in the USA 1997 by
SEVERN HOUSE PUBLISHERS INC., of
595 Madison Avenue, New York, NY 10022.



British Library Cataloguing in Publication Data

Western Movies
1.Western stories
I. Leonard, Elmore, 1925- Title II. Haining, Peter
808.8'3874 [FS]

ISBN 0-7278-5207-8



Typeset by Palimpsest Book Production Limited,
Polmont, Stirlingshire, Scotland.
Printed and bound in Great Britain by
Creative Print and Design Ltd, Ebbw Vale, Wales.

# PROGRAMME



*Note*: This is a list of film titles. The original works on which the movies were based may have had different titles from those given above.

# CREDITS

The Editor and publishers are grateful to the following authors, their agents and publishers for permission to include copyright stories in this collection: *Dime Western Magazine* and Dell Magazines for 'Three-Ten to Yuma' by Elmore Leonard; Headline Publishing Group for 'Buckskin' by Clarence E. Mulford and 'The Great Slave' by Zane Grey; The Estate of Ernest Haycox for 'Stage to Lordsburg' by Ernest Haycox; Golden West Literary Agency for 'Dust Storm' by Max Brand; Macmillan Publishers for 'Happy-Teeth' by Owen Wister; Fleetway Magazines for 'One Man's Honour' by Jack Schaefer and 'The Misfits' by Arthur Miller; Transworld Publishers Ltd for 'The Gift of Cochise' by Louis L'Amour; *Collier's* magazine and McIntosh & Otis for 'A Man Called Horse' by Dorothy M. Johnson; Orion Publishing Group Ltd for 'The Legend of Billy' by Larry McMurtry. While every care has been taken in seeking permission for the use of stories in this anthology, in the case of any accidental infringement interested parties are asked to write to the Editor in care of the publishers.

# PROLOGUE

## *'The Hollywood Trailblazers'*

It is known as 'the town too tough to die' – a place filled with the ghosts of the gunslingers who once fought bloody duels in the street and are now keeping company with the actors who re-enact for visitors the gunfights which have made its name synonymous with the Wild West and classic Western movies. Tombstone, Arizona: home of the OK Corral, where Wyatt Earp and Doc Holliday shot it out with the Clanton gang on the afternoon of 26 October 1881, and which has since become a mecca for Western buffs as well as the location for at least twenty films all inspired by its violent and blood-soaked history.

A lot of Tombstone is still much as it was a century ago when the West really was wild. Many of the original buildings along the main thoroughfare, Allen Street, are as they were in 1881 and still bear the bullet holes of the gunmen who fought and died here and whose likenesses in stiffly posed sepia photographs hang in the houses and saloons where they once lived before becoming enshrouded in legend. There for all to visit is Big Nose Kate's Saloon, once run by Doc Holliday's girlfriend, where whiskey flowed and disputes flared and, nearby, the Bird Cage Theatre, famous for its pretty, high-kicking chorus girls.

In the OK Corral itself, life-sized models of Earp, Holliday and the rest stand rooted to the dusty ground in the same positions they were said to have adopted on that fateful day. Not far off is the infamous Boot Hill cemetery which contains the remains of the Clanton gang: laid side by side under a simple wooden headboard which reads, BILLY CLANTON, TOM MCLAURY, FRANK MCLAURY MURDERED ON THE STREETS of TOMBSTONE, 1881. And, fittingly, the town's newspaper, *The Epitaph*, is still being published a century and more after it began recording the lawlessness of this famous frontier town . . .

It was real-life dramas in places just like Tombstone which inspired the Western novel and, later, the movies which appeared when the cinema was still in its infancy and have continued to enthrall audiences everywhere. It has been said that the genre which was effectively launched by James Fenimore Cooper's *The Pioneers* (1823), recounting the exploits of the frontier scout Natty Bumppo (believed to have been based on the legendary Daniel Boone) has now become the great American myth: as important to the nation's literature as, say, Scandinavian sagas or the Greek epics. Certainly, the Western is America's only truly original art form and has been famously referred to by *Time* magazine as 'The American Morality Play'.

The West certainly threw up its fair share of heroes and villains a hundred years and more ago. Some undoubtedly deserved their notoriety, but others probably owed more to shameless boasting and the eagerness of chroniclers to make legends rather than report facts. But there was no denying the stoicism of the pioneers nor the courage of the Native American Indians, recklessly brave in the face of the white man's superior weapons which drove them from their lands and almost to the point of extinction. Together these two races of men – and a good few of their womenfolk, too – were responsible for projecting the images of wide open spaces, shanty towns and a harsh life grubbed from the soil or over the barrel of a pistol, which became the staple ingredients of the Western.

Despite the bad reputation that the Western novel later earned in some quarters – fuelled by fictions about ruthless gunmen who killed without compunction and the promotion of a conviction that the only good 'Injun' was a dead one – the genre has, in fact, produced its fair share of classic stories: not a few of which have, in turn, inspired outstanding movies. It is a fact that comes as a surprise to many people that one of the very earliest box office successes was a Western, *The Great Train Robbery*, made as early as 1903. Perhaps the very reason for this subject matter being chosen by the embryo film industry just starting to establish itself in Hollywood was its close proximity to the West! In the pages which follow, the reader will find a selection of some of the very best of the short stories that have become films in the intervening years. Those which have not directly inspired movies are included as being typical of their creators' works which *did* inspire Western movies.

The colourful and dramatic stories of good and evil played out against the background of the West by pioneer writers like Owen Wister, Zane Grey and Clarence E. Mulford provided ideal material for the early film makers and their lead has been followed by others whose names now dominate the genre, including Louis L'Amour, Elmore Leonard and Larry McMurtry. Over the years, too, the characters in the Western have become less stereotyped: no longer do all bad men wear black hats while not every Indian is a savage. In today's Western the Native American can be as brave and intelligent as the white man, while the white stetson is just as likely to be worn by a black-hearted villain who never thinks twice about shooting his victims in the back. Even some of the most sacred myths about the so-called heroes of the Wild West like Billy the Kid and Wyatt Earp have been revealed in their true colours.

Undoubtedly, though, both the Western story and movie have bright futures, especially on television, where series set in that great swath of land that lies between the Mississippi River and the Pacific Ocean are appearing with increasing regularity. Although the Western B-movie which was once such a staple of the cinema programme is now a thing of the past, full-length pictures are still being made by the Hollywood studios with a quality and authenticity that owes much to the use of locations like the one I mentioned. Indeed, places such as Tombstone stand today not only as monuments to the *real* West, but also to the literature it generated and the movies it has inspired. In the pages that follow, I believe you will find the best of all three.

PETER HAINING

# THREE-TEN TO YUMA

(Columbia, 1957)
Starring: Glenn Ford, Van Heflin & Felicia Farr
Directed by Delmer Daves
Story 'Three-Ten To Yuma' by Elmore Leonard

**In any discussion of classic Western movies, there are a few absolutely undeniable candidates, including *High Noon*, *Stagecoach*, *Shane* and *Three-Ten To Yuma*. My own favourite is the last named and I therefore make no apology for including the short story upon which it was based as the opening item in this book. Rightly described by a number of critics and countless fans as 'one of the finest Westerns ever made', *Three-Ten To Yuma* is the story of a farmer (Van Heflin) who takes on the unenviable job of escorting a notorious gunslinger (Glenn Ford) to trial, and the tension-filled day they spend together in a hotel room waiting for a train to Yuma certainly makes it the equal of any of the other films I have mentioned. Directed by the veteran Delmer Daves, who had been making Westerns since the Twenties, the picture is also a subtle psychological drama which confirmed the reputations of Ford and Van Heflin in the roles of two totally different characters – one an incorruptible man of the soil and the other a free-wheeling outlaw arrogantly confident he will be rescued by his gang – who are inexorably drawn into a battle of wits with justice as the ultimate prize.**

**Elmore Leonard (1925–), the author of the story on which this classic movie was based, was for almost a decade one of**

**the most popular Western novelists and short-story writers in America. Then he turned his hand to crime fiction and has now become a cult favourite all over the world with his accounts of low-life crime and criminals in Detroit. Leonard contributed his first Western short stories to magazines such as *Dime Western*, *Ten-Story Western* and the revered *Zane Grey Western Magazine*. In 1953 he published his first novel, *The Bounty Hunter*, and two years later one of his short stories, 'The Captives', was filmed as *The Tall T* by Budd Boetticher, starring Randolph Scott (of whom more later) and Maureen O'Sullivan. Other Western movies made from Leonard's work have included *Hombre* (1966), with Paul Newman, Fredric March and Diane Cilento, and *Valdez Is Coming*, which was filmed in 1970. Here, though, is the short story which helped to confirm Leonard's reputation when it first appeared in *Dime Western Magazine* in 1953, and also inspired one of the genre's landmark movies.**

He had picked up his prisoner at Fort Huachuca shortly after midnight and now, in a silent early morning mist, they approached Contention. The two riders moved slowly, one behind the other.

Entering Stockman Street, Paul Scallen glanced back at the open country with the wet haze blanketing its flatness, thinking of the long night ride from Huachuca, relieved that this much was over. When his body turned again, his hand moved over the sawed-off shotgun that was across his lap and he kept his eyes on the man ahead of him until they were near the end of the second block, opposite the side entrance of the Republic Hotel.

He said just above a whisper, though it was clear in the silence, "End of the line."

The man turned in his saddle, looking at Scallen curiously. "The jail's around on Commercial."

"I want you to be comfortable."

Scallen stepped out of the saddle, lifting a Winchester from the boot and walked toward the hotel's side door. A figure stood in the gloom of the doorway, behind the screen, and as Scallen reached the steps the screen door opened.

"Are you the marshal?"

"Yes, sir." Scallen's voice was soft and without emotion. "Deputy, from Bisbee."

"We're ready for you. Two-oh-seven. A corner . . . fronts on Commercial." He sounded proud of the accommodation.

"You're Mr Timpey?"

The man in the doorway looked surprised. "Yeah, Wells Fargo. Who'd you expect?"

"You might have got a back room, Mr Timpey. One with no windows. He swung the shotgun on the man still mounted. "Step down easy, Jim."

The man, who was in his early twenties, a few years younger than Scallen, sat with one hand over the other on the saddle-horn. Now he gripped the horn and swung down. When he was on the ground his hands were still close together, iron manacles holding them three chain lengths apart. Scallen motioned him toward the door with the stubby barrel of the shotgun.

"Anyone in the lobby?"

"The desk clerk," Timpey answered him, "and a man in a chair by the front door."

"Who is he?"

"I don't know. He's asleep . . . got his brim down over his eyes."

"Did you see anyone out on Commercial?"

"No . . . I haven't been out there." At first he had seemed nervous, but now he was irritated and a frown made his face pout childishly.

Scallen said calmly, "Mr Timpey, it was your line this man robbed. You want to see him go all the way to Yuma, don't you?"

"Certainly I do." His eyes went to the outlaw, Jim Kidd, then back to Scallen hurriedly. "But why all the melodrama? The man's under arrest – already been sentenced."

"But he's not in jail till he walks through the gates at Yuma," Scallen said. "I'm only one man, Mr Timpey, and I've got to get him there."

"Well, dammit . . . I'm not the law! Why didn't you bring men with you? All I know is I got a wire from our Bisbee office to get a hotel room and meet you here in the morning of November third. There weren't any instructions that I had to get myself deputised a marshal. That's your job."

"I know it is, Mr Timpey," Scallen said, and smiled, though it was an effort. "But I want to make sure no one knows Jim Kidd's in Contention until after train time this afternoon."

Jim Kidd had been looking from one to the other with a faintly amused grin. Now he said to Timpey, "He means he's afraid somebody's going to jump him." He smiled at Scallen. "That marshal must've really sold you a bill of goods."

"What's he talking about?" Timpey said.

Kidd went on before Scallen could answer. "They hid me in the Huachuca lock-up 'cause they knew nobody could get at me there . . . and finally the Bisbee marshal gets a plan. He and some others hopped the train in Benson last night, heading for Yuma with an army prisoner passed off as me." Kidd laughed, as if the idea were ridiculous.

"Is that right?" Timpey said.

Scallen nodded. "Pretty much right."

"How does he know all about it?"

"He's got ears and ten fingers to add with."

"I don't like it. Why just one man?"

"Every deputy from here down to Bisbee is out trying to scare up the rest of them. Jim here's the only one we caught," Scallen explained – then added, "Alive."

Timpey shot a glance at the outlaw. "Is he the one who killed Dick Moons?"

"One of the passengers swears he saw who did it . . . and he didn't identify Kidd at the trial."

Timpey shook his head. "Dick drove for us a long time. You know his brother lives here in Contention. When he heard about it he almost went crazy." He hesitated, and then said again, "I don't like it."

Scallen felt his patience wearing away, but he kept his voice even when he said, "Maybe I don't either . . . but what you like and what I like aren't going to matter a whole lot, with the marshal past Tucson by now. You can grumble about it all you want, Mr Timpey, as long as you keep it under your breath. Jim's got friends . . . and since I have to haul him clear across this territory, I'd just as soon they didn't know about it."

Timpey fidgeted nervously. "I don't see why I have to get dragged into this. My job's got nothing to do with law enforcement . . ."

"You have the room key?"

"In the door. All I'm responsible for is the stage run between here and Tucson – "

Scallen shoved the Winchester at him. "If you'll take care of this and the horses till I get back, I'll be obliged to you . . . and I know I don't have to ask you not to mention we're at the hotel."

He waved the shotgun and nodded and Jim Kidd went ahead of him through the side door into the hotel lobby. Scallen was a stride behind him, holding the stubby shotgun close to his leg. "Up the stairs on the right, Jim."

Kidd started up, but Scallen paused to glance at the figure in the armchair near the front. He was sitting on his spine with limp hands folded on his stomach and, as Timpey had described, his hat low over the upper part of his face. You've seen people sleeping in hotel lobbies before, Scallen told himself, and followed Kidd up the stairs. He couldn't stand and wonder about it.

Room 207 was narrow and high-ceilinged, with a single window looking down on Commercial Street. An iron bed was placed the long way against one wall and extended to the right side of the window, and along the opposite wall was a dresser with washbasin and pitcher and next to it a rough-board wardrobe. An unpainted table and two straight chairs took up most of the remaining space.

"Lay down on the bed if you want to," Scallen said.

"Why don't you sleep?" Kidd asked. "I'll hold the shotgun."

The deputy moved one of the straight chairs near to the door and the other to the side of the table opposite the bed. Then he sat down, resting the shotgun on the table so that it pointed directly at Jim Kidd sitting on the edge of the bed near the window.

He gazed vacantly outside. A patch of dismal sky showed above the frame buildings across the way, but he was not sitting close enough to look directly down onto the street. He said, indifferently, "I think it's going to rain."

There was a silence, and then Scallen said, "Jim, I don't have anything against you personally . . . this is what I get paid for, but I just want it understood that if you start across the seven feet between us, I'm going to pull both triggers at once – without first asking you to stop. That clear?"

Kidd looked at the deputy marshal, then his eyes drifted out the window again. "It's kinda cold, too." He rubbed his hands together and the three chain links rattled against each other. "The window's open a crack. Can I close it?"

Scallen's grip tightened on the shotgun and he brought the barrel up, though he wasn't aware of it. "If you can reach it from where you're sitting."

Kidd looked at the window sill and said without reaching toward it, "Too far."

"All right," Scallen said, rising. "Lay back on the bed." He worked his gun belt around so that now the Colt was on his left hip.

Kidd went back slowly, smiling. "You don't take any chances, do you? Where's your sporting blood?"

"Down in Bisbee with my wife and three youngsters," Scallen told him without smiling, and moved around the table.

There were no grips on the window frame. Standing with his side to the window, facing the man on the bed, he put the heel of his hand on the bottom ledge of the frame and shoved down hard. The window banged shut and with the slam he saw Jim Kidd kicking up off of his back, his body straining to rise without his hands to help. Momentarily, Scallen hesitated and his finger tensed on the triggers. Kidd's feet were on the floor, his body swinging up and his head down to lunge from the bed. Scallen took one step and brought his knee up hard against Kidd's face.

The outlaw went back across the bed, his head striking the wall. He lay there with his eyes open looking at Scallen.

"Feel better now, Jim?"

Kidd brought his hands up to his mouth, working the jaw around. "Well, I had to try you out," he said. "I didn't think you'd shoot."

"But you know I will the next time."

For a few minutes Kidd remained motionless. Then he began to pull himself straight. "I just want to sit up."

Behind the table, Scallen said, "Help yourself." He watched Kidd stare out the window.

Then, "How much do you make, Marshal?" Kidd asked the question abruptly.

"I don't think it's any of your business."

"What difference does it make?"

Scallen hesitated. "A hundred and fifty a month," he said, finally, "some expenses and a dollar bounty for every arrest against a Bisbee ordinance in the town limits."

Kidd shook his head sympathetically. "And you got a wife and three kids."

"Well, it's more than a cowhand makes."

"But you're not a cowhand."

"I've worked my share of beef."

"Forty a month and keep, huh?" Kidd laughed.

"That's right, forty a month," Scallen said. He felt awkward. "How much do you make?"

Kidd grinned. When he smiled he looked very young, hardly out of his teens. "Name a month," he said. "It varies."

"But you've made a lot of money."

"Enough. I can buy what I want."

"What are you going to be wanting the next five years?"

"You're pretty sure we're going to Yuma."

"And you're pretty sure we're not," Scallen said. "Well, I've got two train passes and a shotgun that says we are. What've you got?"

Kidd smiled. "You'll see." Then he said right after it, his tone changing. "What made you join the law?"

"The money," Scallen answered, and felt foolish as he said it. But he went on, "I was working for a spread over by the Pantano Wash when Old Nana broke loose and raised hell up the Santa Rosa Valley. The army was going around in circles, so the Pima County marshal got up a bunch to help out and we tracked Apaches almost all spring. The marshal and I got along fine, so he offered me a deputy job if I wanted it." He wanted to say that he had started for seventy-five and worked up to the one hundred and fifty, but he didn't.

"And then someday you'll get to be marshal and make two hundred."

"Maybe."

"And then one night a drunk cowhand you've never seen will be tearing up somebody's saloon and you'll go in to arrest him and he'll drill you with a lucky shot before you get your gun out."

"So you're telling me I'm crazy."

"If you don't already know it."

Scallen took his hand off the shotgun and pulled tobacco and paper from his shirt pocket and began rolling a cigarette. "Have you figured out yet what my price is?"

Kidd looked startled, momentarily, but the grin returned. "No, I haven't. Maybe you come higher than I thought."

Scallen scratched a match across the table, lighted the cigarette, then threw it to the floor, between Kidd's boots. "You don't have enough money, Jim."

Kidd shrugged, then reached down for the cigarette. "You've treated me pretty good. I just wanted to make it easy on you."

The sun came into the room after a while. Weakly at first, cold and hazy. Then it warmed and brightened and cast an oblong patch of light between the bed and the table. The morning wore on slowly because there was nothing to do and each man sat restlessly thinking about somewhere else, though it was a restlessness within and it showed on neither of them.

The deputy rolled cigarettes for the outlaw and himself and most of the time they smoked in silence. Once Kidd asked him what time the train left. He told him shortly after three, but Kidd made no comment.

Scallen went to the window and looked out at the narrow rutted road that was Commercial Street. He pulled a watch from his vest pocket and looked at it. It was almost noon, yet there were few people about. He wondered about this and asked himself if it was unnaturally quiet for a Saturday noon in Contention . . . or if it were just his nerves . . .

He studied the man standing under the wooden awning across the street, leaning idly against a support post with his thumbs hooked in his belt and his flat-crowned hat on the back of his head. There was something familiar about him. And each time Scallen had gone to the window – a few times during the past hour – the man had been there.

He glanced at Jim Kidd lying across the bed, then looked out the window in time to see another man moving up next to the one at the post. They stood together for the space of a minute before the second man turned a horse from the tie rail, swung up and rode off down the street.

The man at the post watched him go and tilted his hat against the sun glare. And then it registered. With the hat low on his forehead Scallen saw him again as he had that morning. The man lying in the armchair . . . as if asleep.

He saw his wife, then, and the three youngsters and he could almost feel the little girl sitting on his lap where she had climbed up to kiss him goodbye, and he had promised to bring her something from Tucson. He didn't know why they had come to him all of a sudden. And after he had put them out of his mind, since there was no room now, there was an upset feeling inside as if he had swallowed something that would not go down all the way. It made his heart beat a little faster.

Jim Kidd was smiling up at him. "Anybody I know?"

"I didn't think it showed."

"Like the sun going down."

Scallen glanced at the man across the street and then to Jim Kidd. "Come here." He nodded to the window. "Tell me who your friend is over there."

Kidd half rose and leaned over looking out the window, then sat down again. "Charlie Prince."

"Somebody else just went for help."

"Charlie doesn't need help."

"How did you know you were going to be in Contention?"

"You told the Wells Fargo man I had friends . . . and about the posses chasing around in the hills. Figure it out for yourself. You could be looking out a window in Benson and seeing the same thing."

"They're not going to do you any good."

"I don't know any man who'd get himself killed for a hundred and fifty dollars." Kidd paused. "Especially a man with a wife and young ones . . ."

Men rode to town in something less than an hour later. Scallen heard the horses coming up Commercial, and went to the window to see the six riders pull to a stop and range themselves in a line in the middle of the street facing the hotel. Charlie Prince stood behind them, leaning against the post.

Then he moved away from it, leisurely, and stepped down into the street. He walked between the horses and stopped in front of them just below the window. He cupped his hands to his mouth and shouted, "*Jim!*"

In the quiet street it was like a pistol shot.

Scallen looked at Kidd, seeing the smile that softened his face and was even in his eyes. Confidence. It was all over him. And even with the manacles on you would believe that it was Jim Kidd who was holding the shotgun.

"What do you want me to tell him?" Kidd said.

"Tell him you'll write every day."

Kidd laughed and went to the window, pushing it up by the top of the frame. It raised a few inches. Then he moved his hands under the window and it slid up all the way.

"Charlie, you go buy the boys a drink. We'll be down shortly."

"Are you all right?"

"Sure I'm all right."

Charlie Prince hesitated. "What if you don't come down? He could kill you and say you tried to break . . . Jim, you tell him what'll happen if we hear a gun go off."

"He knows," Kidd said, and closed the window. He looked at Scallen standing motionless with the shotgun under his arm. "Your turn, Marshal."

"What do you expect me to say?"

"Something that makes sense. You said before I didn't mean a thing to you personally – what you're doing is just a job. Well, you figure out if it's worth getting killed for. All you have to do is throw your guns on the bed and let me walk out the door and you can go back to Bisbee and arrest all the drunks you want. Nobody's going to blame you with the odds stacked seven to one. You know your wife's not going to complain . . ."

"You should have been a lawyer, Jim."

The smile began to fade from Kidd's face. "Come on – what's it going to be?"

The door rattled with three knocks in quick succession. Abruptly the room was silent. The two men looked at each other and now the smile disappeared from Kidd's face completely.

Scallen moved to the side of the door, tiptoeing in his high-heeled boots, then pointed his shotgun toward the bed. Kidd sat down.

"Who is it?"

For a moment there was no answer. Then he heard, "Timpey."

He glanced at Kidd who was watching him. "What do you want?"

"I've got a pot of coffee for you."

Scallen hesitated. "You alone?"

"Of course I am. Hurry up, it's hot!"

He drew the key from his coat pocket, then held the shotgun in the crook of his arm as he inserted the key with one hand and turned the knob with the other. The door opened – and slammed against him, knocking him back against the dresser. He went off balance, sliding into the wardrobe, going down on his hands and knees, and the shotgun clattered across the floor to the window. He saw Jim Kidd drop to the floor for the gun . . .

"Hold it!"

A heavyset man stood in the doorway with a Colt pointing out past the thick bulge of his stomach. "Leave that shotgun where it is." Timpey stood next to him with the coffee-pot in his hand. There was coffee down the front of his suit, on the door and on the flooring. He brushed at the front of his coat feebly, looking from Scallen to the man with the pistol.

"I couldn't help it, Marshal – he made me do it. He threatened to do something to me if I didn't."

"Who is he?"

"Bob Moons . . . you know, Dick's brother . . ."

The heavyset man glanced at Timpey angrily. "Shut your damn whining." His eyes went to Jim Kidd and held there. "You know who I am, don't you?"

Kidd looked uninterested. "You don't resemble anybody I know."

"You didn't have to know Dick to shoot him!"

"I didn't shoot that messenger."

Scallen got to his feet, looking at Timpey. "What the hell's wrong with you?"

"I couldn't help it. He forced me."

"How did he know we were here?"

"He came in this morning talking about Dick and I felt he needed some cheering up, so I told him Jim Kidd had been tried and was being taken to Yuma and was here in town . . . on his way. Bob didn't say anything and went out, and a little later he came back with the gun."

"You damn fool." Scallen shook his head wearily.

"Never mind all the talk." Moons kept the pistol on Kidd. "I would've found him sooner or later. This way, everybody gets saved a long train ride."

"You pull that trigger," Scallen said, "and you'll hang for murder."

"Like he did for killing Dick . . ."

"A jury said he didn't do it." Scallen took a step toward the big man. "And I'm damned if I'm going to let you pass another sentence."

"You stay put or I'll pass sentence on you!"

Scallen moved a slow step nearer. "Hand me the gun, Bob."

"I'm warning you – get the hell out of the way and let me do what I came for."

"Bob, hand me the gun or I swear I'll beat you through that wall."

Scallen tensed to take another step, another slow one. He saw Moons's eyes dart from him to Kidd and in that instant he knew it would be his only chance. He lunged, swinging his coat aside with his hand and when the hand came up it was holding a Colt. All in one motion. The pistol went up and chopped an arc across Moons's head before the big man could bring his own gun around. His hat flew off as the barrel swiped his skull and he went back against the wall heavily, then sank to the floor.

Scallen wheeled to face the window, thumbing the hammer back. But Kidd was still sitting on the edge of the bed with the shotgun at his feet.

The deputy relaxed, letting the hammer ease down. "You might have made it, that time."

Kidd shook his head. "I wouldn't have got off the bed." There was a note of surprise in his voice. "You know, you're pretty good . . ."

At two-fifteen Scallen looked at his watch, then stood up, pushing the chair back. The shotgun was under his arms. In less than an hour they would leave the hotel, walk over Commercial to Stockman and then up Stockman to the station. Three blocks. He wanted to go all the way. He wanted to get Jim Kidd on that train . . . but he was afraid.

He was afraid of what he might do once they were on the street. Even now his breath was short and occasionally he would inhale and let the air out slowly to calm himself. And he kept asking himself if it was worth it.

People would be in the windows and the doors though you wouldn't see them. They'd have their own feelings and most of their hearts would be pounding . . . and they'd edge back of the door frames a little more. The man out on the street was something without a human nature or a personality of its own. He was on a stage. The street was another world.

Timpey sat on the chair in front of the door and next to him, squatting on the floor with his back against the wall, was Moons. Scallen had unloaded Moons's pistol and placed it in the pitcher behind him. Kidd was on the bed.

Most of the time he stared at Scallen. His face bore a puzzled expression, making his eyes frown, and sometimes he would cock his head as if studying the deputy from a different angle.

Scallen stepped to the window now. Charlie Prince and another man were under the awning. The others were not in sight.

"You haven't changed your mind?" Kidd asked him seriously.

Scallen shook his head.

"I don't understand you. You risk your neck to save my life, now you'll risk it again to send me to prison."

Scallen looked at Kidd and suddenly felt closer to him than any man he knew. "Don't ask me, Jim," he said, and sat down again.

After that he looked at his watch every few minutes.

At five minutes to three he walked to the door, motioning Timpey aside, and turned the key in the lock. "Let's go, Jim." When Kidd was next to him he prodded Moons with the gun barrel. "Over on the bed, mister, if I see or hear about you on the street before train time, you'll face an attempted murder charge." He motioned Kidd past him, then stepped into the hall and locked the door.

They went down the stairs and crossed the lobby to the front door, Scallen a stride behind with the shotgun barrel almost touching Kidd's back. Passing through the doorway he said as calmly as he could, "Turn left on Stockman and keep walking. No matter what you hear, keep walking."

As they stepped out into Commercial, Scallen glanced at the ramada where Charlie Prince had been standing, but now the saloon porch was an empty shadow. Near the corner, two horses stood under a sign that said EAT in red letters; and on the other side of Stockman the signs continued, lining the rutted main street to make it seem narrower. And beneath the signs, in the shadows, nothing moved. There was a whisper of wind along the ramadas. It whipped sand specks from the street and rattled them against clapboard, and the sound was hollow and lifeless. Somewhere a screen door banged, far away.

They passed the cafe, turning onto Stockman. Ahead, the deserted street narrowed with distance to a dead end at the rail station – a single-store building standing by itself, low and sprawling with most of the platform in shadow. The westbound was there, along the platform, but the engine and most of the cars were hidden by the station-house. White steam lifted above the roof to be lost in the sun's glare.

They were almost to the platform when Kidd said over his shoulder, "Run like hell while you're still able."

"Where are they?"

Kidd grinned, because he knew Scallen was afraid. "How should I know?"

"Tell them to come out in the open!"

"Tell them yourself."

"Dammit, *tell* them!" Scallen clenched his jaw and jabbed the short barrel into Kidd's back. "I'm not fooling. If they don't come out, I'll kill you!"

Kidd felt the gun barrel hard against his spine and suddenly he shouted, "Charlie!"

It echoed in the street, but after there was only the silence. Kidd's eyes darted over the shadowed porches. "Dammit, Charlie – hold on!"

Scallen prodded him up the warped plank steps to the shade of the platform and suddenly he could feel them near. "Tell them again!"

Don't shoot, Charlie!" Kidd screamed the words.

From the other side of the station they heard the trainsman's call trailing off, ". . . Gila Bend. Sentinel, Yuma!"

The whistle sounded loud, wailing, as they passed into the shade of the platform, then out again to the naked glare of the open side. Scallen squinted, glancing toward the station office, but the train dispatcher was not in sight. Nor was anyone. "It's the mail car," he said to Kidd. "The second to last one." Steam hissed from the iron cylinder of the engine, clouding that end of the platform. "Hurry it up!" he snapped, pushing Kidd along.

Then, from behind, hurried footsteps sounded on the planking, and, as the hiss of steam died away – "Stand where you are!"

The locomotive's main rods strained back, rising like the legs of a grotesque grasshopper, and the wheels moved. The connecting rods stopped on an upward swing and couplings clanged down the line of cars.

"Throw the gun away, brother!"

Charlie Prince stood at the corner of the station-house with a pistol in each hand. Then he moved around carefully between the two men and the train. "Throw it far away, and unhitch your belt," he said.

"Do what he says," Kidd said. "They've got you."

The others, six of them, were strung out in the dimness of the platform shed. Grim-faced, stubbles of beard, hat brims low. The man nearest Prince spat tobacco lazily.

Scallen knew fear at that moment as fear had never gripped him before; but he kept the shotgun hard against Kidd's spine. He said, just above a whisper, "Jim – I'll cut you in half!"

Kidd's body was stiff, his shoulders drawn up tightly. "Wait a minute . . ." he said. He held his palms out to Charlie Prince, though he could have been speaking to Scallen.

Suddenly Prince shouted, "Go down!"

There was a fraction of a moment of dead silence that seemed longer. Kidd hesitated. Scallen was looking at the gunman over Kidd's shoulder, seeing the two pistols. Then Kidd was gone, rolling on the planking, and the pistols were coming up, one ahead of the other. Without moving, Scallen squeezed both triggers of the scatter gun.

Charlie Prince was going down, holding his hands tight to his chest, as Scallen dropped the shotgun and swung around drawing his Colt. He fired hurriedly. *Wait for a target!* Words in his mind. He saw the men under the platform shed, three of them breaking for the station office, two going full length to the planks . . . one crouching, his pistol up. *That one! Get him quick!* Scallen aimed and squeezed the heavy revolver and the man went down. *Now get the hell out!*

Charlie Prince was face down. Kidd was crawling, crawling frantically and coming to his feet when Scallen reached him. He grabbed Kidd by the collar savagely, pushing him on and dug the pistol into his back. "Run, damn you!"

Gunfire erupted from the shed and thudded into the wooden caboose as they ran past it. The tram was moving slowly. Just in front of them a bullet smashed a window of the mail car. Someone screamed, "You'll hit Jim!" There was another shot, then it was too late. Scallen and Kidd leaped up on the car platform and were in the mail car as it rumbled past the end of the station platform.

Kidd was on the floor, stretched out along a row of mail sacks. He rubbed his shoulder awkwardly with his manacled hands and watched Scallen who stood against the wall next to the open door.

Kidd studied the deputy for some minutes. Finally he said, "You know, you really earn your hundred and a half."

Scallen heard him, though the iron rhythm of the train wheels and his breathing were loud in his temples. He felt as if all his strength had been sapped, but he couldn't help smiling at Jim Kidd. He was thinking pretty much the same thing.

# HOPALONG CASSIDY

(Paramount Pictures, 1935)
Starring: William Boyd, James Ellison
& George 'Gaby' Hayes
Directed by Harry Sherman
Story 'Buckskin' by Clarence E. Mulford

**It is a fact that one of the earliest and most successful silent movies was a Western, *The Great Train Robbery*, made by Edison in 1903. Directed by Edwin S. Porter, the film, which starred George Barnes, was obviously based on the exploits of Jesse James and the Wild Bunch and enthralled audiences with its scenes of murder on board an express train, several breakneck horseback chases and a dramatic gunfight finale. The success of Porter's Western provided other film makers with a benchmark and similar acclaim greeted later pictures like *The Squaw Man* (1913) with Dustin Farnum, John Ford's epic, *The Iron Horse* (1924), and *The Big Trail* (1930), directed by Raoul Walsh, which gave the young John Wayne his first starring role.**

**In 1935 one of the most popular Western series of all time was launched, *Hopalong Cassidy*, which turned the former screen romantic lead William Boyd into an icon among cowboy heroes while his exploits became the inspiration for countless imitations. Born in Ohio and in reality a poor rider, Boyd soon adapted to the cowboy image and quickly became an excellent horseman on his mount, Topper. With his iron-grey hair, immaculate all-black outfit and determined refusal to drink, swear or smoke, Boyd became a hero to millions of**

**cinemagoers of all ages in a series of 66 movies. The character of Hopalong Cassidy had actually been based on a cowboy in a series of stories about the 'Bar-20' Ranch and its men written for the US monthly magazine *Outing* by Clarence E. Mulford (1883–1956), then a journalist on the *Municipal Journal and Engineer*. However, the Cassidy of these stories was very different from that of the image presented on the screen – he was a red-haired man called Bill and nicknamed 'Hopalong' because of an old bullet wound that caused him to limp. He also swore, smoked, chewed tobacco, spat and killed bad men without a second thought! But after being transformed into the square-jawed, straight-shooting hero of the movies, Hopalong enjoyed unprecedented popularity of the kind that guaranteed regular reshowing of the original movies in cinemas and on TV, plus a further fifty-two half-hour black-and-white episodes made especially for television in the Fifties in which William Boyd again starred. 'Buckskin', which Mulford wrote in 1906, was the story which began this unique Western legend.**

The town lay sprawled over half a square mile of alkali plain, its main street depressing in its width, for those who were responsible for its inception had worked with a generosity born of the knowledge that they had at their immediate and unchallenged disposal the broad lands of Texas and New Mexico on which to assemble a grand total of twenty buildings, four of which were of wood. As this material was scarce, and had to be brought from where the waters of the Gulf lapped against the flat coast, the last-mentioned buildings were a matter of local pride, as indicating the progressiveness of their owners. These creations of hammer and saw were of one storey, crude and unpainted; their cheap weather sheathing, warped and shrunken by the pitiless sun, curled back on itself and allowed unrestricted entrance to alkali dust and air. The other shacks were of adobe, and reposed in that magnificent squalor dear to their owners, Indians and 'Greasers'.

It was an incident of the Cattle Trail, that most unique and stupendous of all modern migrations, and its founders must have been inspired with a malicious desire to perpetrate a crime against geography, or else they revelled in a perverse cussedness, for within a mile on every side lay broad prairies, and two miles to the east flowed the indolent waters of the Rio Pecos itself. The distance separating the town from the river was excusable, for at certain seasons of the year the placid stream swelled mightily and swept down in a broad expanse of turbulent yellow flood.

Buckskin was a town of one hundred inhabitants, located in the valley of the Rio Pecos fifty miles south of the Texas–New Mexico line. The census claimed two hundred, but it was a well-known fact that it was exaggerated. One instance of this is shown at the name of Tom Flynn. Those who once knew Tom Flynn, alias Johnny Redmond, alias Bill Sweeney, alias Chuck Mullen, by all four names, could find them in the census list. Furthermore, he had been shot and killed in the March of the year preceding the census, and now occupied a grave in the young but flourishing cemetery. Perry's Bend, twenty miles up the river, was cognisant of this and other facts, and, laughing in open derision at the padded list, claimed to be the better town in all ways, including marksmanship.

One year before this tale opens, Buck Peters, an example for the more recent Billy the Kid, had paid Perry's Bend a short but busy visit. He had ridden in at the north end of Main street and out at the south. As he came in he was fired at by a group of ugly cowboys from a ranch known as the C 80. He was hit twice, but he unlimbered his artillery, and before his horse had carried him, half dead, out on the prairie, he had killed one of the group. Several citizens had joined the cowboys and added their bullets against Buck. The deceased had been the best bartender in the country, and the rage of the suffering citizens can well be imagined. They swore vengeance on Buck, his ranch and his stamping ground.

The difference between Buck and Billy the Kid is that the former never shot a man who was not trying to shoot him, or who had not been warned by some action against Buck that would call for it. He minded his own business, never picked a quarrel and was quiet and pacific up to a certain point. After that had been passed he became like a raging cyclone in a tenement house, and storm-cellars were much in demand.

'Fanning' is the name of a certain style of gunplay and was universal among the bad men of the West. While Buck was not a bad man, he had to rub elbows with them frequently, and he believed that the sauce for the goose was the sauce for the gander. So he had removed the trigger of his revolver and worked the hammer with the thumb of the 'gun hand' or the thumb of the unencumbered hand. The speed thus acquired was greater than that of the more modern double-action weapon. Six shots in three seconds was his average speed when that number was required, and when it is thoroughly understood that at least five of them found their intended billets it is not difficult to realize that fanning was an operation of danger when Buck was doing it.

He was a good rider, as all cowboys are, and was not afraid of anything that lived. At one time he and his chums, Red Connors and Hopalong Cassidy, had successfully routed a band of fifteen Apaches who wanted their scalps. Of these, twelve never hunted scalps again, nor anything else on this earth, and the other three returned to their tribe with the report that three evil spirits had chased them with 'wheel guns' (cannons).

So now, since his visit to Perry's Bend, the rivalry of the two towns had turned to hatred and an alert and eager readiness to increase the inhabitants of each other's graveyard. A state of war existed, which for a time resulted in nothing worse than acrimonious suggestions. But the time came when the score was settled to the satisfaction of one side, at least.

Four ranches were also concerned in the trouble. Buckskin was surrounded by two, the Bar 20 and the Three Triangle. Perry's Bend was the common point for the C 80 and the Double Arrow. Each of the two ranch contingents accepted the feud as a matter of course, and as a matter of course took sides with their respective towns. As no better class of fighters ever lived, the trouble assumed Homeric proportions and insured a danger zone well worth watching.

Bar 20's northern line was C 80's southern one, and Skinny Thompson took his turn at outriding one morning after the season's round-up. He was to follow the boundary and turn back stray cattle. When he had covered the greater part of his journey he saw Shorty Jones riding toward him on a course parallel to his own and about long revolver range away. Shorty and he had 'crossed trails' the year before and the best of feelings did not exist between them.

Shorty stopped and stared at Skinny, who did likewise at Shorty. Shorty turned his mount around and applied the spurs, thereby causing his indignant horse to raise both heels at Skinny. The latter took it all in gravely and, as Shorty faced him again, placed his left thumb to his nose, wiggling his fingers suggestively. Shorty took no apparent notice of this, but began to shout:

"Yu wants to keep yore busted-down cows on yore own side. They was all over us day afore yisterday. I'm goin' to salt any more what comes over, and don't yu fergit it, neither."

Thompson wigwagged with his fingers again and shouted in reply: "Yu c'n salt all yu wants to, but if I ketch yu adoin' it yu won't have to work no more. An' I kin say right here thet they's more C 80 cows over here than they's Bar 20's over there."

Shorty reached for his revolver and yelled, "Yore a liar!"

Among the cowboys in particular and the Westerners in general at that time, the three suicidal terms, unless one was an expert in drawing quick and shooting straight with one movement, were the words 'liar', 'coward' and 'thief'. Any man who was called one of these in earnest, and he was the judge, was expected to shoot if he could and save his life, for the words were seldom used without a gun coming with them. The movement of Shorty's hand toward his belt before the appellation reached him was enough for Skinny, who let go at long range – and missed.

The two reports were as one. Both urged their horses nearer and fired again. This time Skinny's sombrero gave a sharp jerk and a hole appeared in the crown. The third shot of Skinny's sent the horse of the other to its knees and then over on its side. Shorty very promptly crawled behind it and, as he did so, Skinny began a wide circle, firing at intervals as Shorty's smoke cleared away.

Shorty had the best position for defence, as he was in a shallow coulée, but he knew that he could not leave it until his opponent had either grown tired of the affair or had used up his ammunition. Skinny knew it, too. Skinny also knew that he could get back to the ranch-house and lay in a supply of food and ammunition and return before Shorty could cover the twelve miles he had to go on foot.

Finally, Thompson began to head for home. He had carried the matter as far as he could without it being murder. Too much time had elapsed now, and, besides, it was before breakfast and he was hungry. He would go away and settle the score at some time when they would be on equal terms.

He rode along the line for a mile and chanced to look back. Two C 80 punchers were riding after him, and as they saw him turn and discover them they fired at him and yelled. He rode on for some distance and cautiously drew his rifle out of its long holster at his right leg. Suddenly he turned around in the saddle and fired twice. One of his pursuers fell forward on the neck of his horse, and his comrade turned to help him. Thompson wigwagged again and rode on, reaching the ranch as the others were finishing their breakfast.

At the table Red Connors remarked that the tardy one had a hole in his sombrero, and asked its owner how and where he had received it.

"Had a argument with C 80 out 'n th' line."

"Go 'way! Ventilate enny?"

"One."

"Good boy, sonny! Hey, Hopalong, Skinny perforated C 80 this mawnin'!"

Hopalong Cassidy was struggling with a mouthful of beef. He turned his eyes toward Red without ceasing, and grinning as well as he could under the circumstances managed to grunt out "Gu –", which was as near to "Good" as the beef would allow.

Lanky Smith now chimed in as he repeatedly stuck his knife into a reluctant boiled potato, "How'd yu do it, Skinny?"

"Bet he sneaked up on him," joshed Buck Peters; "did yu ask his pardin, Skinny?"

"Ask nothin'," remarked Red, "he jest nachurly walks up to C 80 an' sez, 'Kin I have the pleasure of ventilatin' yu?' an' C 80 he sez, 'If yu do it easy like,' sez he. Didn't he, Thompson?"

"They'll be some ventilatin' under th' table if yu fellows don't lemme alone; I'm hungry," complained Skinny.

"Say, Hopalong, I bets yu I kin clean up C 80 all by my lonesome," announced Buck, winking at Red.

"Yah! Yu once tried to clean up the Bend, Buckie, an' if Pete an' Billy hadn't afound yu when they come by Eagle Pass that night yu wouldn't be here eatin' beef by th' pound," glancing at the hard-working Hopalong. "It was plum' lucky fer yu that they was acourtin' that time, wasn't it, Hopalong?" suddenly asked Red. Hopalong nearly strangled in his efforts to speak. He gave it up and nodded his head.

"Why can't yu git it straight, Connors? I wasn't doin' no courtin', it was Pete. I runned into him on th' other side o' th' pass. I'd look fine acourtin', wouldn't I?" asked the downtrodden Williams.

Pete Wilson skilfully flipped a potato into that worthy's coffee, spilling the beverage of the questionable name over a large expanse of blue flannel shirt.

"Yu's all right, yu are. Why, when I meets yu, yu was lost in th' arms of yore ladylove. All I could see was yore feet. Go an' git tangled up with a two-hundred-and-forty-pound half-breed squaw an' then try to lay it onter me! When I proposed drownin' yore troubles over at Cowan's, yu went an' got mad over what yu called th' insinooation. An' yu shore didn't look any too blamed fine, neither."

"All th' same," volunteered Thompson, who had taken the edge from his appetite, "we better go over an' pay C 80 a call. I don't like what Shorty said about saltin' our cattle. He'll shore do it, unless I camps on th' line, which same I hain't hankerin' after."

"Oh, he wouldn't stop th' cows that way, Skinny; he was only afoolin'," exclaimed Connors meekly.

"Foolin' yore gran'mother! That there bunch'll do anything if we wasn't lookin'," hotly replied Skinny.

"That's shore nuff gospel, Thomp. They's sore fer mor'n one thing. They got aplenty when Buck went on th' warpath, an' they's hankerin' to git square," remarked Johnny Nelson, stealing the pie, a rare treat, of his neighbour when that unfortunate individual was not looking. He had it half-way to his mouth when its former owner, Jimmy Price, a boy of eighteen, turned his head and saw it going.

"Hi-yi! Yu clay-bank coyete, drap that pie! Did yu ever see such a son-of-a-gun fer pie?" he plaintively asked Red Connors, as he grabbed a mighty handful of apples and crust. "Pie'll kill yu some day, yu bob-tailed jack! I had an uncle that died once. He et too much pie an' he went an' turned green, an' so'll yu if yu don't let it alone."

"Yu ought'r seed th' pie Johnny had down in Eagle Flat," murmured Lanky Smith reminiscently. "She had feet that'd stop a stam*pede*. Johnny was shore loco about her. Swore she was the finest blossom that ever growed." Here he choked and tears of laughter coursed down his weatherbeaten face as he pictured her. "She was a dainty Greaser, about fifteen han's high an' about sixteen han's around. Johnny used to chalk off when he hugged her, usen't yu, Johnny? One night when he had got purty well around on th' second lap he run inter a Greaser jest startin' out on his fust. They hain't caught that Mexican yet."

Nelson was pelted with everything in sight. He slowly wiped off the pie crust and bread and potatoes.

"Anybody'd think I was a busted grub wagon," he grumbled. When he had fished the last piece of beef out of his ear he went out and offered to stand treat. As the round-up was over, they slid into their saddles and raced for Cowan's saloon at Buckskin.

# THE CISCO KID

(20th Century Fox, 1937)
Starring: Cesar Romero, Leo Carrillo & May Arthur
Directed by Warner Cummings
Story 'The Caballero's Way' by O. Henry

**If Hopalong Cassidy had a rival in the cinema then he was probably the ingratiating Latin rogue the Cisco Kid, who made his début on the screen in 1929, but was ensured of lasting fame in the late Thirties when he was transformed into a heroic masked man who rode exclusively on the side of law and order. Always impeccably attired in a richly embroidered black outfit and wearing a huge sombrero, the Kid, accompanied by his sidekick, the fat and crafty Pancho, became a Western legend. As his fame grew, he roamed ever further across the West – sometimes even into his native Mexico – and was as likely to be found wooing a maiden in distress as exchanging gunfire with outlaws and bank robbers. The first actor to play the Kid on screen was Walter Baxter who won an Oscar for his starring role in the movie *In Old Arizona* (1929) which was also the first 'talkie' Western. However, it was Cesar Romero who became the Kid in the public imagination as a result of the series of movies he starred in from 1937 onwards. Later actors to have played the crime-fighting cowboy include Gilbert Roland (in movies) and Duncan Renaldo, who initially played him on the screen and then starred in a long-running TV programme in the Fifties (156 episodes) which has the distinction of being the first TV series to be filmed in colour. For many years,**

**the Cisco Kid was also the hero of a popular comic strip drawn by Jose-Luis Salinas which was syndicated all over the world.**

**Amazingly, the whole legend of *The Cisco Kid* was inspired by a single short story, 'The Caballero's Way', written in 1904 by the American writer who signed himself O. Henry (1862–1910). Born William Sydney Porter in Greensboro, North Carolina, O. Henry spent several years of his youth living in southern Texas, which undoubtedly sparked his interest in cowboy lore. For a time he worked as a farm labourer, pharmacist-assistant and bank clerk. However, when he 'borrowed' some money from the bank to help his consumptive wife and also launch a literary magazine, a scandal blew up, and he fled to South America where he spent some time in the company of the famous bank robber Al Jennings. Returning to visit his dying wife, he gave himself up and during his subsequent three-year prison sentence started to write the ascerbic and often comic stories that he signed 'O. Henry' and which made him famous. 'The Caballero's Way' may be typical of his style, but is unique because of the legendary character it gave birth to in just a few thousand words . . .**

The Cisco Kid had killed six men in more or less fair scrimmages, had murdered twice as many (mostly Mexicans) and had winged a larger number whom he modestly forbore to count. Therefore a woman loved him.

The Kid was twenty-five, looked twenty; and a careful insurance company would have estimated the probable time of his demise at, say, twenty-six. His habitat was anywhere between the Frio and the Rio Grande. He killed for the love of it – because he was quick-tempered – to avoid arrest – for his own amusement – any reason that came to his mind would suffice. He had escaped capture because he could shoot five-sixths of a second sooner than any sheriff or ranger in the service, and because he rode a speckled roan horse that knew every cow-path in the mesquite and pear thickets from San Antonio to Matamoras.

Tonia Perez, the girl who loved the Cisco Kid, was half Carmen, half Madonna, and the rest – oh, yes, a woman who is half Carmen and half Madonna can always be something more – the rest, let us say, was humming-bird. She lived in a grass-roofed *jacal* near a little Mexican settlement at the Lone Wolf Crossing of the Frio. With her lived a father or grandfather, a lineal Aztec, somewhat less than a thousand years old, who herded a hundred goats and lived in a continuous drunken dream from drinking *mescal*. Back of the *jacal* a tremendous forest of bristling pear, twenty feet high at its worst, crowded almost to its door. It was along the bewildering maze of this spinous thicket that the speckled roan would bring the Kid to see his girl. And once, clinging like a lizard to the ridge-pole, high up under the peaked grass roof, he had heard Tonia, with her Madonna face and Carmen beauty and humming-bird soul, parley with the sheriff's posse, denying knowledge of her man in her soft *mélange* of Spanish and English.

One day the adjutant-general of the State, who is, *ex officio*, commander of the ranger forces, wrote some sarcastic lines to Captain Duval of Company X, stationed at Laredo, relative to the serene and undisturbed existence led by murderers and desperadoes in the said captain's territory.

The captain turned the colour of brick dust under his tan, and forwarded the letter, after adding a few comments, per ranger Private Bill Adamson, to ranger Lieutenant Sandridge, camped at a waterhole on the Nueces with a squad of five men in preservation of law and order.

Lieutenant Sandridge turned a beautiful *couleur de rose* through his ordinary strawberry complexion, tucked the letter in his hip pocket and chewed off the ends of his gamboge moustache.

The next morning he saddled his horse and rode alone to the Mexican settlement at the Lone Wolf Crossing of the Frio, twenty miles away.

Six feet two, blond as a Viking, quiet as a deacon, dangerous as a machine-gun, Sandridge moved among the *jacales*, patiently seeking news of the Cisco Kid.

Far more than the law, the Mexicans dreaded the cold and certain vengeance of the lone rider that the ranger sought. It had been one of the Kid's pastimes to shoot Mexicans 'to see them kick': if he demanded from them moribund Terpsichorean feats, simply that he might be entertained, what terrible and extreme penalties would be certain to follow should they anger him! One and all they lounged with upturned palms and shrugging shoulders, filling the air with '*quien sabes*' and denials of the Kid's acquaintance.

But there was a man named Fink who kept a store at the Crossing – a man of many nationalities, tongues, interests and ways of thinking.

"No use to ask them Mexicans," he said to Sandridge. "They're afraid to tell. This *hombre* they call the Kid – Goodall is his name, ain't it? – he's been in my store once or twice. I have an idea you might run across him at – but I guess I don't keer to say, myself. I'm two seconds later in pulling a gun than I used to be, and the difference is worth thinking about. But this Kid's got a half-Mexican girl at the Crossing that he comes to see. She lives in that *jacal* a hundred yards down the arroyo at the edge of the pear. Maybe she – no, I don't suppose she would, but that *jacal* would be a good place to watch, anyway."

Sandridge rode down to the *jacal* of Perez. The sun was low, and the broad shade of the great pear thicket already covered the grass-thatched hut. The goats were enclosed for the night in a brush corral near by. A few kids walked the top of it, nibbling the chaparral leaves. The old Mexican lay upon a blanket on the grass, already in a stupor from his *mescal*, and dreaming, perhaps, of the nights when he and Pizarro touched glasses to their New World fortunes – so old his wrinkled face seemed to proclaim him to be. And in the door of the *jacal* stood Tonia. And Lieutenant Sandridge sat in his saddle staring at her like a gannet agape at a sailorman.

The Cisco Kid was a vain person, as all eminent and successful assassins are, and his bosom would have been ruffled had he known that at a simple exchange of glances two persons, in whose minds he had been looming large, suddenly abandoned (at least for the time) all thought of him.

Never before had Tonia seen such a man as this. He seemed to be made of sunshine and blood-red tissue and clear weather. He seemed to illuminate the shadow of the pear when he smiled, as though the sun were rising again. The men she had known had been small and dark. Even the kid, in spite of his achievements, was a stripling no larger than herself, with black, straight hair and a cold, marble face that chilled the noonday.

As for Tonia, though she sends description to the poorhouse, let her make a millionaire of your fancy. Her blue-black hair, smoothly divided in the middle and bound close to her head, and her large eyes full of the Latin melancholy, gave her the Madonna touch. Her motions and air spoke of the concealed fire and the desire to charm that she had inherited from the *gitanas* of the Basque province. As for the humming-bird part of her, that dwelt in her heart; you could not perceive it unless her bright red skirt and dark blue blouse gave you a symbolic hint of the vagarious bird.

The newly lighted sun-god asked for a drink of water. Tonia brought it from the red jar hanging under the brush shelter. Sandridge considered it necessary to dismount so as to lessen the trouble of her ministrations.

I play no spy; nor do I assume to master the thoughts of any human heart; but I assert, by the chronicler's right, that before a quarter of an hour had sped, Sandridge was teaching her how to plait a six-strand rawhide stake-rope, and Tonia had explained to him that were it not for her little English book that the peripatetic *padre* had given her and the little crippled *chivo*, that she fed from a bottle, she would be very, very lonely indeed.

Which leads to a suspicion that the Kid's fences needed repairing, and that the adjutant-general's sarcasm had fallen upon unproductive soil.

In his camp by the waterhole Lieutenant Sandridge announced and reiterated his intention of either causing the Cisco Kid to nibble the black loam of the Frio country prairies or of haling him before a judge and jury. That sounded businesslike. Twice a week he rode over to the Lone Wolf Crossing of the Frio, and directed Tonia's slim, slightly lemon-tinted fingers among the intricacies of the slowly growing lariata. A six-strand plait is hard to learn and easy to teach.

The ranger knew that he might find the Kid there at any visit. He kept his armament ready, and had a frequent eye for the pear thicket at the rear of the *jacal*. Thus he might bring down the kite and the humming-bird with one stone.

While the sunny-haired ornithologist was pursuing his studies the Cisco Kid was also attending to his professional duties. He moodily shot up a saloon in a small cow village on Quintana Creek, killed the town marshal (plugging him neatly in the centre of his tin badge) and then rode away, morose and unsatisfied. No true artist is uplifted by shooting an aged man carrying an old-style .38 bulldog.

On his way the Kid suddenly experienced the yearning that all men feel when wrongdoing loses its keen edge of delight. He yearned for the woman he loved to reassure him that she was his in spite of it. He wanted her to call his bloodthirstiness bravery and his cruelty devotion. He wanted Tonia to bring him water from the red jar under the brush shelter, and tell him how the *chivo* was thriving on the bottle.

The Kid turned the speckled roan's head up the ten-mile pear flat that stretches along the Arroyo Hondo until it ends at the Lone Wolf Crossing of the Frio. The roan whickered, for he had a sense of locality and direction equal to that of a belt-line street-car horse; and he knew he would soon be nibbling the rich mesquite grass at the end of a forty-foot stake-rope while Ulysses rested his head in Circe's straw-roofed hut.

More weird and lonesome than the journey of an Amazonian explorer is the ride of one through a Texas pear flat. With dismal monotony and startling variety the uncanny and multiform shapes of the cacti lift their twisted trunks, and fat, bristly hands to encumber the way. The demon plant, appearing to live without soil or rain, seems to taunt the parched traveller with its lush grey greenness. It warps itself a thousand times about what look to be open and inviting paths, only to lure the rider into blind and impassable spine-defended 'bottoms of the bad', leaving him to retreat, if he can, with the points of the compass whirling in his head.

To be lost in the pear is to die almost the death of the thief on the cross, pierced by nails and with grotesque shapes of all the fiends hovering about.

But it was not so with the Kid and his mount. Winding, twisting, circling, tracing the most fantastic and bewildering trail ever picked out, the good roan lessened the distance to the Lone Wolf Crossing with every coil and turn that he made.

While they fared the Kid sang. He knew but one tune and sang it, as he knew but one code and lived it and but one girl and loved her. He was a single-minded man of conventional ideas. He had a voice like a coyote with bronchitis, but whenever he chose to sing his song he sang it. It was a conventional song of the camps and trail, running at its beginning as near as may be to these words:

> Don't you monkey with my Lulu girl
> Or I'll tell you what I'll do —

and so on. The roan was inured to it, and did not mind.

But even the poorest singer will, after a certain time, gain his own consent to refrain from contributing to the world's noises. So the Kid, by the time he was within a mile or two of Tonia's *jacal*, had reluctantly allowed his song to die away – not because his vocal performance had become less charming to his own ears, but because his laryngeal muscles were aweary.

As though he were in a circus ring the speckled roan wheeled and danced through the labyrinth of pear until at length his rider knew by certain landmarks that the Lone Wolf Crossing was close at hand. Then, where the pear was thinner, he caught sight of the grass roof of the *jacal* and the hackberry tree on the edge of the arroyo. A few yards farther the Kid stopped the roan and gazed intently through the prickly openings. Then he dismounted, dropped the roan's reins, and proceeded on foot, stooping and silent, like an Indian. The roan, knowing his part, stood still, making no sound.

The Kid crept noiselessly to the very edge of the pear thicket and reconnoitered between the leaves of a clump of cactus.

Ten yards from his hiding place, in the shade of the *jacal*, sat his Tonia calmly plaiting a rawhide lariat. So far she might surely escape condemnation; women have been known, from time to time, to engage in more mischievous occupations. But if all must be told, there is to be added that her head reposed against the broad and comfortable chest of a tall red-and-yellow man, and that his arm was about her, guiding her nimble small fingers that required so many lessons at the intricate six-strand plait.

Sandridge glanced quickly at the dark mass of pear when he heard a slight squeaking sound that was not altogether unfamiliar. A gun scabbard will make that sound when one grasps the handle of a six-shooter suddenly. But the sound was not repeated; and Tonia's fingers needed close attention.

And then, in the shadow of death, they began to talk of their love; and in the still July afternoon every word they uttered reached the ears of the Kid.

"Remember, then," said Tonia, "you must not come again until I send for you. Soon he will be here. A *vaquero* at the *tienda* said today he saw him on the Guadalupe three days ago. When he is that near he always comes. If he comes and finds you here he will kill you. So, for my sake, you must come no more until I send you the word."

"All right," said the ranger. "And then what?"

"And then," said the girl, "you must bring your men here and kill him. If not, he will kill you."

"He ain't a man to surrender, that's sure," said Sandridge. "It's kill or be killed for the officer that goes up against Mr Cisco Kid."

"He must die," said the girl. "Otherwise there will not be any peace in the world for thee and me. He has killed many. Let him so die. Bring your men, and give him no chance to escape."

"You used to think right much of him," said Sandridge.

Tonia dropped the lariat, twisted herself around and curved a lemon-tinted arm over the ranger's shoulder.

"But then," she murmured in liquid Spanish, "I had not beheld thee, thou great, red mountain of a man! And thou art kind and good, as well as strong. Could one choose him, knowing thee? Let him die; for then I will not be filled with fear by day and night lest he hurt thee or me."

"How can I know when he comes?" asked Sandridge.

"When he comes," said Tonia, "he remains two days, sometimes three. Gregorio, the small son of old Luisa, the *lavandera*, has a swift pony. I will write a letter to thee and send it by him, saying how it will be best to come upon him. By Gregorio will the letter come. And bring many men with thee, and have much care, oh, dear red one, for the rattlesnake is not quicker to strike than is '*El Chivato*', as they call him, to send a ball from his *pistola*."

"The Kid's handy with his gun, sure enough," admitted Sandridge, "but when I come for him I shall come alone. I'll get him by myself or not at all. The Cap wrote one or two things to me that make me want to do the trick without any help. You let me know when Mr Kid arrives, and I'll do the rest."

"I will send you the message by the boy Gregorio," said the girl. "I knew you were braver than that small slayer of men who never smiles. How could I ever have thought I cared for him?"

It was time for the ranger to ride back to his camp on the waterhole. Before he mounted his horse he raised the slight form of Tonia with one arm high from the earth for a parting salute. The drowsy stillness of the torpid summer air still lay thick upon the dreaming afternoon. The smoke from the fire in the *jacal*, where the *frijoles* blubbered in the iron pot, rose straight as a plumb-line above the clay-daubed chimney. No sound or movement disturbed the serenity of the dense pear thicket ten yards away.

When the form of Sandridge had disappeared, loping his big dun down the steep banks of the Frio crossing, the Kid crept back to his own horse, mounted him, and rode back along the tortuous trail he had come.

But not far. He stopped and waited in the silent depths of the pear until half an hour had passed. And then Tonia heard the high, untrue notes of his unmusical singing coming nearer and nearer; and she ran to the edge of the pear to meet him.

The Kid seldom smiled; but he smiled and waved his hat when he saw her. He dismounted, and his girl sprang into his arms. The Kid looked at her fondly. His thick, black hair clung to his head like a wrinkled mat. The meeting brought a slight ripple of some undercurrent of feeling to his smooth, dark face that was usually as motionless as a clay mask.

"How's my girl?" he asked, holding her close.

"Sick of waiting so long for you, dear one," she answered. "My eyes are dim with always gazing into that devil's pincushion through which you come. And I can see into it such a little way, too. But you are here, beloved one, and I will not scold. *Que mal muchacho!* not to come to see your *alma* more often. Go in and rest, and let me water your horse and stake him with the long rope. There is cool water in the jar for you."

The Kid kissed her affectionately.

"Not if the court knows itself do I let a lady stake my horse for me," said he. "But if you'll run in, *chica*, and throw a pot of coffee together while I attend to the *caballo*, I'll be a good deal obliged."

Besides his marksmanship the Kid had another attribute for which he admired himself greatly. He was *muy caballero*, as the Mexicans express it, where the ladies were concerned. For them he had always gentle words and consideration. He could not have spoken a harsh word to a woman. He might ruthlessly slay their husbands and brothers, but he could not have laid the weight of a finger in anger upon a woman. Wherefore many of that interesting division of humanity who had come under the spell of his politeness declared their disbelief in the stories circulated about Mr Kid. One shouldn't believe everything one heard, they said. When confronted by their indignant menfolk with proof of the *caballero*'s deeds of infamy, they said maybe he had been driven to it, and that he knew how to treat a lady, anyhow.

Considering this extremely courteous idiosyncrasy of the Kid and the pride that he took in it, one can perceive that the solution of the problem that was presented to him by what he saw and heard from his hiding place in the pear that afternoon (at least as to one of the actors) must have been obscured by difficulties. And yet one could not think of the Kid overlooking little matters of that kind.

At the end of the short twilight they gathered around a supper of *frijoles*, goat steaks, canned peaches and coffee, by the light of a lantern in the *jacal*. Afterward, the ancestor, his flock corralled, smoked a cigarette and became a mummy in a grey blanket. Tonia washed the few dishes while the Kid dried them with the flour-sacking towel. Her eyes shone; she chatted volubly of the inconsequent happenings of her small world since the Kid's last visit; it was as all his other home-comings had been.

Then outside Tonia swung in a grass hammock with her guitar and sang sad *canciones de amor*.

"Do you love me just the same, old girl?" asked the Kid, hunting for his cigarette papers.

"Always the same, little one," said Tonia, her dark eyes lingering upon him.

"I must go over to Fink's," said the Kid, rising, "for some tobacco. I thought I had another sack in my coat. I'll be back in a quarter of an hour."

"Hasten," said Tonia, "and tell me – how long shall I call you my own this time? Will you be gone again tomorrow, leaving me to grieve, or will you be longer with your Tonia?"

"Oh, I might stay two or three days this trip," said the Kid, yawning. "I've been on the dodge for a month, and I'd like to rest up."

He was gone half an hour for his tobacco. When he returned Tonia was still lying in the hammock.

"It's funny," said the Kid, "how I feel. I feel like there was somebody lying behind every bush and tree waiting to shoot me. I never had mullygrubs like them before. Maybe it's one of them presumptions. I've got half a notion to light out in the morning before day. The Guadalupe country is burning up about that old Dutchman I plugged down there."

"You are not afraid – no one could make my brave little one fear."

"Well, I haven't been usually regarded as a jack-rabbit when it comes to scrapping; but I don't want a posse smoking me out when I'm in your *jacal*. Somebody might get hurt that oughtn't to."

"Remain with your Tonia; no one will find you here."

The Kid looked keenly into the shadows up and down the arroyo and toward the dim lights of the Mexican village.

"I'll see how it looks later on," was his decision.

At midnight a horseman rode into the rangers' camp, blazing his way by noisy 'halloes' to indicate a pacific mission. Sandridge and one or two others turned out to investigate the row. The rider announced himself to be Domingo Sales, from the Lone Wolf Crossing. He bore a letter for Señor Sandridge. Old Luisa, the *lavandera*, had persuaded him to bring it, he said, her son Gregorio being too ill of a fever to ride.

Sandridge lighted the camp lantern and read the letter. These were its words:

> *Dear One*: He has come. Hardly had you ridden away when he came out of the pear. When he first talked he said he would stay three days or more. Then as it grew later he was like a wolf or a fox, and walked about without rest, looking and listening. Soon he said he must leave before daylight when it is dark and stillest. And then he seemed to suspect that I be not true to him. He looked at me so strange that I am frightened. I swear to him that I love him, his own Tonia. Last of all he said I must prove to him I am true. He thinks that even now men are waiting to kill him as he rides from my house. To escape he says he will dress in my

clothes, my red skirt and the blue waist I wear and the brown mantilla over the head, and thus ride away. But before that he says that I must put on his clothes, his *pantalones* and *camisa* and hat, and ride away on his horse from the *jacal* as far as the big road beyond the crossing and back again. This before he goes, so he can tell if I am true and if men are hidden to shoot him. It is a terrible thing. An hour before daybreak this is to be. Come, my dear one, and kill this man and take me for your Tonia. Do not try to take hold of him alive, but kill him quickly. Knowing all, you should do that. You must come long before the time and hide yourself in the little shed near the *jacal* where the wagon and saddles are kept. It is dark in there. He will wear my red skirt and blue waist and brown mantilla. I send you a hundred kisses. Come surely and shoot quickly and straight.

THINE OWN TONIA.

Sandridge quickly explained to his men the official part of the missive. The rangers protested against his going alone.

"I'll get him easy enough," said the lieutenant. "The girl's got him trapped. And don't even think he'll get the drop on me."

Sandridge saddled his horse and rode to the Lone Wolf Crossing. He tied his big dun in a clump of brush on the arroyo, took his Winchester from its scabbard and carefully approached the Perez *jacal*. There was only the half of a high moon drifted over by ragged, milk-white gulf clouds.

The wagon shed was an excellent place for ambush; and the ranger got inside it safely. In the black shadow of the brush shelter in front of the *jacal* he could see a horse tied and hear him impatiently pawing the hard-trodden earth.

He waited almost an hour before two figures came out of the *jacal*. One, in man's clothes, quickly mounted the horse and galloped past the wagon shed toward the crossing and village. And then the other figure, in skirt, waist, and mantilla over its head, stepped out into the faint moonlight, gazing after the rider. Sandridge thought he would take his chance then before Tonia rode back. He fancied she might not care to see it.

"Throw up your hands," he ordered loudly, stepping out of the wagon shed with his Winchester at his shoulder.

There was a quick turn of the figure, but no movement to obey, so the ranger pumped in the bullets – one – two – three – and then twice more; for you never could be too sure of bringing down the Cisco Kid. There was no danger of missing at ten paces, even in that half moonlight.

The old ancestor, asleep on his blanket, was awakened by the shots. Listening further, he heard a great cry from some man in mortal distress or anguish, and rose up grumbling at the disturbing ways of moderns.

The tall, red ghost of a man burst into the *facal*, reaching one hand, shaking like a *tule* reed, for the lantern hanging on its nail. The other spread a letter on the table.

"Look at this letter, Perez," cried the man. "Who wrote it?"

"*Ah, Dios!* It is Señor Sandridge," mumbled the old man, approaching. "*Pues, señor*, that letter was written by '*El Chivato*', as he is called – by the man of Tonia. They say he is a bad man; I do not know. While Tonia slept he wrote the letter and sent it by this old hand of mine to Domingo Sales to be brought to you. Is there anything wrong in the letter? I am very old; and I did not know. *Valgame Dios!* It is a very foolish world; and there is nothing in the house to drink – nothing to drink."

Just then all that Sandrige could think of to do was to go outside and throw himself face downward in the dust by the side of his humming-bird, of whom not a feather fluttered.

He was not a *caballero* by instinct, and he could not understand the niceties of revenge.

A mile away the rider who had ridden past the wagon shed struck up a harsh, untuneful song, the words of which began:

Don't you monkey with my Lulu girl
Or I'll tell you what I'll do –

# STAGECOACH

(United Artists, 1939)
Starring: John Wayne, Claire Trevor
& George Bancroft
Directed by John Ford
Story 'Stage to Lordsburg' by Ernest Haycox

**If *Hopalong Cassidy* is the most famous Western series, then there can be little doubt that John Wayne is the genre's most famous star. Despite the success of *The Big Trail* in 1930, Wayne had spent the rest of the decade in B-movies, and but for being cast by John Ford in *Stagecoach*, the former Marion Michael Morrison might have found that this was his lot for the rest of his career instead of the turning-point and the creation of a hero's image that has since reached almost mythic proportions. Wayne played an outlaw, the Ringo Kid, in the story of a dangerous journey across hostile Indian territory by a small, rickety coach carrying a mixed group of passengers including a bank embezzler, a Southern gambler, a whiskey salesman, a drunken doctor, a pregnant military wife and a woman of ill repute. Magnificently filmed against the backdrop of Monument Valley on the Utah-Arizona border, the climactic chase sequence in the picture is now widely acknowledged as one of the high points in cinema – let alone Western – history.**

**The dramatic plot of *Stagecoach* had been adapted by John Ford and scriptwriter Dudley Nichols from a short story, 'Stage to Lordsburg' by Ernest Haycox (1899–1950), at the time regarded as one of the finest Western short-story writers**

**in America, with much of his work being published in the prestigious *Saturday Evening Post*. Born in Portland, Oregon, he served in the US Army during World War One and then tried unsuccessfully for some years to forge a career as a writer. Haycox finally discovered his true métier in the Western, writing first for the pulp magazines before graduating to the *Post* and later still publishing several novels including *The Border Trumpet* (1939) and *Bugles in the Afternoon* (1944). He broke new ground in the Western by creating characters with psychological depth and a moral awareness instead of being just men of action – a lead that many others would follow. Haycox is at the top of his form in "Stage to Lordsburg" and John Ford certainly did it full justice in his classic movie.**

This was one of those years in the Territory when Apache smoke signals spiralled up from the stony mountain summits and many a ranch cabin lay as a square of blackened ashes on the ground and the departure of a stage from Tonto was the beginning of an adventure that had no certain happy ending.

The stage and its six horses waited in front of Weilner's store on the north side of Tonto's square. Happy Stuart was on the box, the ribbons between his fingers and one foot teetering on the brake. John Strang rode shotgun guard and an escort of ten cavalrymen waited behind the coach, half asleep in their saddles.

At four-thirty in the morning this high air was quite cold, though the sun had begun to flush the sky eastward. A small crowd stood in the square, presenting their final messages to the passengers now entering the coach. There was a girl going down to marry an infantry officer, a whiskey drummer from St Louis, an Englishman all length and bony corners and bearing with him an enormous sporting rifle, a gambler, a solid-shouldered cattleman on his way to New

Mexico and a blond young man upon whom both Happy Stuart and the shotgun guard placed a narrow-eyed interest.

This seemed all until the blond man drew back from the coach door; and then a girl known commonly throughout the Territory as Henriette came quietly from the crowd. She was small and quiet, with a touch of paleness in her cheeks and her quite dark eyes lifted at the blond man's unexpected courtesy, showing surprise. There was this moment of delay and then the girl caught up her dress and stepped into the coach.

Men in the crowd were smiling but the blond one turned, his motion like the swift cut of a knife, and his attention covered that group until the smiling quit. He was tall, hollow-flanked and definitely stamped by the guns slung low on his hips. But it wasn't the guns alone; something in his face, so watchful and so smooth, also showed his trade. Afterwards he got into the coach and slammed the door.

Happy Stuart kicked off the brakes and yelled, "Hi!" Tonto's people were calling out their last farewells and the six horses broke into a trot and the stage lunged on its fore and aft springs and rolled from town with dust dripping off its wheels like water, the cavalrymen trotting briskly behind. So they tipped down the long grade, bound on a journey no stage had attempted during the last forty-five days. Out below in the desert's distance stood the relay stations they hoped to reach and pass. Between lay a country swept empty by the quick raids of Geronimo's men.

The Englishman, the gambler and the blond man sat jammed together in the forward seat, riding backward to the course of the stage. The drummer and the cattleman occupied the uncomfortable middle bench; the two women shared the rear seat. The cattleman faced Henriette, his knees almost touching her. He had one arm hooked over the door's window sill to steady himself. A huge gold nugget slid gently back and forth along the watch-chain slung across his wide chest and a chunk of black hair lay below his hat. His eyes considered Henriette, reading something in the girl that caused him to show her a deliberate smile. Henriette dropped her glance to the gloved tips of her fingers, cheeks unstirred.

They were all strangers packed closely together, with nothing in common save a destination. Yet the cattleman's smile and the boldness of his glance were something as audible as speech, noted by everyone except the Englishman, who sat bolt upright with his stony indifference. The army girl, tall and calmly pretty, threw a quick side glance at Henriette and afterwards looked away with a touch of colour. The gambler saw this interchange of glances and showed the cattleman an irritated attention. The whiskey drummer's eyes narrowed a little and some inward cynicism made a faint change on his lips. He removed his hat to show a bald head already beginning to sweat; his cigar smoke turned the coach cloudy and ashes kept dropping on his vest.

The blond man had observed Henriette's glance drop from the cattleman; he tipped his hat well over his face and watched her – not boldly but as though he were puzzled. Once her glance lifted and touched him. But he had been on guard against that and was quick to look away.

The army girl coughed gently behind her hand, whereupon the gambler tapped the whiskey drummer on the shoulder. "Get rid of that." The drummer appeared startled. He grumbled, "Beg pardon," and tossed the smoke through the window.

All this while the coach went rushing down the ceaseless turns of the mountain road, rocking on its fore and aft springs, its heavy wheels slamming through the road ruts and whining on the curves. Occasionally the strident yell of Happy Stuart washed back. "Hi, Nelliel! By God –!" The whiskey drummer braced himself against the door and closed his eyes.

Three hours from Tonto the road, making a last round sweep, let them down upon the flat desert. Here the stage stopped and the men got out to stretch. The gambler spoke to the army girl, gently: "Perhaps you would find my seat, more comfortable." The army girl said, "Thank you," and changed over. The cavalry sergeant rode up to the stage, speaking to Happy Stuart.

"We'll be goin' back now – and good luck to ye."

The men piled in, the gambler taking the place beside Henriette. The blond man drew his long legs together to give the army girl more room, and watched Henriette's face with a soft, quiet care. A hard sun beat fully on the coach and dust began to whip up like fire smoke. Without escort they rolled across a flat earth broken only by cacti standing against a dazzling light. In the far distance, behind a blue heat haze, lay the faint suggestion of mountains.

The cattleman reached up and tugged at the ends of his mustache and smiled at Henriette. The army girl spoke to the blond man. "How far is it to the noon station?" The blond man said courteously: "Twenty miles." The gambler watched the army girl with the strictness of his face relaxing, as though the run of her voice reminded him of things long forgotten.

The miles fell behind and the smell of alkali dust got thicker. Henriette rested against the corner of the coach, her eyes dropped to the tips of her gloves. She made an enigmatic, disinterested shape there; she seemed past stirring, beyond laughter. She was young, yet she had a knowledge that put the cattleman and the gambler and the drummer and the army girl in their exact places; and she knew why the gambler had offered the army girl his seat. The army girl was in one world and she was in another, as everyone in the coach understood. It had no effect on her, for this was a distinction she had learned long ago. Only the blond man broke through her indifference. His name was Malpais Bill and she could see the wildness in the corners of his eyes and in the long crease of his lips; it was a stamp that would never come off. Yet something flowed out of him toward her that was different than the predatory curiosity of other men; something unobtrusively gallant, unexpectedly gentle.

Upon the box Happy Stuart pointed to the hazy outline two miles away. "Injuns ain't burned that anyhow." The sun was directly overhead, turning the light of the world a cruel brass-yellow. The crooked crack of a dry wash opened across the two deep ruts that made this road. Johnny Strang shifted the gun in his lap. "What's Malpais Bill ridin' with us for?"

"I guess I wouldn't ask him," returned Happy Stuart and studied the wash with a troubled eye. The road fell into it roughly and he got a tighter grip on his reins and yelled: "Hang on! Hi, Nellie! God damn you, hi!" The six horses plunged down the rough side of the wash and for a moment the coach stood alone, high and lonely on the break, and then went reeling over the rim. It struck the gravel with a roar, the front wheels bouncing and the back wheels skewing around. The horses faltered but Happy Stuart cursed at his leaders and got them into a run again. The horses lunged up the far side of the wash two and two, their muscles bunching and the soft dirt flying in yellow clouds. The front wheels struck solidly and something cracked like a pistol shot; the stage rose out of the wash, teetered crosswise and then fell ponderously on its side, splintering the coach panels.

Johnny Strang jumped clear. Happy Stuart hung to the handrail with one hand and hauled on the reins with the other; and stood up while the passengers crawled through the upper door. All the men, except the whiskey drummer, put their shoulders to the coach and heaved it upright again. The whiskey drummer stood strangely in the bright sunlight shaking his head dumbly while the others climbed back in. Happy Stuart said, "All right, brother, git aboard."

The drummer climbed in slowly and the stage ran on. There was a low, grey dobe relay station squatted on the desert dead ahead with a scatter of corrals about it and a flag hanging limp on a crooked pole. Men came out of the dobe's dark interior and stood in the shade of the porch gallery. Happy Stuart rolled up and stopped. He said to a lanky man: "Hi, Mack. Where's the God-damned Injuns?"

The passengers were filing into the dobe's dining room. The lanky one drawled: "You'll see 'em before tomorrow night." Hostlers came up to change horses.

The little dining room was cool after the coach, cool and still. A fat Mexican woman ran in and out with the food platters. Happy Stuart said: "Ten minutes," and brushed the alkali dust from his mouth and fell to eating.

The long-jawed Mack said: "Catlin's ranch burned last night. Was a troop of cavalry around here yesterday. Came and went. You'll git to the Cap tonight all right but I do' know about the mountains beyond. A little trouble?"

"A little," said Happy briefly, and rose. This was the end of rest. The passengers followed, with the whisky drummer straggling at the rear, reaching deeply for wind. The coach rolled away again, Mack's voice pursuing them. "Hit it a lick, Happy, if you see any dust rollin' out of the east."

Heat had condensed in the coach and the little wind fanned up by the run of the horses was stifling to the lungs; the desert floor projected its white glitter endlessly away until lost in the smoky haze. The cattleman's knees bumped Henriette gently and he kept watching her, a celluloid toothpick drooped between his lips. Happy Stuart's voice ran back, profane and urgent, keeping the speed of the coach constant through the ruts. The whiskey drummer's eyes were round and strained and his mouth was open and all the colour had gone out of his face. The gambler observed this without expression and without care; and once the cattleman, feeling the sag of the whiskey drummer's shoulder, shoved him away. The Englishman sat bolt upright, staring emotionlessly at the passing desert. The army girl spoke to Malpais Bill: "What is the next stop?"

"Gap Creek."

"Will we meet soldiers there?"

He said: "I expect we'll have an escort over the hills into Lordsburg."

And at four o'clock of this furnace-hot afternoon the whiskey drummer made a feeble gesture with one hand and fell forward into the gambler's lap.

The cattleman shrugged his shoulders and put a head through the window, calling up to Happy Stuart. "Wait a minute." When the stage stopped everybody climbed out and the blond man helped the gambler lay the whiskey drummer in the sweltering patch of shade created by the coach. Neither Happy Stuart nor the shotgun guard bothered to get down. The whiskey drummer's lips moved a little but nobody said anything and nobody knew what to do – until Henriette stepped forward.

She dropped to the ground, lifting the whiskey drummer's shoulders and head against her breasts. He opened his eyes and there was something in them that they could all see, like relief and ease, like gratefulness. She murmured: "You are all right," and her smile was soft and pleasant, turning her lips maternal. There was this wisdom in her, this knowledge of the fears that men concealed behind their manners, the deep hungers that rode them so savagely, and the loneliness that drove them to women of her kind. She repeated, "You are all right," and watched this whiskey drummer's eyes lose the wildness of what he knew.

The army girl's face showed shock. The gambler and the cattleman looked down at the whiskey drummer quite impersonally. The blond man watched Henriette through lids half closed, but the flare of a powerful interest broke the severe lines of his cheeks. He held a cigarette between his fingers; he had forgotten it.

Happy Stuart said: "We can't stay here."

The gambler bent down to catch the whiskey drummer under the arms. Henriette rose and said, "Bring him to me," and got into the coach. The blond man and the gambler lifted the drummer through the door so that he was lying along the back seat, cushioned on Henriette's lap. They all got in and the coach rolled on. The drummer groaned a little, whispering: "Thanks – thanks," and the blond man, searching Henriette's face for every shred of expression, drew a gusty breath.

They went on like this, the big wheels pounding the ruts of the road while a lowering sun blazed through the coach windows. The mountain bulwarks began to march nearer, more definite in the blue fog. The cattleman's eyes were small and brilliant and touched Henriette personally, but the gambler bent toward Henriette to say: "If you are tired – "

"No," she said. "No. He's dead."

The army girl stifled a small cry. The gambler bent nearer the whiskey drummer, and then they were all looking at Henriette; even the Englishman stared at her for a moment, faint curiosity in his eyes. She was remotely smiling, her lips broad and soft. She held the drummer's head with both her hands and continued to hold him like that until, at the swift fall of dusk, they rolled across the last of the desert floor and drew up before Gap Station.

The cattleman kicked open the door and stepped out, grunting as his stiff legs touched the ground. The gambler pulled the drummer up so that Henriette could leave. They all came out, their bones tired from the shaking. Happy Stuart climbed from the box, his face a grey mask of alkali and his eyes bloodshot. He said: "Who's dead?" and looked into the coach. People sauntered from the station yard, walking with the indolence of twilight. Happy Stuart said, "Well, he won't worry about tomorrow," and turned away.

A short man with a tremendous stomach shuffled through the dusk. He said: "Wasn't sure you'd try to git through yet, Happy."

"Where's the soldiers for tomorrow?"

"Other side of the mountains. Everybody's chased out. What ain't forted up here was sent into Lordsburg. You men will bunk in the barn. I'll make out for the ladies somehow." He looked at the army girl and he appraised Henriette instantly. His eyes slid on to Malpais Bill standing in the background and recognition stirred him then and made his voice careful. "Hello, Bill. What brings you this way?"

Malpais Bill's cigarette glowed in the gathering dusk and Henriette caught the brief image of his face, serene and watchful. Malpais Bill's tone was easy, it was soft. "Just the trip."

They were moving on toward the frame house whose corners seemed to extend indefinitely into a series of attached sheds. Lights glimmered in the windows and men moved around the place, idly talking. The unhitched horses went away at a trot. The tall girl walked into the station's big room, to face a soldier in a dishevelled uniform.

He said: "Miss Robertson? Lieutenant Hauser was to have met you here. He is at Lordsburg. He was wounded in a brush with the Apaches last night."

The tall army girl stood very still. She said: "Badly?"

"Well," said the soldier, "yes."

The fat man came in, drawing deeply for wind. "Too bad – too bad. Ladies, I'll show you the rooms, such as I got."

Henriette's dove-coloured dress blended with the background shadows. She was watching the tall army girl's face whiten. But there was a strength in the army girl, a fortitude that made her think of the soldier. For she said quietly, "You must have had a bad trip."

"Nothing – nothing at all," said the soldier and left the room. The gambler was here, his thin face turning to the army girl with a strained expression, as though he were remembering painful things. Malpais Bill had halted in the doorway, studying the softness and the humility of Henriette's cheeks. Afterwards both women followed the fat host of Gap Station along a narrow hall to their quarters.

Malpais Bill wheeled out and stood indolently against the wall of this desert station, his glance quick and watchful in the way it touched all the men loitering along the yard, his ears weighing all the night-softened voices. Heat died from the earth and a definite chill rolled down the mountain hulking so high behind the house. The soldier was in his saddle, murmuring drowsily to Happy Stuart.

"Well, Lordsburg is a long ways off and the dam' mountains are squirmin' with Apaches. You won't have any cavalry escort tomorrow. The troops are all in the field."

Malpais Bill listened to the hoofbeats of the soldier's horse fade out, remembering the loneliness of a man in those dark mountain passes, and went back to the saloon at the end of the station. This was a low-ceilinged shed with a dirt floor and whitewashed walls that once had been part of a stable. Three men stood under a lantern in the middle of this little place, the light of the lantern palely shining in the rounds of their eyes as they watched him. At the far end of the bar the cattleman and the gambler drank in taciturn silence. Malpais Bill took his whiskey when the bottle came, and noted the barkeep's obscure glance. Gap's host put in his head and wheezed, "Second table," and the other men in here began to move out. The barkeep's words rubbed together, one tone above a whisper. "Better not ride into Lordsburg. Plummer and Shanley are there."

Malpais Bill's lips were stretched to the long edge of laughter and there was a shine like wildness in his eyes. He said, "Thanks, friend," and went into the dining room.

When he came back to the yard night lay wild and deep across the desert and the moonlight was a frozen silver that touched but could not dissolve the world's incredible blackness. The girl Henriette walked along the Tonto road, swaying gently in the vague shadows. He went that way, the click of his heels on the hard earth bringing her around.

Her face was clear and strange and incurious in the night, as though she waited for something to come, and knew what it would be. But he said: "You're too far from the house. Apaches like to crawl down next to a settlement and wait for strays."

She was indifferent, unafraid. Her voice was cool and he could hear the faint loneliness in it, the fatalism that made her words so even. "There's a wind coming up, so soft and good."

He took off his hat, long legs braced, and his eyes were both attentive and puzzled. His blond hair glowed in the fugitive light.

She said in a deep breath: "Why do you do that?"

His lips were restless and the sing and rush of strong feeling was like a current of quick wind around him. "You have folks in Lordsburg?"

She spoke in a direct, patient way as though explaining something he should have known without asking. "I run a house in Lordsburg."

"No," he said, "it wasn't what I asked."

"My folks are dead – I think. There was a massacre in the Superstition Mountains when I was young."

He stood with his head bowed, his mind reaching back to fill in that gap of her life. There was a hardness and a rawness to this land and little sympathy for the weak. She had survived and had paid for her survival, and looked at him now in a silent way that offered no explanations or apologies for whatever had been; she was still a pretty girl with the dead patience of all the past years in her eyes, in the expressiveness of her lips.

He said: "Over in the Tonto Basin is a pretty land. I've got a piece of a ranch there – with a house half built."

"If that's your country, why are you here?"

His lips laughed and the rashness in him glowed hot again and he seemed to grow taller in the moonlight. "A debt to collect."

"That's why you're going to Lordsburg? You will never get through collecting those kind of debts. Everybody in the Territory knows you. Once you were just a rancher. Then you tried to wipe out a grudge and then there was a bigger one to wipe out – and the debt kept growing and more men are waiting to kill you. Someday a man will. You'd better run away from the debts."

His bright smile kept constant, and presently she lifted her shoulders with resignation. "No," she murmured, "you won't run." He could see the sweetness of her lips and the way her eyes were sad for him; he could see in them the patience he had never learned.

He said, "We'd better go back," and turned her with his arm. They went across the yard in silence, hearing the undertone of men's drawling talk roll out of the shadows, seeing the glow of men's pipes in the dark corners. Malpais Bill stopped and watched her go through the station door; she turned to look at him once more, her eyes all dark and her lips softly sober, and then passed down the narrow corridor to her own quarters. Beyond her window, in the yard, a man was murmuring to another man: "Plummer and Shanley are in Lordsburg. Malpais Bill knows it." Through the thin partition of the adjoining room she heard the army girl crying with a suppressed, uncontrollable regularity. Henriette stared at the dark wall, her shoulders and head bowed; and afterwards returned to the hall and knocked on the army girl's door and went in.

Six fresh horses fiddled in front of the coach and the fat host of Gap Station came across the yard swinging a lantern against the dead, bitter black. All the passengers filed sleep-dulled and miserable from the house. Johnny Strang slammed the express box in the boot and Happy Stuart gruffly said: "All right, folks."

The passengers climbed in. The cattleman came up and Malpais Bill drawled: "Take the corner spot, mister," and got in, closing the door. The Gap host grumbled: "If they don't jump you on the long grade you'll be all right. You're safe when you get to Al Schrieber's ranch." Happy's bronze voice shocked the black stillness and the coach lurched forward, its leather springs squealing.

They rode for an hour in this complete darkness, chilled and uncomfortable and half asleep, feeling the coach drag on a heavy-climbing grade. Grey dawn cracked through, followed by a sunless light rushing all across the flat desert now far below. The road looped from one barren shoulder to another and at sunup they had reached the first bench and were slamming full speed along a boulder-strewn flat. The cattleman sat in the forward corner, the left corner of his mouth swollen and crushed, and when Henriette saw that her glance slid to Malpais Bill's knuckles. The army girl had her eyes closed, her shoulders pressing against the Englishman, who remained bolt upright with the sporting gun between his knees. Beside Henriette the gambler seemed to sleep, and on the middle bench Malpais Bill watched the land go by with a thin vigilance.

At ten they were rising again, with juniper and scrub pine showing on the slopes and the desert below them filling with the powdered haze of another hot day. By noon they reached the summit of the range and swung to follow its narrow rock-ribbed meadows. The gambler, long motionless, shifted his feet and caught the army girl's eyes.

"Schrieber's is directly ahead. We are past the worst of it."

The blond man looked around at the gambler, making no comment; and it was then that Henriette caught the smell of smoke in the windless air. Happy Stuart was cursing once more and the brake-blocks began to cry. Looking through the angled vista of the window panel Henriette saw a clay and rock chimney standing up like a gaunt skeleton against the day's light. The house that had been there was a black patch on the ground, smoke still rising from pieces that had not been completely burnt.

The stage stopped and all the men were instantly out. An iron stove squatted on the earth, with one section of pipe stuck upright to it. Fire licked lazily along the collapsed fragments of what had been a trunk. Beyond the location of the house, at the foot of a corral, lay two nude figures grotesquely bald, with deliberate knife slashes marking their bodies. Happy Stuart went over there and had his look; and came back.

"Schrieber's. Well – "

Malpais Bill said: "This morning about daylight." He looked at the gambler, at the cattleman, at the Englishman who showed no emotion. "Get back in the coach." He climbed to the coach's top, flattening himself full length there. Happy Stuart and Strang took their places again. The horses broke into a run.

The gambler said to the army girl: "You're pretty safe between those two fellows," and hauled a .44 from a back pocket and laid it over his lap. He considered Henriette more carefully than before, his taciturnity breaking. He said: "How old are you?"

Her shoulders rose and fell, which was the only answer. But the gambler said gently, "Young enough to be my daughter. It is a rotten world. When I call to you, lie down on the floor."

The Englishman had pulled the rifle from between his knees and laid it across the sill of the window on his side. The cattleman swept back the skirt of his coat to clear the holster of his gun.

The little flinty summit meadows grew narrower, with shoulders of grey rock closing in upon the road. The coach wheels slammed against the stony ruts and bounced high and fell again with a jar the springs could not soften. Happy Stuart's howl ran steadily above this rattle and rush. Fine dust turned all things grey.

Henriette sat with her eyes pinned to the gloved tips of her fingers, remembering the tall shape of Malpais Bill cut against the moonlight of Gap Station. He had smiled at her as a man might smile at any desirable woman, with the sweep and swing of laughter in his voice; and his eyes had been gentle. The gambler spoke very quietly and she didn't hear him until his fingers gripped her arm. He said again, not raising his voice: "Get down."

Henriette dropped to her knees, hearing gunfire blast through the rush and run of the coach. Happy Stuart ceased to yell and the army girl's eyes were round and dark. The walls of the canyon had tapered off. Looking upward through the window on the gambler's side, Henriette saw the weaving figure of an Apache warrior reel nakedly on a calico pony and rush by with a rifle raised and pointed in his bony elbows. The gambler took a cool aim; the stockman fired and aimed again. The Englishman's sporting rifle blasted heavy echoes through the coach, hurting her ears, and the smell of powder got rank and bitter. The blond man's boots scraped the coach top and round small holes began to dimple the panelling as the Apache bullets struck. An Indian came boldly abreast the coach and made a target that couldn't be missed. The cattleman dropped him with one shot. The wheels screamed as they slowed around the sharp ruts and the whole heavy superstructure of the coach bounced high into the air. Then they were rushing downgrade.

The gambler said quietly, "You had better take this," handing Henriette his gun. He leaned against the door with his small hands gripping the sill. Pallor loosened his cheeks. He said to the army girl: "Be sure and keep between those gentlemen," and looked at her with a way that was desperate and forlorn and dropped his head to the window's sill.

Henriette saw the bluff rise up and close in like a yellow wall. They were rolling down the mountain without brake. Gunfire fell off and the crying of the Indians faded back. Coming up from her knees then she saw the desert's flat surface far below, with the angular pattern of Lordsburg vaguely on the far borders of the heat fog. There was no more firing and Happy Stuart's voice lifted again and the brakes were screaming on the wheels, and going off, and screaming again. The Englishman stared out of the window sullenly; the army girl seemed in a deep desperate dream; the cattleman's face was shining with a strange sweat. Henriette reached over to pull the gambler up, but he had an unnatural weight to him and slid into the far corner. She saw that he was dead.

At five o'clock that long afternoon the stage threaded Lordsburg's narrow streets of dobe and frame houses, came upon the centre square and stopped before a crowd of people gathered in the smoky heat. The passengers crawled out stiffly. A Mexican boy ran up to see the dead gambler and began to yell his news in shrill Mexican. Malpais Bill climbed off the top, but Happy Stuart sat back on his seat and stared taciturnly at the crowd. Henriette noticed then that the shotgun messenger was gone.

A grey man in a sleazy white suit called up to Happy. "Well, you got through."

Happy Stuart said: "Yeah. We got through."

An officer stepped through the crowd, smiling at the army girl. He took her arm and said, "Miss Robertson, I believe. Lieutenant Hauser is quite all right. I will get your luggage – "

The army girl was crying then, definitely. They were all standing around, bone-weary and shaken. Malpais Bill remained by the wheel of the coach, his cheeks hard against the sunlight and his eyes riveted on a pair of men standing under the board awning of an adjoining store. Henriette observed the manner of their waiting and knew why they were here. The blond man's eyes, she noticed, were very blue and flame burned brilliantly in them. The army girl turned to Henriette, tears in her eyes. She murmured: "If there is anything I can ever do for you – "

But Henriette stepped back, shaking her head. This was Lordsburg and everybody knew her place except the army girl. Henriette said formally, "Goodbye," noting how still and expectant the two men under the awning remained. She swung toward the blond man and said, "Would you carry my valise?"

Malpais Bill looked at her, laughter remote in his eyes, and reached into the luggage pile and got her battered valise. He was still smiling as he went beside her, through the crowd and past the two waiting men. But when they turned into an anonymous and dusty little side street of the town, where the houses all sat shoulder to shoulder without grace or dignity, he had turned sober. He said: "I am obliged to you. But I'll have to go back there."

They were in front of a house no different from its neighbours; they had stopped at its door. She could see his eyes travel this street and comprehend its meaning and the kind of traffic it bore. But he was saying in that gentle, melody-making tone:

"I have watched you for two days." He stopped, searching his mind to find the thing he wanted to say. It came out swiftly. "God made you a woman. The Tonto is a pretty country."

Her answer was quite barren of feeling. "No. I am known all through the Territory. But I can remember that you asked me."

He said: "No other reason?" She didn't answer, but something in her eyes pulled his face together. He took off his hat and it seemed to her he was looking through this hot day to that far-off country and seeing it fresh and desirable. He murmured: "A man can escape nothing. I have got to do this. But I will be back."

He went along the narrow street, made a quick turn at the end of it and disappeared. Heat rolled like a heavy wave over Lordsburg's house tops and the smell of dust was very sharp. She lifted her valise, and dropped it and stood like that, mute and grave before the door of her dismal house. She was remembering how tall he had been against the moonlight at Gap Station.

There were four swift shots beating furiously along the sultry quiet, and a shout, and afterwards a longer and longer silence. She put one hand against the door to steady herself, and knew that those shots marked the end of a man, and the end of a hope. He would never come back; he would never stand over her in the moonlight with the long gentle smile on his lips and with the swing of life in his casual tone. She was thinking of all that humbly and with the patience life had beaten into her . . .

She was thinking of all that when she heard the strike of boots on the street's packed earth; and turned to see him, high and square in the muddy sunlight, coming toward her with his smile.

# DESTRY RIDES AGAIN

(Universal, 1939)
Starring: James Stewart, Marlene Dietrich
& Brian Donlevy
Directed by George Marshall
Story 'Dust Storm' by Max Brand

**In the same year that *Stagecoach* was released, another Western movie destined for legendary status was also filmed: *Destry Rides Again*, starring James Stewart and Marlene Dietrich. The first movie in the genre to combine drama and comedy in equal measure, it has, according to cinema historian Steven H. Scheuer, 'often been copied but never matched'. James Stewart, who came late in his career to Western movies and still gave several of his most memorable performances in pictures like *The Naked Spur* (1953) and *The Man From Laramie* (1955), was unforgettable as Destry the unconventional lawman who refuses to wear a gun but nonetheless manages to bring peace and order to a riotious cowtown. His scenes with Marlene Dietrich remain long in the memory, and the bar-room fight scene between Dietrich and Una Merkel has rightly, I think, been described as one of the most hilariously funny in any Western.**

**The author of *Destry Rides Again* was the hugely prolific Max Brand (1892–1944), then already established as one of the most popular writers in America, having contributed numerous stories to the Western pulp magazines as well as producing hundreds of cowboy novels. But his output did not stop there and some estimates have put**

**his total work in all genres as high as almost 900 stories varying from short-shorts to 90,000-word novels. Born Frederick Schiller Faust in Seattle, Washington, he invented the pen name Max Brand during World War One, and made this famous as a result of his creation of Destry, the secret agent Anthony Hamilton, and the ever popular hospital intern Dr Kildare. During the late Thirties Brand was recruited by Hollywood as a scriptwriter, but following the outbreak of World War Two he signed up as a war correspondent. Never afraid of being close to the heart of the action, he tragically lost his life from shrapnel wounds while reporting on the Italian front. A considerable number of his approximately 400 Western tales have been adapted for the screen – some during his lifetime and many more since his death – and his contribution to the Western genre is immense. 'Dust Storm' is one of Max Brand's least known short stories, well plotted and atmospheric like the very best Western movies . . .**

For seven days the wind came out of the north-east over the Powder Mountains and blew the skirts of a dust storm between Digger Hill and Bender Hill into the hollow where Lindsay was living in his shack. During that week Lindsay waked and slept with a piece of black coat-lining worn across his mouth and nostrils, but the dust penetrated like cosmic rays through the chinks in the walls of the cabin, through the mask and to the bottom of his lungs, so that every night he roused from sleep gasping for breath with a nightmare of being buried alive. Even lamplight could not drive that bad dream farther away than the misty corners of the room.

The blow began on a Tuesday morning, and by twilight of that day he knew what he was in for, so he went out through the whistling murk and led Jenny and Lind, his two mules, and Mustard, his old cream-coloured mustang, from the pasture into the barn. There he had in the mow a good heap of the volunteer hay which he had cut last May on the south-east forty, but the thin silt of the storm soon whitened the hay to such a degree that he had to shake it thoroughly before he fed the stock. Every two hours during that week, he roused himself by an alarm-clock instinct and went out to wash the nostrils and mouths of the stock, prying their teeth open and reaching right in to swab the black off their tongues. On Wednesday, Jenny, like the fool and villainess that she was, closed on his right forearm and raked off eight inches of skin.

Monotony of diet was more terrible to Lindsay than the storm. He had been on the point of riding to town and borrowing money from the bank on his growing crop so as to lay in a stock of provisions, but now he was confined with a bushel of potatoes and the heel of a side of bacon.

Only labour like that of the harvest field could make such food palatable and, in confinement as he was, never thoroughly stretching his muscles once a day, Lindsay began to revolt in belly and then in spirit. He even lacked coffee to give savour to the menu; he could not force himself more than once a day to eat potatoes, boiled or fried in bacon fat, with the dust gritting continually between his teeth.

He had no comfort whatever except for Caesar, his mongrel dog, and half a bottle of whiskey, from which he gave himself a nip once a day. Then in the night of the seventh day, there came to Lindsay a dream of a country where rolling waves of grass washed from horizon to horizon and all the winds of the earth could not blow a single breath of dust into the blue of the sky. He wakened with the dawn visible through the cracks in the shanty walls and a strange expectancy in his mind.

That singular expectation remained in him when he threw the door open and looked across the black of the hills toward the green light that was opening like a fan in the east; then he realised that it was the silence after the storm that seemed more enormous than all the stretch of landscape between him and the Powder Mountains. Caesar ran out past his legs to leap and bark and sneeze until something overawed him, in turn, and sent him skulking here and there with his nose to the ground as though he were following invisible bird trails. It was true that the face of the land was changed.

As the light grew Lindsay saw that the waterhole in the hollow was a black wallow of mud and against the woodshed leaned a sloping mass of dust like a drift of snow. The sight of this started him on the run for his eighty acres of winter-sown summer fallow. From a distance he saw the disaster but could not believe it until his feet were wading deep in the dust. Except for a few marginal strips, the whole swale of the ploughed land was covered with wind-filtered soil, a yard thick in the deepest places.

Two-thirds of his farm was wiped out, two-thirds of it was erased into permanent sterility; and the work of nearly ten years was entombed. He glanced down at the palms of his hands, for he was thinking of the burning, pulpy blisters that had covered them day after day when he was digging holes with the blunt post auger.

He looked up, then, at the distant ridges of the Powder Mountains. Ten years before in the morning light he had been able almost to count the great pines that walked up the slopes and stood on the mountains' crests, but the whole range had been cut over in the interim and the thick coat of forest which bound with its roots the accumulated soil of a million years had been mowed down. That was why the teeth of the wind had found substance they could eat into.

The entire burden of precious loam that dressed the mountains had been blown adrift in recent years and now the worthless underclay, made friable by a dry season, was laid in a stifling coat of silt across the farmlands of the lower valleys and the upper pastures of the range.

Lindsay did not think about anything for a time. His feet, and an automatic impulse that made him turn always to the stock first, took him to the barn, where he turned loose the confined animals. Even the mules were glad enough to kick up their heels a few times, and fifteen years of hard living could not keep Mustard from exploding like a bomb all over the pasture, bucking as though a ghost were on his back and knocking up a puff of dust every time he hit the ground.

Lindsay, standing with feet spread and folded arms, a huge figure in the door of the barn, watched the antics of his old horse with a vacant smile, for he was trying to rouse himself and failing wretchedly. Instead, he could see himself standing in line with signed application slips in his hand, and then in front of a desk where some hired clerk with an insolent face put sharp questions to him. A month hence, when people asked him how things went, he would have to say, "I'm on the county."

When he had gone that far in his thinking, his soul at last rose in him but to such a cold, swift altitude that he was filled with fear, and he found his lips repeating words, stiffly, whispering them aloud, "I'll be damned and dead, first!" The fear of what he would do with his own hands grew stronger and stronger, for he felt that he had made a promise which would be heard and recorded by that living, inmost god of all honest men, his higher self.

Once more, automatically, his feet took him on to the next step in the day: breakfast. Back in the shanty, his lips twitched with disgust as he started frying potatoes; the rank smell of the bacon grease mounted to his brain and gathered in clouds there, but his unthinking hands finished the cookery and dumped the fried potatoes into a tin plate.

A faint chorus came down to him then out of the windless sky. He snatched the loaded pistol from the holster that hung against the wall and ran outside, for sometimes the wild geese, flying north, came very low over the hill as they rose from the marsh south of it, but now he found himself agape like a schoolboy, staring up.

He should have known by the dimness of the honking and by the melancholy harmony which distance added to it that the geese were half a mile up in the sky. Thousands of them were streaming north in a great wedge that kept shuffling and reshuffling at the open ends; ten tons of meat on the wing.

A tin pan crashed inside the shack and Caesar came out on wings with his tail between his legs; Lindsay went inside and found the plate of potatoes overturned on the floor. He called, "Come in here, Caesar, you damned old thief. Come in here and get it, if you want the stuff. I'm better without."

The dog came back, skulking. From the doorway he prospected the face of his master for a moment, slavering with greed: then he sneaked to the food on the floor and began to eat guiltily, but Lindsay already had forgotten him. All through the hollow, which a week before had been a shining tremor of yellow green wheat stalks, the rising wind of the morning was now stirring little airy whirlpools and walking ghosts of dust that made a step or two and vanished.

It seemed to Lindsay that he had endured long enough. He was thirty-five. He had twenty years of hard work behind him. And he would not – by God, he would not – be a government pensioner! The wild geese had called the gun into his hand; he felt, suddenly, that it must be used for one last shot anyway. As for life, there was a stinking savour of bacon that clung inevitably to it. He looked with fearless eyes into the big muzzle of the gun.

Then Mustard whinnied not far from the house and Lindsay lifted his head with a faint smile, for there was a stallion's trumpet sound in the neigh of the old gelding, always, just as there was always an active devil in his heels and his teeth. He combined the savage instincts of a wildcat with the intellectual, patient malevolence of a mule, but Lindsay loved the brute because no winter cold was sharp enough to freeze the big heart in him and no dry summer march was long enough to wither it. At fifteen, the old fellow still could put fifty miles of hard country behind him between dawn and dark. For years Lindsay had felt that those long, mulish ears must eventually point the way to some great destiny.

He stepped into the doorway now and saw that Mustard was whinnying a challenge to a horseman who jogged up the Gavigan Trail with a telltale dust cloud boiling up behind. Mechanical instinct, again, made Lindsay drop the gun into the old leather holster that hung on the wall. Then he stepped outside to wait.

Half a mile off, the approaching rider put his horse into a lope and Lindsay recognised, by his slant in the saddle, that inveterate range tramp and worthless roustabout Gypsy Renner. He reined in at the door of the shack, lifted his bandana from nose and mouth and spat black.

"Got a drink, Bob?" he asked without other greeting.

"I've got a drink for you," said Lindsay.

"I'll get off a minute, then," replied Renner, and swung out of the saddle.

Lindsay poured some whiskey into a tin cup and Renner received it without thanks. Dust was still rising like thick smoke from his shoulders.

"You been far?" asked Lindsay.

"From Boulder," said Renner.

"Much of the range like out yonder?"

"Mostly," said Renner.

He finished the whiskey and held out the cup. Lindsay poured the rest of the bottle.

"If much of the range is like this," said Lindsay, "it's gonna be hell."

"It's gonna be and it is," said Renner. "It's hell already over on the Oliver Range."

"Wait a minute. That's where Andy Barnes and John Street run their cows. What you mean it's hell up there?"

"That's where I'm bound," said Renner. "They're hiring men and guns on both sides. Most of the waterholes and tanks on Andy Barnes's place are filled up with mud, right to the ridge of the Oliver Hills, and his cows are choking. And John Street, his land is clean because the wind kind of funnelled the dust up over the hills and it landed beyond him. Andy has to water those cows and Street wants to charge ten cents a head. Andy says he'll be damned if he pays money for the water that God put free on earth. So there's gonna be a fight."

Lindsay looked through the door at that lumpheaded mustang of his and saw, between his mind and the world, a moonlight night with five thousand head of cattle, market-fat and full of beans, stampeding into the north-east with a thunder and rattle of split hooves and a swordlike clashing of horns. He saw riders galloping ahead, vainly shooting into the face of the herd in the vain hope of turning it, until two of those cowpunchers, going it blind, clapped together and went down, head over heels.

"They used to be friends," said Lindsay. "They come so close to dying together, one night, that they been living side by side ever since; and they used to be friends."

"They got too damn rich," suggested Renner. "A rich man ain't nobody's friend . . . It was you that saved the two hides of them one night in a stampede, ten, twelve years ago, wasn't it?"

Lindsay pointed to Mustard.

"Now I'm gonna tell you something about that," he said. "The fact is that those cows would've washed right over the whole three of us, but I was riding that Mustard horse, and when I turned him back and pointed him at the herd, he just went off like a roman candle and scattered sparks right up to the Milky Way. He pitched so damn hard that he pretty near snapped my head off and he made himself look so big that those steers doggone near fainted and pushed aside from that spot."

Renner looked at the mustang with his natural sneer. Then he said, "Anyway, there's gonna be a fight up there, and it's gonna be paid for."

"There oughtn't be no fight," answered big Bob Lindsay, frowning.

"They're mean enough to fight," said Renner. "Didn't you save their scalps? And ain't they left you to starve here on a hundred and twenty acres of blowsand that can't raise enough to keep a dog fat?"

"Yeah?" said Lindsay. "Maybe you better be vamoosing along."

Renner looked at him, left the shack and swung into the saddle. When he was safely there he muttered, "Ah, to hell with you!" and jogged away.

Lindsay, with a troubled mind, watched him out of sight. An hour later he saddled Mustard and took the way toward the Oliver Hills.

The Oliver Hills lie west of the Powder Mountains, their sides fat with grasslands all the way to the ridge, and right over the crest walked the posts of the fence that separated the holdings of Andy Barnes from those of John Street. Lindsay, as he came up the old Mexican Trail, stopped on a hilltop and took a careful view of the picture.

He had to strain his eyes a little because dust was blowing like battle smoke off the whitened acres of Andy Barnes and over the ridge, and that dust was stirred up by thousands of cattle which milled close to the fence line, drawn by the smell of water. Down the eastern hollows some of the beefs were wallowing in the holes where water once had been and where there was only mud now. But west of the ridge the lands of John Street were clean as green velvet under the noonday sun.

Scattered down the Street side of the fence, a score of riders wandered up and down with significant lines of light balancing across the pommels of the saddles. Those were the rifles. As many more cowpunchers headed the milling cattle of Andy Barnes with difficulty, for in clear view of the cows, but on Street's side of the fence ran a knee-deep stream of silver water that spread out into a quiet blue lake, halfway down the slope.

He found a gate onto the Street land and went through it. Two or three of the line-riders hailed him with waving hats. One of them sang out, "Where's your rifle, brother? Men ain't worth a damn here without they got rifles."

He found John Street sitting on a spectacular black horse just west of a hilltop where the rise of land gave him shelter from ambitious sharpshooters. When he saw Lindsay, he grabbed him by the shoulders and bellowed like a bull in spring, "I knew you'd be over and I knew you'd be on the right side. By God, it's been eleven years since I was as glad to see you as I am today . . . Boys, I wanta tell you what Bob Lindsay here done for me when I got caught in – "

"Shut up, will you?" said Lindsay. "Looks like Andy has got some pretty dry cows, over yonder."

"I hope they dry up till there's nothing but wind in their bellies," said John Street.

"I thought you and Andy been pretty good friends," said Lindsay.

"If he was my brother – if he was two brothers – if he was my son and daughter and my pa and ma, he's so damn mean that I'd see him in hellfire before I'd give him a cup of water to wash the hellfire cinders out of his throat," said John Street, in part.

So Lindsay rode back to the gate and around to the party of Andy Barnes, passing steers with caked, dry mud of the choked waterholes layered around their muzzles. They were red-eyed with thirst and their bellowing seemed to rise like an unnatural thunder out of the ground instead of booming from the skies. Yearlings, already knock-kneed with weakness, were shouldered to the ground by the heavier stock and lay there, surrendering.

Andy Barnes sat cross-legged on the ground inside the rock circle of an old Indian camp on a hilltop, picking the grass, chewing it, spitting it out. He had grown much fatter and redder of face and the fat had got into his eyes, leaving them a little dull and staring.

Lindsay sat down beside him.

"You know something, Bob?" said Andy.

"Know what?" asked Lindsay.

"My wife's kid sister is over to the house," said Andy. "She's just turned twenty-three and she's got enough sense to cook a man steak and onions. As tall as your shoulder and the bluest dam' pair of eyes you ever seen outside a blind horse. Never had bridle or saddle on her and I dunno how she'd go in harness, but you got a pair of hands. What you say? She's heard about Bob Lindsay for ten years, and she don't believe that there's that much man outside of a fairy story."

"Shut up, will you?" said Lindsay. "Seems like ten cents ain't much to pay for the difference between two thousand dead steers and two thousand dogies, all picking grass and fat and happy."

"Look up at that sky," said Andy.

"I'm looking," said Lindsay.

"Look blue?"

"Yeah. Kind of."

"Who put the blue in it?"

"God, maybe."

"Anybody ever pay him for it? And who put the water in the ground and made it leak out again? And why should I pay for *that*?"

"There's a lot of difference," said Lindsay, "between a dead steer on the range and a live steer in Chicago."

"Maybe," dreamed Andy, "but I guess they won't all be dead. You see that yearling over yonder, standing kind of spray-legged, with its nose pretty near on the ground?"

"I see it," said Lindsay.

"When that yearling kneels down," said Andy, "ther's gonna be something happen . . . Ain't that old Mustard?"

"Yeah, that's Mustard," said Lindsay, rising.

"If you ever get through with him," said Andy, "I got a lot of pasture land nothing ain't using where he could just range around and laugh himself to death. I ain't forgot when he was bucking the saddle off his back and knocking splinters out of the stars that night. He must've looked like a mountain to them steers, eh?"

Lindsay got on Mustard and rode over the hill. He went straight up to the fence which divided the two estates and dismounted before it with wire pincers in his hand. He felt scorn and uttermost detestation for the thing he was about to do. Men who cut fences are dirty rustlers and horse thieves and every man jack of them ought to be strung up as high as the top of the Powder Mountains; but the thirsty uproar of the cattle drove him on to what he felt was both a crime and a sin.

It had been a far easier thing, eleven years ago, to save Barnes and Street from the stampeding herd than it was to save them now from the petty hatred that had grown up between them without cause, without reason. The posts stood at such distance apart that the wires were strung with an extra heavy tension. When the steel edges cut through the topmost strand, it parted with a twang and leaped back to either side, coiling and tangling like thin, bright metallic snakes around the posts.

Yelling voices of protest came shouting through the dusty wind. Lindsay could see men dropping off their horses and lying prone to level their rifles at him; and all at once it seemed to him that the odour of frying bacon grease was thickening in his nostrils again and that this was the true savour of existence.

He saw the Powder Mountains lifting their sides from brown to blue in the distant sky with a promise of better lands beyond that horizon but the promise was a lie, he knew. No matter what he did, he felt assured that ten years hence he would be as now, a poor unrespected squatter on the range, slaving endlessly, not even for a monthly pay cheque, but merely to fill his larder with – bacon and Irish potatoes! Hope, as vital to the soul as breath to the nostrils, had been subtracted from him, and therefore what he did with his life was of no importance whatever. He leaned a little and snapped the pincers through the second wire of the fence.

He did not hear the sharp twanging sound of the parting strand, for a louder noise struck at his ear, a ringing rifle report full of resonance, like two heavy sledge-hammers struck face to face. At his feet a riffle of dust lifted; he heard the bullet hiss like a snake through the grass. Then a whole volley crashed. Bullets went by him on rising notes of enquiry; and just behind him a slug spatted into the flesh of Mustard. Sometimes an axe makes a sound like that when it sinks into green wood.

He turned and saw Mustard sitting down like a dog, with his long, mulish ears pointing straight ahead and a look of pleased expectancy in his eyes. Out of a hole in his breast blood was pumping in long, thin jets.

Lindsay leaned and cut the third and last wire.

When he straightened again he heard the body of Mustard slump down against the ground with a squeaking, jouncing noise of liquids inside his belly. He did not lie on his side but with his head outstretched and his legs doubled under him as though he were playing a game and would spring up again in a moment.

Lindsay looked toward the guns. They never should have missed him the first time except that something like buck fever must have shaken the marksmen. He walked right through the open gap in the fence to meet the fire with a feeling that the wire clipper in his hand was marking him down like a cattle thief for the lowest sort of a death.

Then someone began to scream in a shrill falsetto. He recognised the voice of Big John Street, transformed by hysterical emotion. Street himself broke over the top of the hill with the black horse at a full gallop, yelling for his men to stop firing.

The wind of the gallop furled up the wide brim of his sombrero and he made a noble picture, considering the rifles of Andy Barnes, which must be sighting curiously at him by this time; then a hammer stroke clipped Lindsay on the side of the head. The Powder Mountains whirled into a mist of brown and blue; the grass spun before him like running water; he dropped to his knees, and down his face ran a soft, warm stream.

Into his dizzy view came the legs and the sliding hooves of the black horse, cutting shallow furrows in the grass as it slid to a halt, and he heard the voice of John Street, dismounted beside him, yelling terrible oaths. He was grabbed beneath the armpits and lifted.

"Are you dead, Bob?" yelled Street.

"I'm gonna be all right," said Lindsay. He ran a fingertip through the bullet furrow in his scalp and felt the hard bone of the skull all the way. "I'm gonna be fine," he stated, and turned toward the uproar that was pouring through the gap he had cut in the fence.

For the outburst of rifle fire had taken the attention of Barnes's men from their herding and the cattle had surged past them toward water. Nothing now could stop that hungry stampede as they crowded through the gap with rattling hooves and the steady clashing of horns. Inside the fence the stream divided right and left and rushed on toward water, some to the noisy, white cataract, some to the wide blue pool.

"I'm sorry, John," said Lindsay, "but those cows looked kind of dry to me."

Then a nausea of body and a whirling dimness of mind overtook him and did not clear away again until he found himself lying with a bandaged head on the broad top of a hill. John Street was on one side of him and Andy Barnes on the other. They were holding hands like children and peering down at him anxiously.

"How are you, Bob, old son?" asked Andy.

"Fine," said Lindsay, sitting up. "Fine as a fiddle," he added, rising to his feet.

Street supported him hastily by one arm and Barnes by the other. Below him he could see the Barnes cattle thronging into the shallow water of the creek.

"About that ten cents a head," said Andy, "it's all right with me."

"Damn the money," said Street. "I wouldn't take money from you if you were made of gold . . . I guess Bob has paid for the water like he paid for our two hides eleven years ago. Bob, don't you give a hang about nothing? Don't you care nothing about your life?"

"The cows seemed kind of dry to me," said Lindsay, helplessly.

"You're comin' home with me," said Street.

"I got *two* females in my place to look after him," pointed out Andy Barnes.

"I got a cook that's a doggone sight better than a doctor," said Street.

"I don't need any doctor," said Lindsay. "You two just shut up and say goodbye to me, will you? I'm going home. I got work to do tomorrow."

This remark produced a silence out of which Lindsay heard, from the surrounding circle of cowmen, a voice that murmured, "He's gonna go home!" And another said, "He's got the chores to do, I guess."

Andy looked at John Street.

"He's gonna go, John," he said.

"There ain't any changing him," said John Street sadly. "Hey, Bob, take this here horse of mine, will you?"

"Doncha do it!" shouted Barnes. "Hey, Mickie, bring up that grey, will you? . . . Look at that piece of grey sky and wind, Bob, will you?"

"They're a mighty slick pair," said Lindsay. "I never seen a more upstanding pair of hellcats in my life. It would take a lot of barley and oats to keep them sleeked up so's they shine like this . . . But if you wanta wish a horse onto me, how about that down-headed, wise-lookin' cayuse over there? He's got some bottom to him and the hellfire is kind of worked out of his eyes."

He pointed to a brown gelding which seemed to have fallen half asleep. Another silence was spread by this remark. Then someone said: "He's picked out Slim's cuttin' horse . . . He's gone and picked out old Dick."

"Give them reins to Bob, Slim!" commanded Andy Barnes, "and leave the horse tied right onto the reins, too."

Lindsay said, "Am I parting you from something, Slim?"

Slim screwed up his face and looked at the sky.

"Why, I've heard about you, Lindsay," he said, "and today I've seen you. I guess when a horse goes to you, he's just going home; and this Dick horse of mine, I had the making of him and he sure rates a home . . . If you just ease him along the first half-hour, he'll be ready to die for you all the rest of the day."

"Thanks," said Lindsay, shaking hands. "I'm gonna value him, brother."

He swung into the saddle and waved his adieu. John Street followed him a few steps, and so did Andy Barnes.

"Are you gonna be comin' over? Are you gonna be comin' back, Bob?" they asked him.

"Are you two gonna stop being damn fools?" he replied.

They laughed and waved a cheerful agreement and they were still waving as he jogged Dick down the hill. The pain in his head burned him to the brain with every pulse of his blood but a strange feeling of triumph rose in his heart. He felt he never would be impatient again, for he could see that he was enriched for ever.

The twilight found him close to home and planning the work of the next days. If he put a drag behind the two mules he could sweep back the dust where it thinned out at the margin and so redeem from total loss a few more acres. With any luck, he would get seed for the next year; and as for food, he could do what he had scorned all his days – he could make a kitchen garden and irrigate it from the windmill.

It was dark when he came up the last slope and the stars rose like fireflies over the edge of the hill. Against them he made out Jenny and Lind waiting for him beside the door of the shack. He paused to stare at the vague silhouettes and remembered poor Mustard with a great stroke in his heart.

Caesar came with a shrill howl of delight to leap about his master and bark at the new horse, but Dick merely pricked his ears with patient understanding as though he knew he had come home indeed.

Inside the shanty the hand of Lindsay found the lantern. Lighting it brought a suffocating odor of kerosene fumes, but even through this Lindsay could detect the smell of fried bacon and potatoes in the air. He took a deep breath of it for it seemed to him the most delicious savour in the world.

# WESTERN UNION

(20th Century Fox, 1941)
Starring: Randolph Scott, Robert Young
& Dean Jagger
Directed by Budd Boetticher
Story 'The Great Slave' by Zane Grey

**Zane Grey was an author almost as prolific as Max Brand, enjoying huge popularity with Western readers and cinema fans, as well as writing in several other genres, too. Among the dozens of movies based on his novels and short stories, *Western Union* has been among the most highly praised and certainly ranks high on my own listing, for it starred my favourite Western actor, the laconic, steely-eyed, straight-shooting Randolph Scott. The story, based on the laying of the first transcontinental Western Union wire in 1861, allowed Scott to give one of his best performances as a stoical, heroic figure going his own way and for ever true to his own code. It was the sort of role which Scott made his own in movie after movie, and which caused millions of cinemagoers – myself included – to rank him among the screen immortals. *Western Union* is regularly reshown on television where it is rightly described as a classic.**

**The author, Zane Grey (1872–1939) was born Pearl Zane Grey in Zanesville, Ohio, a town named after his pioneering great-great-grandfather. Although trained to be a dentist, it was as a result of a trip to the West that he began writing stories of cowboys and Indians and then came**

**to public attention with *Riders of the Purple Sage* in 1912 which has to date sold over five million copies. Readers and film producers eagerly snapped up his subsequent novels, and it is claimed that with his total sales in excess of 150 million, Zane Grey is the second-best-selling Western writer of all time – only Louis L'Amour (who is also represented in this collection) has sold more. Such, in fact, has been Grey's popularity that since his death two of his sons, Romer and Loren, have continued writing novels about his major characters; a TV series, *Zane Grey Theatre*, has screened 145 half-hour episodes based on his work; and a Zane Grey Museum has been established in his birthplace. Despite criticism that his style is now rather dated, all of Zane Grey's stories were based on detailed research into the peoples of the West, and 'The Great Slave' is a powerful evocation of Indian life – a theme which particularly appealed to him because of what he saw as years of mistreatment of the Native Americans at the hands of government administrators.**

A voice on the wind whispered to Siena the prophecy of his birth. "A chief is born to save the vanishing tribe of Crows! A hunter to his starving people!" While he listened, at his feet swept swift waters, the rushing, green-white, thundering Athabasca, spirit-forsaken river; and it rumbled his name and murmured his fate. "Siena! Siena! His bride will rise from a wind kiss on the flowers in the moonlight! A new land calls to the last of the Crows! Northward where the wild goose ends its flight Siena will father a great people!"

So Siena, a hunter of the leafy trails, dreamed his dreams; and at sixteen he was the hope of the remnant of a once powerful tribe, a stripling chief, beautiful as a bronzed autumn god, silent, proud, forever listening to voices on the wind.

To Siena the lore of the woodland came as flight comes to the strong-winged wildfowl. The secrets of the forests were his, and of the rocks and rivers.

He knew how to find the nests of the plover, to call the loon, to net the heron and spear the fish. He understood the language of the whispering pines. Where the deer came down to drink and the caribou browsed on moss and the white rabbit nibbled in the grass and the bear dug in the logs for grubs – all these he learned; and also when the black flies drove the moose into the water and when the honk of the geese meant the approach of the north wind.

He lived in the woods, with his bow, his net and his spear. The trees were his brothers. The loon laughed for his happiness, the wolf mourned for his sadness. The bold crag above the river, Old Stoneface, heard his step when he climbed there in the twilight. He communed with the stern god of his ancestors and watched the flashing Northern Lights and listened.

From all four corners came his spirit guides with steps of destiny on his trail. On all the four winds breathed voices whispering of his future; loudest of all called the Athabasca, god-forsaken river, murmuring of the bride born of a wind kiss on the flowers in the moonlight.

It was autumn, with the flame of leaf fading, the haze rolling out of the hollows, the lull yielding to moan of coming wind. All the signs of a severe winter were in the hulls of the nuts, in the fur of the foxes, in the flight of waterfowl. Siena was spearing fish for winter store. None so keen of sight as Siena, so swift of arm; and as he was the hope, so he alone was the provider for the starving tribe. Siena stood to his knees in a brook where it flowed over its gravelly bed into the Athabasca. Poised high was his wooden spear. It glinted downward swift as a shaft of sunlight through the leaves. Then Siena lifted a quivering whitefish and tossed it upon the bank where his mother

Ema, with other women of the tribe, sun-dried the fish upon a rock.

Again and again, many times, flashed the spear. The young chief seldom missed his aim. Early frosts on the uplands had driven the fish down to deeper water, and as they came darting over the bright pebbles Siena called them by name.

The oldest squaw could not remember such a run of fish. Ema sang the praises of her son; the other women ceased the hunger chant of the tribe.

Suddenly a hoarse shout pealed out over the waters.

Ema fell in a fright; her companions ran away; Siena leaped upon the bank, clutching his spear. A boat in which were men with white faces drifted down toward him.

"Hal-loa!" again sounded the hoarse cry.

Ema cowered in the grass. Siena saw a waving of white hands; his knees knocked together and he felt himself about to flee. But Siena of the Crows, the saviour of a vanishing tribe, must not fly from visible foes.

"Palefaces," he whispered, trembling, yet stood his ground ready to fight for his mother. He remembered stories of an old Indian who had journeyed far to the south and had crossed the trails of the dreaded white men. There stirred in him vague memories of strange Indian runners telling campfire tales of white hunters with weapons of lightning and thunder.

"Naza! Naza!" Siena cast one fleeting glance to the north and a prayer to his god of gods. He believed his spirit would soon be wandering in the shades of the other Indian world.

As the boat beached on the sand Siena saw men lying with pale faces upward to the sky, and voices in an unknown tongue greeted him. The tone was friendly, and he lowered his threatening spear. Then a man came up to the bank, his hungry eyes on the pile of fish, and he began to speak haltingly in mingled Cree and Chippewayan language:

"Boy – we're white friends – starving – let us buy fish – trade for fish – we're starving and we have many moons to travel."

"Siena's tribe is poor," replied the lad. "Sometimes they starve too. But Siena will divide his fish and wants no trade."

His mother, seeing the white men intended no evil, came out of her fright and complained bitterly to Siena of his liberality. She spoke of the menacing winter, of the frozen streams, the snow-bound forest, the long night of hunger. Siena silenced her and waved the frightened braves and squaws back to their wigwams.

"Siena is young," he said simply; "but he is chief here. If we starve – we starve."

Whereupon he portioned out a half of the fish. The white men built a fire and sat around it feasting like famished wolves around a fallen stag. When they had appeased their hunger they packed the remaining fish in the boat, whistling and singing the while. Then the leader made offer to pay, which Siena refused, though the covetous light in his mother's eyes hurt him sorely.

"Chief," said the leader, "the white man understands; now he offers presents as one chief to another."

Thereupon he proffered bright beads and tinselled trinkets, yards of calico and strips of cloth. Siena accepted with a dignity in marked contrast to the way in which the greedy Ema pounced upon the glittering heap. Next the paleface presented a knife which, drawn from its scabbard, showed a blade that mirrored its brightness in Siena's eyes.

"Chief, your woman complains of a starving tribe," went on the white man. "Are there not many moose and reindeer?"

"Yes. But seldom can Siena creep within range of his arrow."

"A-ha! Siena will starve no more," replied the man, and from the boat he took a long iron tube with a wooden stock.

"What is that?" asked Siena.

"The wonderful shooting stick. Here, boy, watch! See the bark on the campfire. Watch!"

He raised the stick to his shoulder. Then followed a streak of flame, a puff of smoke, a booming report; and the bark of the campfire flew into bits.

The children dodged into the wigwams with loud cries, the women ran screaming, Ema dropped in the grass wailing that the end of the world had come, while Siena, unable to move hand or foot, breathed another prayer to Naza of the northland.

The white man laughed and, patting Siena's arm, he said: "No fear." Then he drew Siena away from the bank, and began to explain the meaning and use of the wonderful shooting stick. He reloaded it and fired again and yet again, until Siena understood and was all aflame at the possibilities of such a weapon.

Patiently the white man taught the Indian how to load it, sight and shoot, and how to clean it with ramrod and buckskin. Next he placed at Siena's feet a keg of powder, a bag of lead bullets and boxes full of caps. Then he bade Siena farewell, entered the boat with his men and drifted round a bend of the swift Athabasca.

Siena stood alone upon the bank, the wonderful shooting stick in his hands, and the wail of his frightened mother in his ears. He comforted her, telling her the white men were gone, that he was safe, and that the prophecy of his birth had at last begun its fulfilment. He carried the precious ammunition to a safe hiding place in a hollow log near his wigwam and then he plunged into the forest.

Siena bent his course toward the runways of the moose. He walked in a kind of dream, for he both feared and believed. Soon the glimmer of water, splashes and widening ripples, caused him to crawl stealthily through the ferns and grasses to the border of a pond. The familiar hum of flies told him of the location of his quarry. The moose had taken to the water, driven by the swarms of black flies, and were standing neck deep, lifting their muzzles to feed on the drooping poplar branches. Their wide-spreading antlers, tipped back into the water, made the ripples.

Trembling as never before, Siena sank behind a log. He was within fifty paces of the moose. How often in that very spot had he strung a feathered arrow and shot it vainly! But now he had the white man's weapon, charged with lightning and thunder. Just then the poplars parted above the shore, disclosing a bull in the act of stepping down. He tossed his antlered head at the cloud of humming flies, then stopped, lifting his nose to scent the wind.

"Naza!" whispered Siena in his swelling throat.

He rested the shooting stick on the log and tried to see over the brown barrel. But his eyes were dim. Again he whispered a prayer to Naza. His sight cleared, his shaking arms stilled, and with his soul waiting, hoping, doubting, he aimed and pulled the trigger.

Boom!

High the moose flung his ponderous head, to crash down upon his knees, to roll in the water and churn a bloody foam, and then lie still.

"Siena! Siena!"

Shrill the young chief's exultant yell pealed over the listening waters, piercing the still forest, to ring back in echo from Old Stoneface. It was Siena's triumphant call to his forefathers, watching him from the silence.

The herd of moose ploughed out of the pond and crashed into the woods, where, long after they had disappeared, their antlers could be heard cracking the saplings.

When Siena stood over the dead moose his doubts fled; he was indeed god-chosen. No longer chief of a starving tribe!

Reverently and with immutable promise he raised the shooting stick to the north, toward Naza who had remembered him; and on the south, where dwelt the enemies of his tribe, his dark glance brooded wild and proud and savage.

Eight times the shooting stick boomed out in the stillness and eight moose lay dead in the wet grasses. In the twilight Siena wended his way home and placed eight moose tongues before the whimpering squaws.

"Siena is no longer a boy," he said. "Siena is a hunter. Let his women go bring in the meat."

Then to the rejoicing and feasting and dancing of his tribe he turned a deaf ear, and in the night passed alone under the shadow of Old Stoneface, where he walked with the spirits of his ancestors and believed the voices on the wind.

Before the ice locked the ponds Siena killed a hundred moose and reindeer. Meat and fat and oil and robes changed the world for the Crow tribe.

Fires burned brightly all the long winter; the braves awoke from their stupor and chanted no more; the women sang of the Siena who had come, and prayed for summer wind and moonlight to bring his bride.

Spring went by, summer grew into blazing autumn, and Siena's fame and wonder of the shooting stick spread through the length and breadth of the land.

Another year passed, then another, and Siena was the great chief of the rejuvenated Crows. He had grown into a warrior's stature, his face had the beauty of the god-chosen, his eye the falcon flash of the Sienas of old. Long communion in the shadow of Old Stoneface had added wisdom to his other gifts; and now to his worshipping tribe all that was needed to complete the prophecy of his birth was the coming of an alien bride.

* * *

It was another autumn, with the wind whipping the tamaracks and moaning in the pines, and Siena stole along a brown, fern-lined trail. The dry smell of fallen leaves filled his nostrils; he tasted snow in the keen breezes. The flowers were dead, and still no dark-eyed bride sat in his wigwam. Siena sorrowed and strengthened his heart to wait. He saw her flitting in the shadows around him, a wraith with dusky eyes veiled by dusky wind-blown hair, and ever she hovered near him, whispering from every dark pine, from every waving tuft of grass.

To her whispers he replied: "Siena waits."

He wondered of what alien tribe she would come. He hoped not of the unfriendly Chippewayans or the far-distant Blackfeet; surely not of the hostile Crees, life enemies of his tribe, destroyers of its once puissant strength, jealous now of its resurging power.

Other shadows flitted through the forest, spirits that rose silently from the graves over which he trod, and warned him of double steps on his trail, of unseen foes watching him from the dark coverts. His braves had repeated gossip, filterings from stray Indian wanderers, hinting of plots against the risen Siena. To all these he gave no heed, for was not he Siena, god-chosen, and had he not the wonderful shooting stick?

It was the season that he loved, when dim forest and hazy fernland spoke most impellingly. The tamaracks talked to him, the poplars bowed as he passed, and the pines sang for him alone. The dying vines twined about his feet and clung to him, and the brown ferns, curling sadly, waved him a welcome that was a farewell. A bird twittered a plaintive note and a loon whistled a lonely call. Across the wide grey hollows and meadows of white moss moaned the north wind, bending all before it, blowing full into Siena's face with its bitter promise. The lichen-covered rocks and the rugged-barked trees and the creatures that moved among them – the whole world of earth and air heard Siena's step on the rustling leaves and a thousand voices hummed in the autumn stillness.

So he passed through the shadowy forest and over the grey muskeg flats to his hunting place. With his birch-bark horn he blew the call of the moose. He alone of hunting Indians had the perfect moose call. There, hidden within a thicket, he waited, calling and listening till an angry reply bellowed from the depths of a hollow, and a bull moose, snorting fight, came cracking the saplings in his rush. When he sprang fierce and bristling into the glade, Siena killed him. Then, laying his shooting stick over a log, he drew his knife and approached the beast.

A snapping of twigs alarmed Siena and he whirled upon the defensive, but too late to save himself. A band of Indians pounced upon him and bore him to the ground. One wrestling heave Siena made, then he was overpowered and bound. Looking upward, he knew his captors, though he had never seen them before; they were the lifelong foes of his people, the fighting Crees.

A sturdy chief, bronze of face and sinister of eye, looked grimly down upon his captive. "Baroma makes Siena a slave."

Siena and his tribe were dragged far southward to the land of the Crees. The young chief was bound upon a block in the centre of the village where hundreds of Crees spat upon him, beat him and outraged him in every way their cunning could devise. Siena's gaze was on the north and his face showed no sign that he felt the torments.

At last Baroma's old advisers stopped the spectacle, saying: "This is a man!"

Siena and his people became slaves of the Crees. In Baroma's lodge, hung upon caribou antlers, was the wonderful shooting stick with Siena's powder horn and bullet pouch, objects of intense curiosity and fear.

None knew the mystery of this lightning-flashing, thunder-dealing thing; none dared touch it.

The heart of Siena was broken; not for his shattered dreams or the end of his freedom, but for his people. His fame had been their undoing. Slaves to the murderers of his forefathers! His spirit darkened, his soul sickened; no more did sweet voices sing to him on the wind, and his mind dwelt apart from his body among shadows and dim shapes.

Because of his strength he was worked like a dog at hauling packs and carrying wood; because of his frame he was set to cleaning fish and washing vessels with the squaws. Seldom did he get to speak a word to his mother or any of his people. Always he was driven.

One day, when he lagged almost fainting, a maiden brought him water to drink. Siena looked up, and all about him suddenly brightened, as when sunlight bursts from cloud.

"Who is kind to Siena?" he asked, drinking.

"Baroma's daughter," replied the maiden.

"What is her name?"

Quickly the maiden bent her head, veiling dusky eyes with dusky hair. "Emihiyah."

"Siena has wandered on lonely trails and listened to voices not meant for other ears. He has heard the music of Emihiyah on the winds. Let the daughter of Siena's great foe not fear to tell of her name."

"Emihiyah means a wind kiss on the flowers in the moonlight," she whispered shyly and fled.

Love came to the last of the Sienas and it was like a glory. Death shuddered no more in Siena's soul. He saw into the future, and out of his gloom he rose again, god-chosen in his own sight, with such added beauty to his stern face and power to his piercing eye and strength to his lofty frame that the Crees quailed before him and marvelled. Once more sweet voices came to him, and ever on the soft winds were songs of the dewy moorlands to the northward, songs of the pines and the laugh of the loon and of the rushing, green-white, thundering Athabasca, god-forsaken river.

Siena's people saw him strong and patient, and they toiled on, unbroken, faithful. While he lived, the pride of Baroma was vaunting. "Siena waits" were the simple words he said to his mother, and she repeated them as wisdom. But the flame in his eye was like the leaping Northern Lights, and it kept alive the fire deep down in their breasts.

In the winter when the Crees lolled in their wigwams, when less labour fell to Siena, he set traps in the snow trails for silver fox and marten. No Cree had ever been such a trapper as Siena. In the long months he captured many furs, with which he wrought a robe the like of which had not before been the delight of a maiden's eye. He kept it by him for seven nights, and always during this time his ear was turned to the wind. The seventh night was the night of the midwinter feast, and when the torches burned bright in front of Baroma's lodge Siena took the robe and, passing slowly and stately till he stood before Emihiyah, he laid it at her feet.

Emihiyah's dusky face paled, her eyes that shone like stars drooped behind her flying hair, and all her slender body trembled.

"Slave!" cried Baroma, leaping erect. "Come closer that Baroma may see what kind of a dog approaches Emihiyah."

Siena met Baroma's gaze, but spoke no word. His gift spoke for him. The hated slave had dared to ask in marriage the hand of the proud Baroma's daughter. Siena towered in the firelight with something in his presence that for a moment awed beholders. Then the passionate and untried braves broke the silence with a clamour of the wolf pack.

Tillimanqua, wild son of Baroma, strung an arrow to his bow and shot into Siena's hip, where it stuck, with feathered shaft quivering.

The spring of the panther was not swifter than Siena; he tossed Tillimanqua into the air and, flinging him down, trod on his neck and wrenched the bow away. Siena pealed out the long-drawn war whoop of his tribe that had not been heard for a hundred years, and the terrible cry stiffened the Crees in their tracks.

Then he plucked the arrow from his hip and, fitting it to the string, pointed the gory flint head at Tillimanqua's eyes and began to bend the bow. He bent the tough wood till the ends almost met, a feat of exceeding great strength, and thus he stood with brawny arms knotted and stretched.

A scream rent the suspense. Emihiyah fell upon her knees. "Spare Emihiyah's brother!"

Siena cast one glance at the kneeling maiden, then, twanging the bowstring, he shot the arrow toward the sky.

"Baroma's slave is Siena," he said, with scorn like the lash of a whip. "Let the Cree learn wisdom."

Then Siena strode away, with a stream of dark blood down his thigh, and went to his brush tepee, where he closed his wound.

In the still watches of the night, when the stars blinked through the leaves and the dew fell, when Siena burned and throbbed in pain, a shadow passed between his weary eyes and the pale light. And a voice that was not one of the spirit voices on the wind called softly over him, "Siena! Emihiyah comes."

The maiden bound the hot thigh with a soothing balm and bathed his fevered brow.

Then her hands found his in tender touch, her dark face bent low to his, her hair lay upon his cheek. "Emihiyah keeps the robe," she said.

"Siena loves Emihiyah," he replied.

"Emihiyah loves Siena," she whispered.

She kissed him and stole away.

On the morrow Siena's wound was as if it had never been; no eye saw his pain. Siena returned to his work and his trapping. The winter melted into spring, spring flowered into summer, summer withered into autumn.

Once in the melancholy days Siena visited Baroma in his wigwam. "Baroma's hunters are slow. Siena sees a famine in the land."

"Let Baroma's slave keep his place among the squaws," was the reply.

That autumn the north wind came a moon before the Crees expected it; the reindeer took their annual march farther south; the moose herded warily in open groves; the whitefish did not run, and the seven-year pest depleted the rabbits.

When the first snow fell Baroma called a council and then sent his hunting braves far and wide.

One by one they straggled back to camp, footsore and hungry, and each with the same story. It was too late.

A few moose were in the forest, but they were wild and kept far out of range of the hunter's arrows, and there was no other game.

A blizzard clapped down upon the camp, and sleet and snow whitened the forest and filled the trails. Then winter froze everything in icy clutch. The old year drew to a close.

The Crees were on the brink of famine. All day and all night they kept up their chanting and incantations and beating of tom-toms to conjure the return of the reindeer. But no reindeer appeared.

It was then that the stubborn Baroma yielded to his advisers and consented to let Siena save them from starvation by means of his wonderful shooting stick.

Accordingly Baroma sent word to Siena to appear at his wigwam.

Siena did not go, and said to the medicine men: "Tell Baroma soon it will be for Siena to demand."

Then the Cree chieftain stormed and stamped in his wigwam and swore away the life of his slave. Yet again the wise medicine men prevailed. Siena and the wonderful shooting stick would be the salvation of the Crees. Baroma, muttering deep in his throat like distant thunder, gave sentence to starve Siena until he volunteered to go forth and hunt, or let him be the first to die.

The last scraps of meat, except a little hoarded in Baroma's lodge, were devoured, and then began the boiling of bones and skins to make a soup to sustain life. The cold days passed and a silent gloom pervaded the camp. Sometimes a cry of a bereaved mother, mourning for a starved child, wailed through the darkness. Siena's people, long used to starvation, did not suffer or grow weak so soon as the Crees. They were of hardier frame, and they were upheld by faith in their chief. When he would sicken it would be time for them to despair. But Siena walked erect as in the days of his freedom, nor did he stagger under the loads of firewood, and there was a light on his face. The Crees, knowing of Baroma's order that Siena should be the first to perish of starvation, gazed at the slave first in awe, then in fear. The last of the Sienas was succoured by the spirits.

But god-chosen though Siena deemed himself, he knew it was not by the spirits that he was fed in this time of famine. At night in the dead stillness, when even no mourning of wolf came over the frozen wilderness, Siena lay in his brush tepee close and warm under his blanket. The wind was faint and low, yet still it brought the old familiar voices. And it bore another sound – the soft fall of a moccasin on the snow. A shadow passed between Siena's eyes and the pale light.

"Emihiyah comes," whispered the shadow and knelt over him.

She tendered a slice of meat which she had stolen from Baroma's scanty hoard as he muttered and growled in uneasy slumber. Every night since her father's order to starve Siena, Emihiyah had made this perilous errand.

And now her hand sought his and her dusky hair swept his brow. "Emihiyah is faithful," she breathed low.

"Siena only waits," he replied.

She kissed him and stole away.

Cruel days fell upon the Crees, before Baroma's pride was broken. Many children died and some of the mothers were beyond help. Siena's people kept their strength, and he himself showed no effect of hunger. Long ago the Cree women had deemed him superhuman, that the Great Spirit fed him from the happy hunting grounds.

At last Baroma went to Siena. "Siena may save his people and the Crees."

Siena regarded him long, then replied: "Siena waits."

"Let Baroma know. What does Siena wait for? While he waits we die."

Siena smiled his slow, inscrutable smile and turned away.

Baroma sent for his daughter and ordered her to plead for her life.

Emihiyah came, fragile as a swaying reed, more beautiful than a rose choked in a tangled thicket, and she stood before Siena with doe eyes veiled. "Emihiyah begs Siena to save her and the tribe of Crees."

"Siena waits," replied the slave.

Baroma roared his fury and bade his braves lash the slave. But the blows fell from feeble arms and Siena laughed at his captors.

Then, like a wild lion unleashed from long thrall, he turned upon them: "Starve! Cree dogs! Starve! When the

Crees all fall like leaves in autumn, then Siena and his people will go back to the north."

Baroma's arrogance left him then, and on another day, when Emihiyah lay weak and palid in his wigwam and the pangs of hunger gnawed at his own vitals, he again sought Siena. "Let Siena tell for what he waits."

Siena rose to his lofty height and the leaping flame of the Northern Light gathered in his eyes. "Freedom!" One word he spoke and it rolled away on the wind.

"Baroma yields," replied the Cree, and hung his head.

"Send the squaws who can walk and the braves who can crawl out upon Siena's trail."

Then Siena went to Baroma's lodge and took up the wonderful shooting stick and, loading it, he set out upon snowshoes into the white forest. He knew where to find the moose yards in the sheltered corners. He heard the bulls pounding the hard-packed snow and cracking their antlers on the trees. The wary beasts would not have allowed him to steal close, as a warrior armed with a bow must have done, but Siena fired into the herd at long range. And when they dashed off, sending the snow up like a spray, a huge black bull lay dead. Siena followed them as they floundered through the drifts, and whenever he came within range he shot again. When five moose were killed he turned upon his trail to find almost the whole Cree tribe had followed him and were tearing the meat and crying out in a kind of crazy joy. That night the fires burned before the wigwams, the earthen pots steamed and there was great rejoicing. Siena hunted the next day, and the next, and for ten days he went into the white forest with his wonderful shooting stick, and eighty moose fell to his unerring aim.

The famine was broken and the Crees were saved.

When the mad dances ended and the feasts were over, Siena appeared before Baroma's lodge. "Siena will lead his people northward."

Baroma, starving, was a different chief from Baroma well fed and in no pain. All his cunning had returned. "Siena goes free. Baroma gave his word. But Siena's people remain slaves."

"Siena demanded freedom for himself and his people," said the younger chief.

"Baroma heard no word of Siena's tribe. He would not have granted freedom for them. Siena's freedom was enough."

"The Cree twists the truth. He knows Siena would not go without his people. Siena might have remembered Baroma's cunning. The Crees were ever liars."

Baroma stalked before his fire with haughty presence. About him in the circle of light sat his medicine men, his braves and squaws. "The Cree is kind. He gave his word. Siena is free. Let him take his wonderful shooting stick and go back to the north."

Siena laid the shooting stick at Baroma's feet and likewise the powder horn and bullet pouch. Then he folded his arms, and his falcon eyes looked far beyond Baroma to the land of the changing lights and the old home on the green-white, rushing Athabasca, god-forsaken river. "Siena stays."

Baroma started in amazement and anger. "Siena makes Baroma's word idle. Begone!"

"Siena stays!"

The look of Siena, the pealing reply, for a moment held the chief mute. Slowly Baroma stretched wide his arms and lifted them, while from his face flashed a sullen wonder. "Great Slave!" he thundered.

So was respect forced from the soul of the Cree, and the name thus wrung from his jealous heart was one to live for ever in the lives and legends of Siena's people.

Baroma sought the silence of his lodge, and his medicine men and braves dispersed, leaving Siena standing in the circle, a magnificent statue facing the steely north.

* * *

From that day insult was never offered to Siena, nor word spoken to him by the Crees, nor work given. He was free to come and go where he willed, and he spent his time in lessening the tasks of his people.

The trails of the forest were always open to him, as were the streets of the Cree village. If a brave met him, it was to step aside; if a squaw met him, it was to bow her head; if a chief met him, it was to face him as warriors faced warriors.

One twilight Emihiyah crossed his path, and suddenly she stood as once before, like a frail reed about to break in the wind. But Siena passed on. The days went by and each one brought less labour to Siena's people, until that one came wherein there was no task save what they set themselves. Siena's tribe were slaves, yet not slaves.

The winter wore by and the spring and the autumn, and again Siena's fame went abroad on the four winds. The Chippewayans journeyed from afar to see the Great Slave, and likewise the Blackfeet and the Yellow Knives. Honour would have been added to fame; councils called; overtures made to the sombre Baroma on behalf of the Great Slave, but Siena passed to and fro among his people, silent and cold to all others, true to the place which his great foe had given him. Captive to a lesser chief, they said; the Great Slave who would yet free his tribe and gather to him a new and powerful nation.

Once in the late autumn Siena sat brooding in the twilight by Ema's tepee. That night all who came near him were silent. Again Siena was listening to voices on the wind, voices that had been still for long, which he had tried to forget. It was the north wind, and it whipped the spruces and moaned through the pines. In its cold breath it bore a message to Siena, a hint of coming winter and a call from Naza, far north of the green-white, thundering Athabasca, river without a spirit.

In the darkness when the camp slumbered Siena faced the steely north. As he looked a golden shaft, arrow-shaped and arrow-swift, shot to the zenith.

"Naza!" he whispered to the winds. "Siena watches."

Then the gleaming, changing Northern Lights painted a picture of gold and silver bars, of flushes pink as shell, of opal fire and sunset red; and it was a picture of Siena's life from the moment the rushing Athabasca rumbled his name, to the far distant time when he would say farewell to his great nation and pass for ever to the retreat of the winds. God-chosen he was, and had power to read the story in the sky.

Seven nights Siena watched in the darkness; and on the seventh night, when the golden flare and silver shafts faded in the north, he passed from tepee to tepee, awakening his people. "When Siena's people hear the sound of the shooting stick let them cry greatly: Siena kills Baroma! Siena kills Baroma!"

With noiseless stride Siena went among the wigwams and along the lanes until he reached Baroma's lodge. Entering the dark he groped with his hands upward to a moose's antlers and found the shooting stick. Outside he fired it into the air.

Like a lightning bolt the report ripped asunder the silence, and the echoes clapped and reclapped from the cliffs. Sharp on the dying echoes Siena bellowed his war whoop, and it was the second time in a hundred years for foes to hear that terrible, long-drawn cry.

Then followed the shrill yells of Siena's people: "Siena kills Baroma . . . Siena kills Baroma . . . Siena kills Baroma!"

The slumber of the Crees awoke to a babel of many voices; it rose hoarsely on the night air, swelled hideously into a deafening roar that shook the earth.

In this din of confusion and terror when the Crees were lamenting the supposed death of Baroma and screaming in each other's ears, "The Great Slave takes his freedom!" Siena ran to his people and, pointing to the north, drove them before him.

Single file, like a long line of flitting spectres, they passed out of the fields into the forest. Siena kept close on their trail, ever looking backward, and ready with the shooting stick.

The roar of the stricken Crees softened in his ears and at last died away.

Under the black canopy of whispering leaves, over the grey, mist-shrouded muskeg flats, around the glimmering reed-bordered ponds, Siena drove his people.

All night Siena hurried them northward and with every stride his heart beat higher. Only he was troubled by a sound like a voice that came to him on the wind.

But the wind was now blowing in his face, and the sound appeared to be at his back. It followed on his trail as had the step of destiny. When he strained his ears he could not hear it, yet when he had gone on swiftly, persuaded it was only fancy, then the voice that was not a voice came haunting him.

In the grey dawn Siena halted on the far side of a grey flat and peered through the mists on his back trail. Something moved out among the shadows, a grey shape that crept slowly, uttering a mournful cry.

"Siena is trailed by a wolf," muttered the chief.

Yet he waited, and saw that the wolf was an Indian. He raised the fatal shooting stick.

As the Indian staggered forward, Siena recognised the robe of silver fox and marten, his gift to Emihiyah. He laughed in mockery. It was a Cree trick. Tillimanqua had led the pursuit disguised in his sister's robe. Baroma would find his son dead on the Great Slave's trail.

"Siena!" came the strange, low cry.

It was the cry that had haunted him like the voice on the wind. He leaped as a bounding deer.

Out of the grey fog burned dusky eyes half veiled by dusky hair, and little hands that he knew wavered as fluttering leaves. "Emihiyah comes," she said.

"Siena waits," he replied.

Far to the northward he led his bride and his people, far beyond the old home on the green-white, thundering Athabasca, god-forsaken river; and there, on the lonely shores of an inland sea, he fathered the Great Slave Tribe.

# THE VIRGINIAN

(Paramount, 1946)
Starring: Joel McCrea, Brian Donlevy
& Sonny Tufts
Directed by Victor Fleming
Story 'Happy-Teeth' by Owen Wister

*The Virginian* by Owen Wister may well be the most filmed and televised of all Western novels. Published in 1902, the story of the bloody struggle between some ranchers and a band of rustlers and the mysterious horseman who comes to their assistance was first brought to the cinema screen in 1914 with Dustin Farnum, then in 1930 with the young Gary Cooper in an early role and again in 1946 with Joel McCrea as the eponymous Virginian. Almost twenty years later, NBC turned *The Virginian* into a highly successful TV series which ran for seven seasons and seventy-four episodes starring James Drury, with Doug McClure as his friend Trampas, and Charles Bickford (later Lee J. Cobb) as the judge. Many leading actors guested in the series – including George C. Scott, Robert Redford and Charles Bronson – which later inspired a twenty-four-part sequel, *The Men from Shiloh* (1970), in which Stewart Granger joined James Drury and Doug McClure.

Although little remembered today, Owen Wister (1860–1938) has a place of honour in the history of Western fiction because of the remarkable success of *The Virginian* – subtitled 'A Horseman of the Plains' – which was heaped with praise by critics on both sides of the Atlantic when it

**was first published. Among the most lauditory reviews was that of W. L. Courtney in the *Daily Telegraph*, who called the book 'a remarkable piece of work' and described the hero as 'a man so real and vital, so throbbing with the red blood in his veins, that we should recognise him if we ever had the good fortune to meet him'. Some praise for a novel in the genre usually ignored by the press! Wister was born in Philadelphia and studied music at Havard before suffering a nervous breakdown and being sent to the West to improve his health. The memories of that time never left him and later inspired his first short stories, followed by *The Virginian* – in all of which he portrayed his cowboy heroes as knight-errant characters fighting the forces of lawlessness and moral degeneration. The following story, 'Happy-Teeth', is particularly significant in that it was first published in 1901 and marks the debut in print of 'The Virginian' who, a year later, would become the hero of a classic novel and thereafter one of the most enduring characters in both films and on TV . . .**

Scipio Le Moyne lay in bed, held together with bandages. His body had need for many bandages. A Bar-Circle-Zee three-year-old had done him violent mischief at the forks of Stinking Water. But for the fence, Scipio might have swung clear of the wild, rearing animal. When they lifted his wrecked frame from the ground, one of them had said: "A spade's all he'll need now."

Overhearing this with some still unconquered piece of his mind, Scipio made one last remark: "I ain't going to die for years and years."

Upon this his head had rolled over, and no further statements came from him for – I forget how long. Yet somehow, we all believed that last remark of his.

"Since I've known him," said the Virginian, "I have found him a truthful man."

"Which don't mean," Honey Wiggin put in, "that he can't lie when he ought to."

Judge Henry always sent his hurt cowpunchers to the nearest surgical aid, which in this case was the hospital on the reservation. Here then, one afternoon, Scipio lay, his body still bound tight at a number of places, but his brain needing no bandages whatever; he was able to see one friend for a little while each day. It was almost time for this day's visitor to go, and the visitor looked at his watch.

"Oh, don't do that!" pleaded the man in bed. "I'm not sick any more."

"You will be sick some more if you keep talking," replied the Virginian.

"Thinkin' is a heap more dangerous, if y'u can't let it out," Scipio urged. "I'm not half through tellin' y'u about Horacles."

"Did his mother name him that?" enquired the Virginian.

"Naw! but his mother brought it on him. Didn't y'u know? Of course you don't often get so far north in the Basin as the Agency. His name is Horace Pericles Byram. Well, the Agent wasn't going to call his assistant store-clerk all that, y'u know, not even if he *has* got an uncle in the Senate of the United States. Couldn't spare the time. Days not long enough. Not even in June. So everybody calls him Horacles now. He's reconciled to it. But I ain't. It's too good for him. A heap too good. I've knowed him all my life, and I can't think of a name that's not less foolish than he is. Well, where was I? I was tellin' y'u how back in Gallipo*leece* he couldn't understand anything. Not dogs. Not horses. Not girls."

"Do you understand girls?" the Virginian interrupted.

"Better'n Horacles. Well, now it seems he can't understand Indians. Here he is sellin' goods to 'em across the counter at the Agency store. I could sell twiced what he does, from what they tell me. I guess the Agent has begun to discover what a trick the Uncle played him when he unloaded Horacles on him. Now why did the Uncle do that?"

Scipio stopped in his rambling discourse, and his brows knitted as he began to think about the Uncle. The Virginian once again looked at his watch, but Scipio, deep in his thoughts, did not notice him. "Uncle," he resumed to himself, half aloud, "Uncle was the damnedest scoundrel in Gallipol*eece*. – Say!" he exclaimed suddenly, and made an eager movement to sit up. "Oh Lord!" he groaned, sinking back. "I forgot – what's your hurry?"

But the Virginian had seen the pain transfix his friend's face, and though that face had instantly smiled, it was white. He stood up. "I'd ought to get kicked from here to the ranch," he said, remorsefully. "I'll get the doctor."

Vainly the man in bed protested; his visitor was already at the door.

"I've not told y'u about his false teeth!" shrieked Scipio, hoping this would detain him. "And he does tricks with a rabbit and a bowl of fish."

But the guest was gone. In his place presently the Post surgeon came, and was not pleased. Indeed, this excellent army doctor swore. Still, it was not the first time that he had done so, nor did it prove the last; and Scipio, it soon appeared, had given himself no hurt. But in answer to a severe threat, he whined: "Oh, ain't y'u goin' to let me see him tomorro'?"

"You'll see nobody tomorrow except me."

"Well, that'll be seein' nobody," whined Scipio, more grievously.

The doctor grinned. "In some ways you're incurable. Better go to sleep now." And he left him.

Scipio did not go to sleep then, though by morning he had slept ten healthful hours, waking with the Uncle still at the centre of his thoughts. It made him again knit his brows.

"No, you can't see him today," said the doctor, in reply to a request.

"But I hadn't finished sayin' something to him," Scipio protested. "And I'm well enough to see my dead grandmother."

"That I'll not forbid," answered the doctor. And he added that the Virginian had gone back to Sunk Creek with some horses.

"Oh, yes," said Scipio. "I'd forgot. Well, he'll be coming through on his way to Billings next week. You been up to the Agency lately? Yesterday? Well, there's going to be something new happen. Agent seem worried or anything?"

"Not that I noticed. Are the Indians going on the warpath?"

"Nothing like that. But why does a senator of the United States put his nephew in that store? Y'u needn't to tell me it's to provide for him, for it don't provide. I thought I had it figured out last night, but Horacles don't fit. I can't make him fit. He don't understand Injuns. That's my trouble. Now the Uncle must know Horacles don't understand. But if he didn't know?" pursued Scipio, and fell to thinking.

"Well," said the doctor indulgently, as he rose, "it's good you can invent these romances. Keeps you from fretting, shut up here alone."

"There'd be no romances here," retorted Scipio. "Uncle is exclusively hard cash." The doctor departed.

At his visit next morning, he was pleased with his patient's condition. "Keep on," said he, "and I'll let you sit up Monday for ten minutes. Any more romances?"

"Been thinkin' of my past life," said Scipio.

The doctor laughed long. "Why, how old are you, anyhow?" he asked at length.

"Oh, there's some lovely years still to come before I'm thirty. But I've got a whole lot of past life, all the same." Then he pointed a solemn, oracular finger at the doctor. "What white man savvys the Injun? Not you. Not me. And I've drifted around some, too. The map of the United States has been my home. Been in Arizona and New Mexico and among the Siwashes – seen all kinds of Injun – but I don't savvy 'em. I know most any Injun's better'n most any white man till he meets the white man. Not smarter, y'u know, but better. And I do know this: you take an Injun and let him be a warrior and a chief and a grandfather who has killed heaps of white men in his day – but all that don't make him grown up. Not like we're grown up. He stays a child in some respects till he's dead. He'll believe things and be scared at things that ain't nothin' to you and me. You take Old High Bear right on this reservation. He's got hair like snow and eyes like an eagle's and he can sing a war-song about fights that happened when our fathers were kids. But if you want to deal with him, you got to remember he's a child of five."

"I do know all this," said the doctor, interested. "I've not been twenty years on the frontier for nothing."

"Horacles don't know it," said Scipio. "I've saw him in the store all season."

"Well," said the doctor, "see you tomorrow. I've some new patients in the ward."

"Soldiers?"

"Soldiers."

"Guess I know why they're here."

"Oh, yes," sighed the doctor. "You know. Few come here for any other reason." The doctor held views about how a military post should be regulated, which popular sentiment will never share. "Can I do anything for you?" he inquired.

"If I could have some newspapers?" said Scipio.

"Why didn't you tell me before?" said the doctor. After that he saw to it that Scipio had them liberally.

With newspapers the patient sat surrounded deep, when the Virginian, passing north on his way to Billings, looked in for a moment to give his friend the good word. That is what he came for, but what he said was: "So he has got false teeth?"

Scipio, hearing the voice at the door, looked over the top of his paper at the visitor.

"Yes," he replied, precisely as if the visitor had never been out of the room.

"What d' y'u know?" inquired the Virginian.

"Nothing; what do you?"

"Nothing."

After all, such brief greetings cover the ground.

"Better sit down," suggested Scipio.

The Virginian sat, and took up a paper. Thus for a little while they both read in silence.

"Did y'u stop at the Agency as y'u came along?" asked Scipio, not looking up from his paper.

"No."

There was silence again as they continued reading. The Virginian, just come from Sunk Creek, had seen no newspapers as recent as these. When two friends on meeting after absence can sit together for half an hour without a word passing between them, it is proof that they really enjoy each other's company. The gentle air came in the window, bringing the tonic odour of the sage-brush. Outside the window stretched a yellow world to distant golden hills. The talkative voice of a magpie somewhere near at hand was the only sound.

"Nothing in the newspapers in particular," said Scipio, finally.

"You expaictin' something particular?" the Virginian asked.

"Yes."

"Mind sayin' what it is?"

"Wish I knew what it is."

"Always Horacles?"

"Always him – and Uncle. I'd like to spot Uncle."

Mess call sounded from the parade ground. It recalled the flight of time to the Virginian.

"When you get back from Billings," said Scipio, "you're liable to find me up and around."

"Hope so. Maybe you'll be well enough to go with me to the ranch."

But when the Virginian returned, a great deal had happened all at once, as is the custom of events.

Scipio's vigorous convalescence brought him in the next few days to sitting about in the open air, and then enlarged his freedom to a crutch. He hobbled hither and yon, paying visits, many of them to the doctor. The doctor it was, and no newspaper, who gave to Scipio the first grain of that 'something particular' which he had been daily seeking and never found. He mentioned a new building that was being put up rather far away down in the corner of the reservation. The rumor in the air was that it had something to do with the Quartermaster's department. The odd thing was that the Quartermaster himself had heard nothing about it. The Agent up at the Agency store considered this extremely odd. But a profound absence of further explanations seemed to prevail. What possible need for a building was there at that inconvenient, isolated spot?

Scipio slapped his leg. "I guess what y'u call my romance is about to start."

"Well," the doctor admitted, "it may be. Curious things are done upon Indian reservations. Our management of them may be likened to putting the Lord's Prayer and the Ten Commandments into a bag and crushing them to powder. Let our statesmen at Washington get their hands on an Indian reservation, and not even honour among thieves remains."

"Say, doc," said Scipio, "when d' y'u guess I can get off?"

"Don't be in too much of a hurry," the doctor cautioned him. "If you go to Sunk Creek – "

"Sunk Creek! I only want to go to the Agency."

"Oh, well, you could do that today – but don't you want to see the entertainment? Conjuring tricks are promised."

"I want to see Horacles."

"But he is the entertainment. Supper comes after he's through."

Scipio stayed. He was not repaid, he thought. "A poor show," was his comment as he went to bed. He came later to be very glad indeed that he had gone to that entertainment.

The next day found him seated in the Agency store, being warmly greeted by his friends the Indians. They knew him well; perhaps he understood them better than he had said. By Horacles he was not warmly greeted; perhaps Horacles did not wish to be understood – and then, Scipio, in his comings and goings through the reservation, had played with Horacles for the benefit of bystanders. There is no doubt whatever that Horacles did not understand Scipio. He was sorry to notice how the Agent, his employer, shook Scipio's hand and invited him to come and stop with him till he was fit to return to his work. And Scipio accepted this invitation. He sat him down in the store, and made himself at home. Legs stretched out on one chair, crutch within reach, hands comfortably clasped round the arms of the chair he sat in, head tilted back, eyes apparently studying the goods which hung from the beams overhead, he visibly sniffed the air.

"Smell anything you don't like?" enquired the clerk, tartly – and unwisely.

"Nothin' except you, Horacles," was the perfectly amiable rejoinder. "It's good," Scipio then confessed, "to be smellin' buckskin and leather and groceries instead of ether and iodoform."

"Guess you were pretty sick," observed the clerk, with relish.

"Yes. Oh, yes. I was pretty sick. That's right. Yes." Scipio had continued through these slowly drawled remarks to look at the ceiling. Then his glance dropped to the level of Horacles, and keenly fixed that unconscious youth's plump little form, pink little face and mean little mustache. Behind one ear stuck a pen, behind the other a pencil, as the assistant clerk was arranging some tins of Arbuckle's Arioso coffee. Then Scipio took aim and fired: "So you're going to quit your job?"

Horacles whirled round. "Who says so?"

The chance shot – if there ever is such a thing, if such shots are not always the result of visions and perceptions which lie beyond our present knowledge – this chance shot had hit.

"First I've heard of it," then said Horacles, sulkily. "Guess you're delirious still." He returned to his coffee, and life grew more interesting than ever to Scipio.

Instead of trickling back, health began to rush back into his long imprisoned body, and though he could not fully use it yet, and though if he hobbled a hundred yards he was compelled to rest it, his wiry mind knew no fatigue. How athletic his brains were was easily perceived by the Indian Agent. The convalescent would hobble over to the store after breakfast and hail the assistant clerk at once. "Morning, Horacles," he would begin; "how's Uncle?" – "Oh, when are you going to give us a new joke?" the worried Horacles would retort. – "Just as soon as you give us a new Uncle, Horacles. Or any other relation to make us feel proud we know you. What did his letter last night say?" The second or third time this had been asked still found Horacles with no better repartee than angry silence. "Didn't he send me his love?" Scipio then said; and still the hapless Horacles said nothing. "Well, y'u give him mine when you write him this afternoon." – "I ain't writing this afternoon," snapped the clerk. – "You're not! Why, I thought you wrote each other every day!" This was so near the truth that Horacles flared out: "I'd be ashamed if I'd nothing better to do than spy on other people's mails."

Thus by dinner time generally an audience would be gathered round Scipio where he sat with his legs on the chair, and Horacles over his ledger would be furiously muttering that "Some day they would all see."

Horacles asked for a couple of days' holiday, and got it. He wished to hunt, he said. But the Agent happened to find that he had been to the railroad about some freight. This he mentioned to Scipio. "I don't know what he's up to," he said. He had found that worrying Horacles was merely one of the things that Scipio's brains were good for; Scipio had advised him prudently about a sale of beeves, and had introduced a simple contrivance for luring to the store the customers whom Horacles failed to attract. It was merely a free lunch counter – cheese and crackers every day, and deviled ham on pay-day – but it put up the daily receipts.

And next, one evening after the mail was in, Scipio, sitting alone in the front of the store, saw the Agent, sitting alone in the back of the store, spring suddenly from his chair, crush a newspaper into his pocket, and stride out to his house. At breakfast the Agent spoke thus to Scipio: "I must go to Washington. I shall be back before they let you and your leg run loose. Will you do something for me?"

"Name it. Just name it."

"Run the store while I'm gone."

"D' y'u think I can?"

"I know you can. There'll be no trouble under you. You understand Indians."

"But suppose something turns up?"

"I don't think anything will before I'm back. I'd sooner leave you than Horacles in charge here. Will you do it and take two dollars a day?"

"Do it for nothing. Horacles'll be compensation enough."

"No, he won't – and see here, he can't help being himself."

"Enough said. I'll strive to pity him. None of us was consulted about being born. And I'll keep remembering that we was both raised at Gallipol*eece*, Ohio, and that he inherited a bigger outrage of a name than I did. That's what comes of havin' a French ancestor – only, he used to steal my lunch at school." And Scipio's bleached blue eye grew cold. Later injuries one may forgive, but school ones never.

"Didn't you whale him?" asked the Agent.

"Every time," said Scipio, "till he told Uncle. Uncle was mayor of Gallipol*eece* then. So I wasn't ready to get expelled – I got ready later; nothin' is easier than gettin' expelled – but I locked up my lunch after that."

"Uncle's pretty good to him," muttered the Agent. "Got him this position – well, nobody will expel you here. Look after things. I'll feel easy to think you're on hand."

For that newspaper which the Agent had crushed into his pocket, Scipio searched cracks and corners, but searched in vain. A fear quite unreasoning possessed him for a while: could he but learn what was in the paper that had so stirred his patron, perhaps he could avert whatever the thing was that he felt in the air, threatening some sort of injury. He knew himself resourceful. Dislike of Horacles and Uncle had been enough to start his wish to thwart them – if there was anything to thwart; but now pride and gratitude fired him; he had been trusted; he cared more to be trusted than for anything on earth; he must rise equal to it now! The Agent had evidently taken the paper away with him – and so Scipio absurdly read all the papers. He collected old ones, and laid his hands upon the new the moment they were out of the mailbag. It may be said that he lived daily in a wrapping of newspapers.

"Why, you have got Horacles laughing at you."

This the observant Virginian pointed out to Scipio immediately on his arrival from Billings. Scipio turned a sickened look upon his friend. The look was accompanied by a cold wave in his stomach.

"Y'u cert'nly have," the remorseless friend pursued. "I reckon he must have had a plumb happy time watchin' y'u still-hunt them newspapers. Now who'd ever have foretold you would afford Horacles enjoyment?"

In a weak voice Scipio essayed to fight it off. "Don't you try to hoodwink me with any of your frog lies."

"No need," said the Virginian. "From the door as I came in I saw him at his desk lookin' at y'u easy-like. 'Twas a right quaint pictyeh – him smilin' at the desk, and your nose tight agaynst the Omaha *Bee*. I thought first y'u didn't have a handkerchief."

"I wonder if he has me beat?" muttered poor Scipio.

The Virginian now had a word of consolation. "Don't y'u see," he again pointed out, "that no newspaper could have helped you? If it could why did he go away to Washington without tellin' you? He don't look for you to deal with troubles he don't mention to you."

"I wonder if Horacles has me beat?" said Scipio once more.

The Virginian standing by the seated, brooding man clapped him twice on the shoulders, gently. It was enough. They were very fast friends.

"I know," said Scipio in response. "Thank y'u. But I'd hate for him to have me beat."

It was the doctor who now furnished information that would have relieved any reasonable man from a sense of failure. The doctor was excited because his view of our faith in Indian matters was again justified by a further instance.

"Oh, yes! he said. "Just give those people at Washington time, and every step they've taken from the start will be in the mud puddle of a lie. Uncle's in the game all right. He's been meditating how to serve his country and increase his income. There's a railroad at the big end of his notion, but the entering wedge seems only to be a new store down in the corner of this reservation. You see, it has been long settled by the sacredest compacts that two stores shall be enough here – the Post-trader's and the Agent's – but the dear Indians need a third, Uncle says. He has told the Senate and the Interior Department and the White House that a lot of them have to travel too far for supplies. So now Washington is sure the Indians need a third store. The Post-trader and the Agent are stopping at the Post tonight. They got East too late to hold up the job. If Horacles opens that new store, the Agent might just as well shut up his own."

"Ain't y'u going to look at my leg?" was all the reply that Scipio made.

The doctor laughed. It was to examine the leg that he had come, and he had forgotten all about it. "You can forget all about it, too," he told Scipio when he had finished. "Go back to Sunk Creek when you like. Go back to full work next week, say. Your wicked body is sound again. A better man would unquestionably have died."

But the cheery doctor could not cheer the unreasonable Scipio. In the morning the complacent little Horacles made known to all the world his perfected arrangements. Directly the Agent had safely turned his back and gone to Washington, his disloyal clerk had become doubly busy. He had at once perceived that this was a comfortable time for him to hurry his new rival store into readiness and be securely established behind its counter before his betrayed employer should return. In this last he might not quite succeed; the Agent had come back a day or two sooner than Horacles had calculated, but it was a trifle; after all, he had carried through the small part of his uncle's scheme which he had been sent here to do. Inside that building in the far corner of the reservation, once rumoured to be connected with the Quartermaster's department, he would now sell luxuries and necessities to the Indians at a price cheaper than his employer's, and his employer's store would henceforth be empty of customers. Perhaps the sweetest moment that Horacles had known for many weeks was when he said to Scipio: "I'm writing Uncle about it today."

That this should have gone on under his nose while he sat searching the papers was to Scipio utterly unbearable. His mind was in a turmoil, feeling about helplessly but furiously for vengeance; and the Virginian's sane question – What could he have done to stop it if he had discovered it? – comforted him not at all. They were outside the store, sitting under a tree, waiting for the returning Agent to appear. But he did not come, and the suspense added to Scipio's wretchedness.

"He put me in charge," he kept repeating.

"The driver ain't responsible when a stage is held up," reasoned the Virginian.

Scipio hardly heard him. "He put me in charge," he said. Then he worked round to Horacles again. "He ain't got strength. He ain't got beauty. He ain't got riches. He ain't got brains. He's just got sense enough for parlour conjuring tricks – not good ones, either. And yet he has me beat."

"He's got an uncle in the Senate," said the Virginian.

The disconsolate Scipio took a pull at his cigar – he had taken one between every sentence. "Damn his false teeth."

The Virginian looked grave. "Don't be hasty. Maybe the day will come when you and me'll need 'em to chew our tenderloin."

"We'll be old. Horacles is twenty-five."

"Twenty-five is certainly young to commence eatin' by machinery," admitted the Virginian.

"And he's proud of 'em," whined Scipio. "Proud! Opens his bone box and sticks 'em out at y'u on the end of his tongue."

"I hate an immodest man," said the Virginian.

"Why, he hadn't any better sense than to do it over to the officers' club right before the ladies and everybody the other night. The KO's wife said it gave her the creeps – and she don't look sensitive."

"Well," said the Virginian, "if I weighed three hundred pounds I'd be turrable sensitive."

"She had to leave," pursued Scipio. "Had to take her little girl away from the show. Them teeth comin' out of

Horacles's mouth the way they did sent the child into hysterics. Y'u could hear her screechin' halfway down the line."

The Virginian looked at his watch. "I wonder if that Agent is coming here at all today?"

Scipio's worried face darkened again. "What can I do? What *can* I?" he demanded. And he rose and limped up and down where the ponies were tied in front of the store. The fickle Indians would soon be tying these ponies in front of the rival store. "I received this business in good shape," continued Scipio, "and I'll hand it back in bad."

Horacles looked out of the door. He wore his hat tilted to make him look like the daredevil that he was not; daredevils seldom have soft pink hands, red eyelids and a fluffy mustache. He smiled at Scipio, and Scipio smiled at him, sweetly and dangerously.

"Would you mind keeping store while I'm off?" enquired Horacles.

"Sure not!" cried Scipio, with heartiness. "Goin' to have your grand opening this afternoon?"

"Well, I *was*," Horacles replied, enjoying himself every moment. "But Mr Forsythe" (this was the Agent) "can't get over from the Post in time to be present this afternoon. It's very kind of him to want to be present when I start my new enterprise, and I appreciate it, boys, I can tell you. So I sent him word I wouldn't think of opening without him, and it's to be tomorrow morning."

While Horacles was speaking thus, the Indians had gathered about to listen. It was plain that they understood that this was a white man's war; their great, grave, watching faces showed it. Young squaws, half-hooded in their shawls, looked on with bright eyes; a boy who had been sitting out on the steps playing a pipe, stopped his music, and came in; the aged Pounded Meat, wrapped in scarlet and shrunk with years to the appearance of a dried apple, watched with eyes that still had in them the primal fire of life; tall in a corner stood the silver-haired High Bear, watching too. Did they understand the white man's war lying behind the complacent smile of Horacles and the dangerous smile of the lounging Scipio? The red man is grave when war is in question; all the Indians were perfectly still.

"Wish you boys could be there to give me a good send-off," continued Horacles.

The pipe-playing Indian boy must have caught some flash of something beneath Scipio's smile, for his eye went to Scipio's pistol – but it returned to Scipio's face.

Horacles spoke on. "Fine line of fresh Eastern goods, dry goods, candies, and – hee-hee! – free lunch. Mr Le Moyne, I want to thank you publicly for that idea."

"Y'u're welcome to it. Guess I'll hardly be over tomorrow, though. With such a competitor as you, I expect I'll have to stay with my job and hustle."

"Ah, well," simpered Horacles, "I couldn't have done it by myself. My Uncle – say, boys!" (Horacles in the elation of victory now melted to pure goodwill) "Do come see me tomorrow. It's all business, this, you know. There's no hard feelings?"

The pipe boy couldn't help looking at the pistol again.

"Not a feeling!" cried Scipio. And he clapped Horacles between his little round shoulders. With head on one side, he looked down along his lengthy, jocular nose at Horacles for a moment. Then his eye shone upon the company like the edge of a knife – and they laughed at him because he was laughing so contagiously at them; a soft laugh, like the fall of moccasins. Often the Indian will join, like a child, in mirth which he does not comprehend. High Bear's smile shone from his corner at young Scipio, whom he fancied so much that he had offered him his fourteenth daughter to wed as soon as his leg should be well. But Scipio had sorrowfully explained to the father that he was already married – which was true, but which I fear would in former days have proved no impediment to him. Perhaps some day I may tell you of the early marriages of Scipio as Scipio in hospital narrated them to me.

"Hey!" said High Bear now, to Scipio. "New store. Pretty good. Heap cheap."

"Yes, High Bear. Heap cheap. You savvy why?"

With a long arm and an outstretched finger, Scipio suddenly pointed to Horacles. At this the Virginian's hitherto unchanging face wakened to curiosity and attention. Scipio was now impressively and mysteriously nodding at the silver-haired chief in his bright, green blanket, and his long, fringed, yellow, soft buckskins.

"No savvy," said High Bear, after a pause, with a tinge of caution. He had followed Scipio's pointing finger to where Horacles was happily practising a trick with a glass and a silver dollar behind the counter.

"Heap cheap," repeated Scipio, "because" (here he leaned close to High Bear and whispered) "because his uncle medicine-man. He big medicine-man, too."

High Bear's eyes rested for a moment on Horacles. Then he shook his head. "Ah, nah," he grunted. "He not medicine-man. He fall off horse. He no catch horse. My little girl catch him. Ah, nah!" High Bear laughed profusely at 'Sippo's' joke. 'Sippo' was the Indians' English name for their vivacious friend. In their own language they called him something complimentary in several syllables, but it was altogether too intimate and too plain-spoken for me to repeat aloud. Into his whisper Scipio now put more electricity. "He's big medicine-man," he hissed again, and he drilled his bleached blue eye into the brown one of the savage. "See him now!" He stretched out a vibrating finger.

It was a pack of cards that Horacles was lightly manipulating. He fluttered it open in the air and fluttered it shut again, drawing it out like a concertina and pushing it flat like an opera hat – nor did a card fall to the ground.

High Bear watched it hard; but soon High Bear laughed. "He pretty good," he declared. "All same tin-horn monte-man. I see one Miles City."

"Maybe monte-man medicine-man too," suggested Scipio.

"Ah, nah!" said High Bear. Yet nevertheless Scipio saw him shoot one or two more doubtful glances at Horacles as that happy clerk continued his activities.

Horacles had an audience (which he liked), and he held his audience – and who could help liking that? The bucks and squaws watched him, sometimes nudging one another, and they smiled and grunted their satisfaction at his news. Cheaper prices was something which their primitive minds could take in as well as any of us.

"Why you not sell cheap like him?" they asked their friend 'Sippo'. "We stay then. Not go his store." This was the burden of their chorus, soft, laughing, a little mocking, floating among them like a breeze, voice after voice:

"We like buy everything you, we like buy everything cheap."

"You make cheap, we buy heap shirts."

"Buy heap tobacco."

"Heap cartridge."

"You not sell cheap, we go."

"Ah!"

The chorus laughed like pleased children.

Scipio looked at them solemnly. He explained how much he would like to sell cheap, if only he were a medicine-man like Horacles.

"You medicine-man?" they asked the assistant clerk.

"Yes," said Horacles, pleased. "I big medicine-man."

"Ah, nah!" The soft, mocking words ran among them like the flight of a moth.

Soon with their hoods over their heads they began to go home on their ponies, blanketed, feathered, many-coloured, moving and dispersing wide across the sage-brush to their far-scattered tepees.

High Bear lingered last. For a long while he had been standing silent and motionless. When the chorus spoke he had not; when the chorus laughed he had not. Now his head moved; he looked about him and saw that for a moment he was alone in a way. He saw the Virginian reading a newspaper, and his friend 'Sippo' bending down and attending to his leg. Horacles had gone into an inner room. Left on the counter lay the pack of cards. High Bear went quickly to the cards, touched them, lifted them, set them down and looked about him again. But the Virginian was reading still, and Scipio was still bent down, having some trouble with his boot. High Bear looked at the cards, shook his head sceptically, laughed a little, grunted once, and went out where his pony was tied. As he was throwing his soft buckskin leg over the saddle, there was Scipio's head thrust out of the door and nodding strangely at him.

"Goodnight, High Bear. He big medicine-man."

High Bear gave a quick slash to his pony, and galloped away into the dusk.

Then Scipio limped back into the store, sank into the first chair he came to, and doubled over. The Virginian looked up from his paper at this mirth, scowled, and turned back to his reading. If he was to be 'left out' of the joke, he would make it plain that he was not in the least interested in it.

Scipio now sat up straight, bursting to share what was in his mind; but he instantly perceived how it was with the Virginian. At this he redoubled his silent symptoms of delight. In a moment Horacles had come back from the inner room with his hair wet with ornamental brushing.

"Well, Horacles," began Scipio in the voice of a purring cat, "I expect y'u have me beat."

The flattered clerk could only nod and show his bright, false teeth.

"Y'u have me beat," repeated Scipio. "Y'u have for a fact."

"Not you, Mr Le Moyne. It's not you I'm making war on. I do hope there's no hard feelings – "

"Not a feelin', Horacles! How can y'u entertain such an idea?" Scipio shook him by the hand and smiled like an angel at him – a fallen angel. "What's the use of me keepin' this store open tomorrow? Nobody'll be here to spend a cent. Guess I'll shut up, Horacles, and come watch the Injuns all shoppin' like Christmas over to your place."

The Virginian sustained his indifference, and added to Scipio's pleasure. But during breakfast the Virginian broke down.

"Reckon you're ready to start today?" he said.

"Start? Where for?"

"Sunk Creek, y'u fool! Where else?"

"I'm beyond y'u! I'm sure beyond y'u for once!" screeched Scipio, beating his crutch on the floor.

"Oh, eat your grub, y'u fool."

"I'd have told y'u last night," said Scipio, remorselessly, "only y'u were so awful anxious not to *be* told."

As the Virginian drove him across the sage-brush, not to Sunk Creek, but to the new store, the suspense was once more too much for the Southerner's curiosity. He pulled up the horses as the inspiration struck him.

"You're going to tell the Indians you'll undersell him!" he declared, over-hastily.

"Oh, drive on, y'u fool," said Scipio.

The baffled Virginian grinned. "I'll throw you out," he said, "and break all your laigs and bones and things fresh."

"I wish Uncle was going to be there," said Scipio.

Nearly everybody else was there: the Agent, bearing his ill fortune like a philosopher, some officers from the Post, and the doctor; some enlisted men, blue-legged with yellow stripes; civilians male and female, honourable and shady; and then the Indians. Wagons were drawn up, ponies stood about, the littered plain was populous. Horacles moved behind the counter, busy and happy; his little mustache was combed, his ornamental hair was damp. He smiled and talked, and handled and displayed his abundance: the bright calicoes, the shining knives, the clean six-shooters and rifles, the bridles, the fishing-tackle, the gum-drops and chocolates – all his plenty and its cheapness.

Squaws and bucks young and old thronged his establishment, their soft footfalls and voices made a gentle continuous sound, while their green and yellow blankets bent and stood straight as they inspected and purchased. High Bear held an earthen crock with a luxury in it – a dozen of fresh eggs. "Hey!" he said when he saw his friend 'Sippo' enter. "Heap cheap." And he showed the eggs to Scipio. He cherished the crock with one hand and arm while with the other hand he helped himself to the free lunch.

To Scipio Horacles 'extended' a special welcome; he made it otentatious in order that all the world might know how perfectly absent 'hard feelings' were. And Scipio on his side wore openly the radiance of brotherhood and well-wishing. He went about admiring everything, exclaiming now and then over the excellence of the goods, or the cheapness of their price. His presence was soon no longer a cause of curiosity, and they forgot to watch him – all of them except the Virginian. The hours passed on, the little fires, where various noon meals were cooked, burnt out, satisfied individuals began to depart after an entertaining day, the Agent himself was sauntering toward his horse.

"What's your hurry?" said Scipio.

"Well, the show is over," said the Agent.

"Oh, no, it ain't. Horacles is goin' to entertain us a whole lot."

"Better stay," said the Virginian.

The Agent looked from one to the other. Then he spoke anxiously. "I don't want anything done to Horacles."

"Nothing will be done," stated Scipio.

The Agent stayed. The magnetic current of expectancy passed, none could say how, through the assembled people.

No one departed after this, and the mere loitering of spectators turned to waiting. Particularly expectant was the Virginian, and this he betrayed by mechanically droning in his strongest accent a little song that bore no reference to the present occasion:

> "Of all my fatheh's familee
>   I love myself the baist,
> And if Gawd will just look afteh me
>   The devil may take the raist."

The sun grew lower. The world outside was still full of light, but dimness had begun its subtle pervasion of the store. Horacles thanked the Indians and every one for their generous patronage on this his opening day, and intimated that it was time to close. Scipio rushed up and whispered to him: "My goodness, Horacles! You ain't going to send your friends home like that?"

Horacles was taken aback. "Why," he stammered, "what's wrong?"

"Where's your vanishing handkerchief, Horacles? Get it out and entertain 'em some. Show you're grateful. Where's that trick dollar? Get 'em quick – I tell you," he declaimed aloud to the Indians, "he big medicine-man. Make come. Make go. You no see. Nobody see. Make jack-rabbit in hat – "

"I couldn't tonight," simpered Horacles. "Needs preparation, you know." And he winked at Scipio.

Scipio struggled upon the counter, and stood up above their heads to finish his speech. "No jack-rabbit this time," he said.

"Ah, nah!" laughed the Indians. "No catch um."

"Yes, catch um any time. Catch anything. Make anything. Make all this store" – Scipio moved his arms about – "that's how make heap cheap. See that!" He stopped dramatically, and clasped his hands together. Horacles tossed a handkerchief in the air, caught it, shut his hand upon it with a kneading motion, and opened the hand empty. "His fingers swallow it, all same mouth!" shouted Scipio. "He big medicine-man. You see. Now other hand spit out." But Horacles varied the trick. Success and the staring crowd elated him; he was going to do his best. He opened both hands empty, felt about him in the air, clutched space suddenly, and drew two silver dollars from it. Then he threw them back into space, again felt about for them in the air, made a dive at High Bear's eggs, and brought handkerchief and dollars out of them.

"Ho!" went High Bear, catching his breath. He backed away from the reach of Horacles. He peered down into the crock among his eggs. Horacles whispered to Scipio: "Keep talking till I'm ready."

"Oh, I'll talk. Go get ready quick – High Bear, what I tell you?" But High Bear's eye was now fixedly watching the door through which Horacles had withdrawn; he did not listen as Scipio proceeded. "What I tell everybody? He do handkerchief. He do dollar. He do heap more. See me. I no can do like him. I not medicine-man. I throw handkerchief and dollar in the air, look! See! they tumble on floor no good – thank you, my kind noble friend from Virginia, you pick my fool dollar and my fool handkerchief up for me, *muy pronto*. Oh, thank you, blackhaired, green-eyed son of Dixie, you have the manners of a queen, but I no medicine-man, I shall never turn a skunk into a watermelon, I innocent, I young, I helpless babe, I suck bottle when I can get it. Fire and water will not obey me. Old man Makes-the-Thunder does not know my name and address. He spit on me Wednesday night last, and there are no dollars in this man's hair." (The Virginian winced beneath Scipio's vicious snatch at his scalp, and the Agent and the doctor retired to a dark corner and laid their heads in each other's waistcoats.) "Hal he comes! Big medicine-man comes. See him, High Bear! His father, his mother, his aunts all twins, he ninth dog-pup in three sets of triplets, and the great white Ram-of-the-Mountains fed him on punkin-seed – sick 'em, Horacles."

The burning eye of High Bear now blazed with distended fascination, riveted upon Horacles, whom it never left. Darkness was gathering in the store.

"Hand all same foot," shouted Scipio, with gestures, "mouth all same hand. Can eat fire. Can throw ear mile off and listen you talk." Here Horacles removed a dollar from the hair of High Bear's fourteenth daughter, threw it into one boot, and brought it out of the other. The daughter screamed and burrowed behind her sire. All the Indians had drawn close together, away from the counter, while Scipio on top of the counter talked high and low, and made gestures without ceasing. "Hand all same mouth. Foot all same head. Take off head, throw it out window, it jump in door. See him, see big medicine-man!" And Scipio gave a great shriek.

A gasp went among the Indians; red fire was blowing from the jaws of Horacles. It ceased, and after it came slowly, horribly, a long red tongue, and riding on the tongue's end glittered a row of teeth. There was a crash upon the floor. It was High Bear's crock. The old chief was gone. Out of the door he flew, his blanket over his face, and up on his horse he sprang, wildly beating the animal. Squaws and bucks flapped after him like poultry, rushing over the ground, leaping on their ponies, melting away into the dusk. In a moment no sign of them was left but the broken eggs, oozing about on the deserted floor.

The white men there stood tearful, dazed and weak with laughter.

"'Happy-Teeth' should be his name," said the Virginian. "It sounds Injun." And Happy-Teeth it was. But Horacles did not remain long in the neighbourhood after he realised what he had done; for never again did an Indian enter, or even come near, that den of flames and magic. They would not even ride past it; they circled it widely. The idle merchandise that filled it was at last bought by the Agent at a reduction.

"Well," said Scipio bashfully to the Agent, "I'd have sure hated to hand y'u back a ruined business. But he'll never understand Injuns."

# SHANE

(Paramount, 1953)
Starring: Alan Ladd, Van Heflin & Jean Arthur
Directed by George Stevens
Story 'One Man's Honour' by Jack Schaefer

***Shane* is an epic movie – some critics have called it the greatest Western of all time – but notwithstanding any arguments, it is certainly one of the most *satisfying* pictures whether or not you are a fan of the Western. The story is almost classically simple. It is told through the eyes of a young boy who sees a stranger come riding into the Wyoming valley where he lives and there help a group of homesteaders against evil men before riding away once again. Beautifully photographed against the harsh background of Jackson's Hole in Wyoming, the movie was further enhanced by the outstanding performances of Alan Ladd as the world-weary stranger, Shane; Van Heflin as the ineffectual leader of the homesteaders; and Jean Arthur as his wife full of fortitude, patience and unspoken yearning. The result is a picture that offers fresh insights every time it is viewed.**

**Despite becoming famous as an archetypal Western author, Jack Schaefer (1907–1991) was actually born in Cleveland, Ohio, and worked as a reporter, publisher and editor in the East before his interest in the West and his research into the frontier years through old diaries and newspaper cuttings lead to the writing of *Shane* in 1949. Greeted as 'the almost perfect Western', the book became a huge best-seller and, with the film a few years later, enabled**

**Schaefer to buy a ranch in New Mexico and write full time. Here he produced several more successful novels – including *First Blood* (1953) and *Monte Walsh* (1963) – and a steady flow of short stories. Shortly before his death, however, Schaefer revealed in an interview that *Shane* was far from being his favourite book (he placed *Monte Walsh* and *The Canyon* (1953) much higher) and argued that George Raft would have made a better Shane than 'that little shrimp Alan Ladd'. He even said he would like to rewrite the original book with the hero on the *other* side – because the homesteaders were actually the ones destroying the West by introducing modern civilisation, 'a creeping, deadly blight', in his words. The strong opinions and values that shaped Jack Schaefer's life and fiction are also evident in 'One Man's Honour', another dramatic tale of intriguing characters that is surely worthy of filming.**

Late afternoon sun slanted over one of the higher ridges and shone on the sparse beginnings of a homestead claim. Clear and hot in the clean air, it shone on a long strip of shallow-ploughed ground; on a sagging pole corral where an old milk cow and two stocky ungainly draught horses drooped in motionless rest; and on the shelter, half-dugout, half-timbered with scrub logs. Trimmed branches corded together and plastered over with clay formed the roof and a rusting stovepipe rose from it.

On the split-log doorstep sat a little girl. Her short, scratched, sunburnt legs barely reached the ground. Her light brown hair, sun-bleached in lighter streaks, curled softly down to frame a round snub-nosed face whose dark eyes, unmasked by the light lashes, were wide and bright. A twenty-foot length of rope was tied round her waist and fastened to a staple driven into the door-jamb. She was small and serious and very quiet and she smoothed the skirt of her small flour-sacking dress down over her bare knees and poked, earnest and intent, one small moccasined foot at an ant scurrying in the dooryard dust.

Behind her, in the dim recess of the one-windowed shelter, a tall, flat-bodied man stooped over a rumpled bed and laid a moistened cloth across the forehead of a woman lying there.

His voice was low and harsh with irritation but the touch of his hand was gentle. "What's got into ye?" he said.

The woman stared up at him, apology plain on her thin flushed face. "I don't know," she whispered. "It just came on me sudden-like." Her voice came faint and wavering. "You'll have to do the food. There's soup in the kettle."

The man brushed one hand impatiently at the flies hovering over the bed. "Ye'll be better in the morning," he said. Abruptly he turned and went to the stove set against the wall.

The woman watched him. She tried to speak and could not. She lay still a moment and summoned strength to rise on her elbows and send her voice across the room to him. "Wait," she said. "Wait. You'll have to do the game with her. It's her fun. It helps her learn."

The man swung his head to look at the doorway. The little girl sat still, her back to him, her head bent forward as she peered at something by her feet. The last sun slanting over the ridge filtered through the tangled curls along her neck.

Slowly the lines of worry and irritation faded from the man's face and the tightness round his mouth eased. He went to the doorway and leaned low to untie the rope round her waist.

She stood up, small and soft beside his hard height, and stretched back her head to look up at him. She raised one small hand and reached to put it in one of his big calloused hands. Together they went along the front of the shelter towards the corral.

Near the corner the man stopped. He slapped his free hand on the side of the shelter. "This," he said.

Gravely the little girl regarded the shelter. A triumphant smile crinkled her small face. "Hullo, house," she said.

"Right," the man said. They moved on and stopped by an old wagon pulled in close alongside the shelter. The man reached under and pulled out an empty milk pail and held it up.

Gravely the little girl regarded it. Her small eyebrows drew down in a frown. She looked up at the man in doubt and back at the object in his hand. "Hullo," she said slowly, "hullo, buck-et."

"That's it!" The man grinned down at her and reached to put the pail back under the wagon.

They moved on to the sagging poles of the corral. The man pointed over the poles at the cow, and the little girl peered through them beside him. She spoke at once, quick and proud. "Hullo, cow."

"Mighty smart ye're getting to be," the man said. He pointed over the poles at the draught horses standing together in a corner.

The little girl tossed her head. "Hullo, horse."

"No," the man said. "There's two of them. Hor-ses."

The little girl looked up at him, small and earnest and intent. She looked back through the poles across the corral. "Hullo, hor-ses."

Forty-three miles to the south and five miles west of the meagre town on the river, where the ground dipped in a hollow some ten feet below the level expanse around, a saddled horse stood alone, ground-reined, patiently waiting. A wide-brimmed weatherworn hat hung on the saddle-horn.

Several hundred yards away the river road followed the bank, a dust track running west into fading distance and east towards the low hills hiding the town. Close by the roadside two small rocks jutted out of the ground, butted against each other. The late afternoon sun slanted down on them and they made a small lengthening patch of shade.

Beside them, stretched out, head and shoulders into the shade, a man lay flat, belly down, pressed against the ground. Beside him lay a rifle. Its barrel had been rubbed with dirt to remove all shine. He was a short man, short and thick, with a head that seemed small, out of proportion to the thick body, set too close into the hunched shoulders. His hair was a dirty black, close-cropped with the rough scissor slashes of his own cutting plainly marked, and it merged with no break into the dark unshaven stubble down his cheeks and round his narrow, tight-lipped mouth.

He raised his head higher to sight along the road to the west through the cleft where the tops of the two rocks joined. Pushing with his toes in worn, scarred, old knee-length boots, he hitched his body a few inches to the left so that it lay almost parallel to the road, invisible to anyone approaching from the west.

As he moved, the hammer of the revolver in a holster at his side made a tiny groove in the ground and he reached to test the firmness of its seat in the holster and free it of any clinging dirt. His voice was a low murmur lost in the vast empty reaches of space, the flat inflectionless voice of a man accustomed to being alone and to talking to himself.

"Last place they'd be expecting trouble," he said.

He lay flat, his head relaxed on its side with one ear against the ground, and the sun dropped slowly down the sky and the patch of shade of the rocks spread down his back and reached the brass-studded cartridge belt round his waist, and far out along the road to the west a tiny puff of dust appeared and crept closer, barely seeming to move, only to grow imperceptibly larger.

Faint tremors in the ground came to the man's ear. He raised his head and sighted through the rock cleft. He rolled on his side and pulled the tattered old bandana tied loosely round his neck up over his face, up to the bridge of his nose so that only his eyes and forehead showed over it. He rolled back into position and took the rifle and eased the barrel forward through the cleft. Propped on his elbows, with the curved butt of the rifle against his right shoulder and his right cheek under the bandana against the stock, he watched the puff of dust far out along the road.

It was no longer just a puff of dust. Emerging from it, yet never escaping, and always emerging as the dust rose under the hooves, was a light, fast freight wagon drawn by two stout horses at a steady trot. Two men sat on the board-backed seat, the driver and another man with a shotgun between his knees, the butt on the floorboard, the barrel pointing at the sky.

The man behind the rocks waited. He waited until the wagon was little more than one hundred feet away, and in a few seconds he would begin to be visible over the top of the rocks, and his finger tightened on the trigger of the rifle and with the crash of the shot the man with the shotgun jolted hard against the back of the wagon seat and the horses reared, beating upwards with their front hooves and trying to swing away, and the man with the shotgun dropped it clattering on the floorboard and struggled to stand on the swaying platform and toppled sideways into the road dust and lay still.

The man behind the rocks let the rifle stock fall to the ground and leapt up and in the leaping took the revolver from the holster at his side. He moved out and round the rocks and closer to the wagon and watched the driver fighting with the horses to quiet them. He watched the driver pull them to quivering stillness and become aware of him and the gun in his hand and stiffen in a tight silence.

"That's right," he said. "Keep your hands on those reins where I can see them." He moved closer and to the right side of the wagon and with his left hand took the shotgun from the floorboard and tossed it back from the road. He moved out and round the horses to the left side of the wagon and took the driver's revolver from its holster and threw it towards the river. He stepped back, away from the wagon.

"Now," he said. "Take it slow. Wrap the reins round that brake. Put your hands up behind your head."

The driver hesitated. His lips were pale, pressed tight together, and a slow flush crept up his cheeks. He reached slowly and looped the reins over the brake handle and raised his hands and clasped them together at the back of his head.

The man with the gun stepped up by the body of the wagon. He was careful to stand facing part way forward so that the driver was always within his angle of vision. With his left hand he unfastened the rope lashed over the wagon and pulled away the light canvas dust-cover. Four square boxes and several small crates and half a dozen sacks of potatoes were exposed to view.

He chuckled, a strange, harsh sound in the wide silence. "Mighty little load to be packing a guard," he said.

He swung his head for a quick check of the load and back to look straight at the driver.

His voice was suddenly sharp and biting. "Where is it? I know you're carrying it."

The driver had pivoted his body at the hips to watch him and stared at him and said nothing.

The man with the gun grunted and reached with his left hand to yank aside one of the sacks of potatoes. He reached again and heaved to move aside the one that had been beneath the first. He plunged the hand into the hole opened to the bed of the wagon and felt around and pulled out a small metal box. He stepped back and again his strange, harsh chuckle sounded in the silence.

The voice of the driver broke through the tight line of his lips. "You'll never get away with it, Kemp. I'd know that gunbelt anywhere."

The man with the gun let the metal box fall and pulled the bandana down from his face. "Too bad," he said.

He raised his right hand and the gun in it bucked with the shot, and the driver rose upright off the seat, arching his back in sudden agony, and fell sideways over the footboard to strike on the wagon tongue and bounce to the ground between the harness rugs and with the roar of the shot the horses were rearing and they plunged ahead and the wheels crunched over the driver's body as they rolled forward along the road.

The man with the gun took one leap after the wagon and stopped. He raised the gun again and in almost aimless haste fired the four remaining bullets in it at the plunging horses. The horses drove forward, goaded by several flesh wounds, and the reins ripped off the brake handle and the wagon careened after them and swerved to the left, and the left front wheel struck against the rocks behind which the man had been hiding. The wagon bounced upwards as the wheel cracked and the harness traces snapped and the horses, freed of the weight, surged in frantic gallop along the road.

The man threw the empty revolver to the ground. He raced to the wagon and round it to the rocks and leapt over them and grabbed the rifle. He dropped to his right knee and braced his left elbow on his left knee to steady his aim and fired and one of the horses staggered and fell, and the other, pulled sideways by the falling weight, lashed frantically with its hoofs and the harness parted and the horse galloped ahead alone along the road. Already it was a far shape, dwindling into distance, and the man fired again and again until the magazine of the rifle was emptied and the bullets kicked small spurts of dust and the horse galloped on unhit into the low hills.

The man threw down the rifle and stood erect. He was shaking with a tense fury. He stood still, forcing himself to quiet, driving the shaking out of his body. He drew a long breath. "That'll tell 'em too damn soon," he said.

Quickly he took up the rifle and opened the breech and blew through the barrel and loaded the magazine with bullets from the pocket of his faded old shirt. He hurried back to where he had dropped the metal box. The two bodies lay near in the road dust and already the flies were gathering and he paid no attention to them.

He picked up the revolver and loaded it with bullets from the brass-studded belt round his waist. He reached down and blasted the lock of the metal box with a single shot and ripped the top open and took out two small, plump leather bags and a sheaf of notes and jammed these into the pockets of his old patched pants. At a steady run he moved away from the road, across the level expanse, to the hollow several hundred yards away and the waiting horse.

With swift, sure gestures he slapped the hat on his head and pushed the rifle into its saddle scabbard and transferred the two small bags and the notes to the saddlebag. He swung up and yanked the horse round, lifting it into a fast lope, and headed north through the red-brown reaches of distance.

* * *

Early morning sun slanted in from the east on the homestead shelter. It made a narrow triangular patch of brightness on the packed dirt floor through the open doorway and pushed a soft glow farther into the room. On the edge of a low, short truckle cot against the back wall by the foot of the big bed the little girl sat, her body bent forward, her small face puckered in a frown as she concentrated on the problem of putting the right little moccasin on the right foot.

On the bed itself the woman lay thin and motionless. Her eyes were closed. At intervals the eyelids twitched and flickered and were still. Her mouth was partly open and her breath drew through it in long, slow, straining gasps.

On the floor beside the bed, stretched on an old quilt folded over, the man lay asleep, fully dressed except for his short, thick boots.

The little girl finished with the moccasins. She slid to the floor and turned and tried to smooth the old blanket on her cot. She took hold of the cot and tugged at it to pull it a few inches out from the wall. She went to the end of it away from the bed and turned her small back to it and against it and pushed with her feet to move it along the floor and slide it under the bed.

The scratching sound of the cot runners scraping on the hard dirt floor roused the man. He bent his body at the waist to sit up and wavered and fell back. He pushed against the floor with both hands and was up to the sitting position. He looked round, his eyes glassy and staring, and saw the boots and his attention focused on them and he reached for them and struggled to get them on. He heaved himself over on one hip and pushed against the floor and stood swaying on his feet. Sweat streamed down his face and his body shook as with a chill.

He took a step and staggered and fell towards the wall and clutched at it for support. He moved along it to the head of the bed. Leaning his weight on one hand on the bed, he reached with the other to the woman's shoulder and gently shook her. Her head wobbled limply at the pressure and her eyes remained closed. He straightened against the wall. Slowly he wiped one hand down over his damp face and let it fall to his side.

The little girl stood by the foot of the bed and looked up at him. Slowly his attention focused on her. He stared at her for a long moment and she looked up at him and a small smile of greeting touched her face and was gone.

He drew a long, slow, sobbing breath and by sheer effort of will pushed out from the wall. His feet dragged and he moved in a strange lurching walk. He took the old quilt from the floor and reached under the bed to take the old blanket from the cot and pulled a pile of empty flour sacks down from a shelf. With these in his arms he staggered to the doorway and out and along the front of the shelter to the old wagon beside it. He heaved his load into the body of the wagon and leaned panting on the side to reach in and spread out the sacks and put the blanket and quilt over them.

Weakness took him and he swayed against one of the wagon wheels and hung over it while sweat dripped in tiny glistening beads from his chin to the ground below. He pushed out from the wheel and veered to the shelter wall and hitched his way along towards the door.

The little girl was in the doorway and she backed away inside and he held to the door-jamb and pulled himself round and in and a short way along the inside wall and reached for the team harness hanging on two wooden pegs, and in the reaching suddenly sagged in a limp helplessness and collapsed doubling forward to bump against the wall and slide to the floor. His body stretched out and rolled over and his unseeing eyes stared upward a few seconds and the lids dropped and no motion stirred in him except the long slow heaving of his chest.

The little girl stared at the man lying still and silent and her eyebrows drew together in a frown. She looked at the woman on the bed and back at the man on the floor. She turned away and went to the table under the one window in the right wall and climbed on the chair beside it and then on to the table.

Standing on tiptoe and leaning out she reached one hand into an earthenware jar on the shelf by the window and took it out with a cracker clutched in her fingers. She climbed down to the chair and sat on it with her short, sunburnt legs swinging over the edge. Gravely she regarded the biscuit in her hand. "Hullo, crack-er," she said in a soft, hushed voice. Gravely she bit off a corner and began to chew it.

A mile and a half to the south-east the early morning sun sent long shadows streaming out from a man and a horse climbing the rough slope of a twisting, boulder-strewn ridge. The man rode with his short, thick body hunched forward, and the sun glinted on the brass studdings of the cartridge belt round his waist. The horse was sweat-streaked, tired, taking the slope in short spurts as the man kicked it forward.

They topped the ridge and dropped a short way down the near side and stopped. The man swung to the ground. He took off his weatherworn hat and slapped at himself with it to knock some of the dust off his clothes and hung it on the saddle-horn. He turned back to the top of the ridge and lay flat on the blunt, bare rock to peer over. No motion anywhere disturbed the empty distance.

He turned his head to look at the horse standing with braced legs apart, head hanging, grateful for the rest. He settled himself more comfortably on the rock and watched over the ridge top. The shadows of the boulders down the slope shrank slightly as the sun crept upward and far out along his back trail, round a swelling shoulder of wind-piled sand, a straggling line of seven tiny figures crawled into view.

"Damn funny," he said in a flat inflectionless voice. "Can't shake 'em."

The seven tiny figures crawled closer, increasing in size, seeming to increase in pace as the distance dwindled, and they were seven men on horseback, six in a ragged, relatively compact group and one alone in the lead.

The man on the ridge top shaded his eyes against the slanting sun and studied the figure in the lead, distinguishable now across the dwindling distance, a lean, long-armed figure wearing a buckskin shirt, slim and straight in the saddle on a tall grey horse. He wore no hat and his hair, iron-grey and long, caught the sun clearly in the bobbing rhythm of riding. He rode at a fast trot and at intervals pulled his horse to a brief walk and leaned in the saddle to check the ground beside and ahead.

The man on the ridge top smacked a clenched fist on the rock. "That's it," he said. "Thought he'd left for the mines." He licked his dry lips and spat out the dust-dirty saliva. "Can't just keep running," he said. "Not with him after me."

He crawled down from the ridge top a few feet and turned squatting on his heels to look down the near slope. Down where it slipped into a level expanse of red-brown ground and sparse silver-green of sagebrush, a few score feet out from the base, a stony, dry stream bed followed the twisting formation of the ridge. To the right, swinging in along the level from around a curving twist of the ridge and cutting across the dry stream bed to push in a long arc towards a far break in the next ridge, ran the wagon trace. Plain in the sand dust of the trace, visible from the height, were the day-old, unending ribbon ruts of wheel tracks and the hoofprints of many horses heading north.

The man's eyes brightened. He leapt down the slope to his horse and took the rifle from the saddle scabbard and was back on his belly at the ridge top. The seven figures, suddenly larger, made grotesque in the clear, clean brightness of sun by the long shadows streaming sideways from them, were little more than half a mile away.

Deliberately, in slow succession, careless of exact aim at the range, he fired once at the figure in the lead and twice at the group behind and a strange harsh chuckle came from him as he saw them scatter and swing their horses and gallop back and cluster again in a jumble round the lean man on the grey horse.

"That'll do it," he said. "They'll take time working up this hill."

He pulled back from the ridge top and ran to the horse and jammed the rifle into the scabbard and slammed the hat on his head and swung into the saddle. At a hard run he drove the horse angling down the slope, across the first few score feet of level stretch, across the dry stream bed and angling on across the level to the wagon trace.

He rode along the trace thirty feet, forty, and eased the horse to a slow stop. Holding it steady, headed north, he backed it along the trace, back to where he had angled in and past, back to the crossing of the dry stream bed.

Gripping the reins short and pulling up hard on the horse's head so that it rose on its hind legs, front hooves pawing the air, he yanked its head savagely to the left and slammed the heels of his heavy old boots into its flanks and it leapt, twisting sideways, and was off the trace on the dry stones of the stream bed and he clamped down hard on the reins to hold it from breaking into a surging gallop. Head bent to one side, peering down in steady concentration, he walked the horse along the stream bed, picking his way, holding to the side where the rolled, loose stone lay thickest.

He turned his head to look back and up at the ridge top where he had been. Faintly, over the high rock, came the sound of a shot and then another. He looked ahead where the stream bed, following the ridge, curved left with it and disappeared from sight. He urged the horse into a trot and he was round the bend, out of sight of the wagon trace behind. He pulled the horse to the right and out of the stream bed and on the easier sand-silt ground he pushed it into a lope, moving west as the ground rose and swinging north-westward as it dropped again.

The morning sun, higher now, shone clear and hot on the homestead shelter and beat slanting against the high ridge behind and beyond. A quarter of a mile away, up past the long, shallow-ploughed strip by the almost dry stream bed, close in by the base of the ridge, a man sat, short and thick and hunched in the saddle, on a tired, sweat-streaked horse. He held the wide brim of his weather-worn hat low over his eyes with one hand as he studied the whole scene before him.

Not a sound that he could hear disturbed the empty silence. Not a living thing moved anywhere in sight except the two horses and the old cow in the corral twitching in patient endurance at the flies. He dropped the hand from his hat and reached to take the rifle from its scabbard and hold it ready across the saddle in front of him. He urged the horse into a slow walk, along the base of the ridge and swinging to come to the shelter from the rear.

Fifty feet from the low, blank, rear wall of the shelter he stopped the horse and dismounted. Quietly he slipped the rifle back into the scabbard and took off his hat and hung it on the saddle-horn and in the same gesture flowing onward took the revolver from the holster at his side.

Quietly he walked to the rear wall of the shelter. He moved along the rear wall to the right corner and leaned to peer round and then to look across the short space at the corral. He saw that the horses were heavy draught animals and he shook his head in disgust and he saw the swelling udders of the cow, and a puzzled frown showed through the dark stubble on his face, and the cow, sighting him, pressed against the poles of the corral and lowed with a soft, sighting moan. At the sound he leapt back, close against the rear wall, and the empty silence regained and held and he relaxed and moved again, forward and round the corner.

He was moving past the wagon drawn in by the side of the shelter when he stopped and dropped below the wagon level and listened. Faint, from inside the shelter, he heard a slow creaking sound, then again and yet again and continuing in slow steady rhythm.

He waited. The sound stopped and in the silence there was another sound, not heard, below hearing, sensed or felt, and the slow creaking began again and continued, deliberate, unhurried.

Cautiously he moved, forward, round the front corner, along the blank wall towards the open doorway. Half-crouched, gun raised and ready, he swung swiftly round the door-jamb and into the doorway and there, halfway across the room and confronting him, perched on the seat edge of an old rocking chair and swinging her small body to make the chair roll on its rockers, was a little girl.

Caught, rigid in a kind of frantic immobility, he stared at her; and her eyes widened at the sight of him and her small body stiffened, swaying gently to the dying motion of the chair. Gravely she regarded him. Her lips lifted slightly in a suggestion of a smile. "Hullo, man," she said.

Slowly he straightened. He turned his head and saw the woman motionless on the bed and the man limp on the floor and heard the other sound, audible now inside the room, the long, slow, unconscious gaspings for breath.

He looked back at the little girl and suddenly he was aware of the gun in his hand and he turned his body sideways to her. As he turned, his head remained towards her, swivelling on his short, thick neck and with a quick, furtive motion he slid the gun into its holster. He stood still a long moment, his head fixed in its sidelong, tipped slant over his shoulder, and looked down at her, and gravely she watched him and he seemed unable to look away.

Abruptly he jerked his head round straight, swinging his eyes to inspect the room. He went to the shelf by the one window and took a nearly empty flour sack from the floor beneath and laid this on the table. He reached to the shelf and snatched the few cans there and dropped them into the sack.

He stopped, silent and tense, his jaws clenched together, the cords in his neck standing out in strain. He swung round and leaned against the table and jutted his head forward and down at her.

His voice struck at her with an angry intensity. "There'll be people coming! They'll untangle my trail! They'll get here some time!"

She stared at him, understanding or not understanding unknown on her face, and he pulled himself round and scooped the bag off the table. He strode to the doorway and out and along the front wall of the shelter and round and back to his horse.

He jammed the old hat on his head and fumbled in the saddlebag until he found a short piece of cord and with this tied the flour sack close up to the saddle-horn. He mounted and the horse, stronger for the rest, responded as he pulled it round and headed off north-westward, angling towards the high ridge.

He rode slowly, head down, hunched in the saddle, letting the horse find its own pace. There was no urging along the reins, no drumming of heels on its flanks, and the horse stopped. The man sat still in the saddle.

He drew a long breath and let it out with a sighing sound. His voice came, flat, inflectionless. "Maybe they won't," he said.

Suddenly an explosive fury seemed to burst inside him and strike outwards into action. Viciously he yanked the horse round to the right and kicked it into headlong gallop, heading north-eastward towards a far lowering of the ridge.

The fury in him dwindled with the wind of movement and a quietness came over him. He was aware of the horse straining under him, of its heavy breathing. He pulled it to a steady jogging.

He rode on: a short, thick man on a tired horse, dirty, unshaven, dingy in old, stained clothes except for the glintings of brass on the cartridge belt round his waist. He rode on: a small moving blot in the vast red-brown reaches of distance, and he passed over the far lowering of the ridge and down the long gradual slope beyond and up a wide groundswell of shifting sand and before him, stretching out of distance into distance, was the wagon trace and a third of a mile away, headed north along it, moving away from him, were seven men on horseback . . .

The lean man on the grey horse and another man were in the lead, one on each side of the trace, bent in their saddles, studying the ground as they moved ahead, and the other five followed.

The man on the groundswell of shifting sand stopped his horse and took the rifle from its scabbard. A strange, harsh chuckle sounded in the sun-hot silence and was cut short by the shot and he saw the spurt of dust beside the lean man's horse and all of them halt with sudden, startled jerks and swing in their saddles to look towards him.

He jammed the rifle back into its scabbard and lifted his horse, rearing to wheel it round, and drove it at a fast gallop back down the groundswell of sand the way he had come. He was well up the long, gradual slope towards the lowering of the ridge when he looked back and saw them coming over the groundswell and lining out in full gallop behind him.

Savagely he beat at the horse and it surged up and over the lowering of the ridge and as it raced down the other side towards the long level stretch to the homestead shelter he felt the first falterings in its stride, the slight warning stumblings and recoveries, and he took hold of the sack tied to the saddle-horn and snapped the cord with a lurch and let the sack fall.

The horse drove on, frantic in lessening rushes of strength, and again he looked back. They were coming steadily, no closer than before, coming with steady intensity of purpose. He saw them pull, sliding to a bunched brief stop by the sack, and one swing down and grab it and shake out the contents in a flurry of flour, and in the stopping he increased his lead.

The shelter was just ahead now and he yanked the horse to a skidding stop in front of it and whipped the revolver from the holster at his side and fired two shots towards the doorway, low, into the doorstep. He caught a flashing glimpse of the little girl inside shrinking back from the roar of the shots and he was beating the horse forward again, past the corral, across the shallow-ploughed strip, angling back towards the high ridge.

He reached the base and started up and the horse, faltering often now, laboured into the climb. It stopped, legs braced and quivering, ribs heaving, a bloody froth bubbling in its nostrils. He pivoted to the right in the saddle and looked back.

Riderless horses stood in front of the shelter and the lean man in the buckskin shirt near them directing the others. One man ran towards the closest brackish pool in the almost dry stream bed with a bucket in his hand. Another strode towards the corral with the team harness over his shoulder. Another heaved at the tongue of the old wagon to swing it out from the side wall of the shelter. And yet another mounted one of the saddled horses and swung off south-eastward.

The man on the ridge slope checked each in the one swift, sliding glance and stared intently at the blank walls of the shelter as if trying to force vision through them. Suddenly, as thought and bodily awareness coincided, he pivoted round and to the left in the saddle.

Two of them had not stopped by the shelter, had galloped on past and swept in a wide arc towards him. They were little more than three hundred yards away. One of them had stopped and was raising a rifle to his shoulder.

The man on the ridge yanked upward on his reins trying to lift the horse into motion and even before he heard the shot he felt the horse leap shuddering and its forelegs doubled under and he jumped free as it collapsed forward and sideways on the slope. He leaned down and jerked the rifle free and crouched behind the still quivering body of the horse and sent a single shot crashing down towards the level and saw the two men circle back to a safer distance and turn their horses sideways towards him and dismount to stand behind them with the barrels of rifles resting over the saddles.

He reached with one hand into the pocket of his old shirt and with fumbling fingers counted the rifle bullets there. He turned his head to study the slope rising behind him. Fifty feet higher it levelled in a small ledge that had caught several large stones in age-gone descent. Above were other small ledges.

He looked back over the body of the horse and sent another shot crashing down and leapt up crouching and scrambled towards the first ledge above and a barrage of shots battered from the two men below and out, and a bullet smashed into his left shoulder and spun him falling and he rolled back behind the body of the horse and hitched himself round to hold the rifle with his right hand over it. The sun beat clean and hot upon him and the two men and he lay quiet watching them.

Down and across the level expanse the lean man in the buckskin shirt stepped out from the doorway of the shelter and round the corner for a clear view of the ridge and the body of the horse, small at the distance yet distinct against the rock. His eyes narrowed as he made out the deadliness of the rifle barrel pointing over the body. He walked to the tall grey horse, ground-reined in front of the shelter, and took his rifle from the saddle.

Quietly, paying no attention to the harnessing of the draught horses to the old wagon, he walked round the other side of the shelter and started back towards the ridge directly behind. He came on tracks, hoofprints in the loose earth heading south-west into the distance towards the far lowering of the ridge. He stopped and looked down at these a long moment and moved on and came to the base of the ridge and climbed until he was almost parallel on it to the man behind the body of the horse not quite a half mile away.

He lay flat on a slight levelling of the slope and adjusted the sights on his rifle and pushed the barrel out in front of him and settled into position and waited.

Several shots came from the two men out on the level expanse and the man behind the body of the horse hunched himself forward and up to reply to them and the man in the buckskin shirt tightened his finger on his trigger in a slow, steady squeeze.

He saw the man behind the body of the horse jerk convulsively and try to rise and fall forward over the body of the horse and lie still. He saw the two men out on the level mount and start towards the ridge. He stood up and walked towards the shelter.

The wagon was ready. Two of the saddled horses were tied behind it and a blanket had been rigged over the wagon body for shade. Under it lay the man and the woman from inside the shelter. The little girl, small and shrinking and silent, sat on the seat between two of the other men.

"Take it easy but aimin' for time," the man in the buckskin shirt said. "Hit for the trace then towards town. Maybe the doc'll meet you part way."

The draught team, fresh and strong, leaned into the harness and the traces tightened and the wagon moved away. The man in the buckskin shirt turned to watch the two men who had ridden to the ridge approach leading their horses. An old battered saddle and a bridle hung bouncing from the saddle-horn of one of the horses. The body of a man, short and thick with a brass-studded cartridge belt round its waist, hung limply over the saddle of the other horse.

"Did you get it?" said the man in the buckskin shirt.

"Yes," said one of the men. "In the saddle-bag there."

The man in the buckskin shirt stepped forward and bent to slip a shoulder close against the saddle up under the body of the man in the brass-studded belt and lifted it away and went and heaved it over the saddle of the tall grey horse.

He stepped into the shelter and came out carrying a spade in one hand. He took the reins of the tall grey horse with the other hand and led it away.

Head low, staring at the ground before him, he led it past the corral, across the almost dry stream bed, and stopped at last by the straggling row of stunted cottonwoods.

He looked up. The other men had followed him.

"Don't be a fool," one of the other men said. "Drag him out somewheres and let the buzzards and coyotes have him. He wasn't no more'n an animal himself."

"No," the man in the buckskin shirt said. He looked back past the shelter, on into the vast empty distance where the trail of a tired horse led north-eastward towards the far lowering of the ridge and returned. "He was a murderin', thievin' son-of-a-bitch. But he was a man."

Quietly, bending to the hot task in the clean sun, the man in the buckskin shirt struck the spade into the red-brown earth.

# HONDO

(United Artists, 1954)
Starring: John Wayne, James Arness
& Geraldine Page
Directed by John Sturges
Story 'The Gift of Cochise' by Louis L'Amour

**This picture might well be described as 'the biggest star in Western movies meets the genre's top-selling author.' The making of *Hondo,* based on the Louis L'Amour story, resulted in what Steven H. Scheuer has described as 'one of Hollywood's best adult Westerns – strong in human relationships with a minimum of violence'. Scheuer, like a number of other film critics, believes that it is a 'much underrated' picture in the pantheon of top Western movies. Wayne, in fact, gave a perfectly measured performance as the tough, trail-hardened cowboy whose sympathies for a woman captured by Apaches (Geraldine Page, then a Broadway actress making her outstanding film début) run much deeper than he expects. Louis L'Amour considered *Hondo* one of the best screen adaptations of his work.**

**Louis Dearborn L'Amour (1908–1988) was of French-Irish descent and could trace his family in North America back to the early sixteen-hundreds and follow their growth thereafter on the wild frontier. He himself grew up in Jamestown, North Dakota, and there absorbed the facts of his family's heritage – especially the story of his great-grandfather, who had been scalped by Sioux warriors. Louis left home at the age of fifteen and after various jobs as a seaman, lumberjack, miner,**

**skinner of dead cattle and professional boxer (he won fifty-one of fifty-nine fights) he turned to writing, and began producing short stories about the Western frontier for the popular fiction magazines of the day. In the mid-Fifties he produced the first of his hundred novels, all drawn from the land he knew so intimately and the research he carried out so painstakingly. At the time of writing, all of his titles are still in print and have sold around 230 million copies worldwide. Among the many awards conferred on Louis L'Amour, was that of being the first novelist ever to be awarded the Congressional Gold Medal by the United States Congress in honour of his life's work. 'The Gift of Cochise' is a gem among his remarkable output and serves as a reminder of both L'Amour's contribution to fiction as well as to Western movies . . .**

Tense, and white to the lips, Angie Lowe stood in the door of her cabin with a double-barreled shotgun in her hands. Beside the door was a Winchester '73, and on the table inside the house were two Walker Colts.

Facing the cabin were twelve Apaches on ragged calico ponies, and one of the Indians had lifted his hand, palm outward. The Apache sitting on the white-splashed bay pony was Cochise.

Beside Angie were her seven-year-old son Jimmy and her five-year-old daughter Jane.

Cochise sat on his pony in silence; his black, unreadable eyes studied the woman, the children, the cabin and the small garden. He looked at the two ponies in the corral and the three cows. His eyes strayed to the small stack of hay cut from the meadow, and to the few steers farther up the canyon.

Three times the warriors of Cochise had attacked this solitary cabin and three times they had been turned back. In all, they had lost seven men, and three had been wounded. Four ponies had been killed. His braves reported that there was no man in the house, only a woman and two children, so Cochise had come to see for himself this woman who was so certain a shot with a rifle and who killed his fighting men.

These were some of the same fighting men who had outfought, outguessed and outrun the finest American army on record, an army outnumbering the Apaches by a hundred to one. Yet a lone woman with two small children had fought them off, and the woman was scarcely more than a girl. And she was prepared to fight now. There was a glint of admiration in the old eyes that appraised her. The Apache was a fighting man, and he respected fighting blood.

"Where is your man?"

"He has gone to El Paso." Angie's voice was steady, but she was frightened as she had never been before. She recognised Cochise from descriptions, and she knew that if he decided to kill or capture her it would be done. Until now, the sporadic attacks she had fought off had been those of casual bands of warriors who raided her in passing.

"He has been gone a long time. How long?"

Angie hesitated, but it was not in her to lie. "He has been gone four months."

Cochise considered that. No one but a fool would leave such a woman, or such fine children. Only one thing could have prevented his return. "Your man is dead," he said.

Angie waited, her heart pounding with heavy, measured beats. She had guessed long ago that Ed had been killed but the way Cochise spoke did not imply that Apaches had killed him, only that he must be dead or he would have returned.

"You fight well," Cochise said. "You have killed my young men."

"Your young men attacked me." She hesitated, then added, "They stole my horses."

"Your man is gone. Why do you not leave?"

Angie looked at him with surprise. "Leave? Why, this is my home. This land is mine. This spring is mine. I shall not leave."

"This was an Apache spring," Cochise reminded her reasonably.

"The Apache lives in the mountains," Angie replied. "He does not need this spring. I have two children, and I do need it."

"But when the Apache comes this way, where shall he drink? His throat is dry and you keep him from water."

The very fact that Cochise was willing to talk raised her hopes. There had been a time when the Apache made no war on the white man. "Cochise speaks with a forked tongue," she said. "There is water yonder." She gestured toward the hills, where Ed had told her there were springs. "But if the people of Cochise come in peace they may drink at this spring."

The Apache leader smiled faintly. Such a woman would rear a nation of warriors. He nodded at Jimmy. "The small one – does he also shoot?"

"He does," Angie said proudly, "and well, too!" She pointed to an upthrust leaf of prickly pear. "Show them, Jimmy."

The prickly pear was an easy two hundred yards away, and the Winchester was long and heavy, but he lifted it eagerly and steadied it against the door-jamb as his father had taught him, held his sight an instant, then fired. The bud on top of the prickly pear disintegrated.

There were grunts of appreciation from the dark-faced warriors. Cochise chuckled. "The little warrior shoots well. It is well you have no man. You might raise an army of little warriors to fight my people."

"I have no wish to fight your people," Angie said quietly. "Your people have your ways, and I have mine. I live in peace when I am left in peace. I did not think," she added with dignity, "that the great Cochise made war on women!"

The Apache looked at her, then turned his pony away. "My people will trouble you no longer," he said. "You are the mother of a strong son."

"What about my two ponies?" she called after him. "Your young men took them from me."

Cochise did not turn or look back, and the little cavalcade of riders followed him away. Angie stepped back into the cabin and closed the door. Then she sat down abruptly, her face white, the muscles in her legs trembling.

When morning came, she went cautiously to the spring for water. Her ponies were back in the corral. They had been returned during the night.

Slowly, the days drew on. Angie broke a small piece of the meadow and planted it. Alone, she cut hay in the meadow and built another stack. She saw Indians several times, but they did not bother her. One morning, when she opened her door, a quarter of antelope lay on the step, but no Indian was in sight. Several times, during the weeks that followed, she saw moccasin tracks near the spring.

Once, going out at daybreak, she saw an Indian girl dipping water from the spring. Angie called to her, and the girl turned quickly, facing her. Angie walked toward her, offering a bright red silk ribbon. Pleased, the Apache girl left.

And the following morning there was another quarter of antelope on her step – but she saw no Indian.

Ed Lowe had built the cabin in West Dog Canyon in the spring of 1871, but it was Angie who chose the spot, not Ed. In Santa Fe they would have told you that Ed Lowe was good-looking, shiftless and agreeable. He was, also, unfortunately handy with a pistol.

Angie's father had come from County Mayo to New York and from New York to the Mississippi, where he became a tough, brawling river boatman. In New Orleans, he met a beautiful Cajun girl and married her. Together, they started west for Santa Fe, and Angie was born en route. Both parents died of cholera when Angie was fourteen. She lived with an Irish family for the following three years, then married Ed Lowe when she was seventeen.

Santa Fe was not good for Ed, and Angie kept after him until they started south. It was Apache country, but they kept on until they reached the old Spanish ruin in West Dog. Here there were grass, water and shelter from the wind.

There was fuel, and there were piñons and game. And Angie, with an Irish eye for the land, saw that it would grow crops.

The house itself was built on the ruins of the old Spanish building, using the thick walls and the floor. The location had been admirably chosen for defence. The house was built in a corner of the cliff, under the sheltering overhang, so that approach was possible from only two directions, both covered by an easy field of fire from the door and windows.

For seven months, Ed worked hard and steadily. He put in the first crop, he built the house and proved himself a handy man with tools. He repaired the old plough they had bought, cleaned out the spring and paved and walled it with slabs of stone. If he was lonely for the carefree companions of Santa Fe, he gave no indication of it. Provisions were low, and when he finally started off to the south, Angie watched him go with an ache in her heart.

She did not know whether she loved Ed. The first flush of enthusiasm had passed, and Ed Lowe had proved something less than she had believed. But he had tried, she admitted. And it had not been easy for him. He was an amiable soul, given to whittling and idle talk, all of which he missed in the loneliness of the Apache country. And when he rode away, she had no idea whether she would ever see him again. She never did.

Santa Fe was far and away to the north, but the growing village of El Paso was less than a hundred miles to the west, and it was there Ed Lowe rode for supplies and seed.

He had several drinks – his first in months – in one of the saloons. As the liquor warmed his stomach, Ed Lowe looked around agreeably. For a moment, his eyes clouded with worry as he thought of his wife and children back in Apache country, but it was not in Ed Lowe to worry for long. He had another drink and leaned on the bar, talking to the bartender. All Ed had ever asked of life was enough to eat, a horse to ride, an occasional drink and companions to talk with. Not that he had anything important to say. He just liked to talk.

Suddenly a chair grated on the floor, and Ed turned. A lean, powerful man with a shock of uncut black hair and a torn, weather-faded shirt stood at bay. Facing him across the table were three hard-faced young men, obviously brothers.

Ches Lane did not notice Ed Lowe watching from the bar. He had eyes only for the men facing him. "You done that deliberate!" The statement was a challenge.

The broad-chested man on the left grinned through broken teeth. "That's right, Ches. I done it deliberate. You killed Dan Tolliver on the Brazos."

"He made the quarrel." Comprehension came to Ches. He was boxed, and by three of the fighting, blood-hungry Tollivers.

"Don't make no difference," the broad-chested Tolliver said. "'Who sheds a Tolliver's blood, by a Tolliver's hand must die!'"

Ed Lowe moved suddenly from the bar. "Three to one is long odds," he said, his voice low and friendly. "If the gent in the corner is willin', I'll side him."

Two Tollivers turned toward him. Ed Lowe was smiling easily, his hand hovering near his gun. "You stay out of this!" one of the brothers said harshly.

"I'm in," Ed replied. "Why don't you boys light a shuck?"

"No, by –!" The man's hand dropped for his gun, and the room thundered with sound.

Ed was smiling easily, unworried as always. His gun flashed up. He felt it leap in his hand, saw the nearest Tolliver smashed back and he shot him again as he dropped. He had only time to see Ches Lane with two guns out and another Tolliver down when something struck him through the stomach and he stepped back against the bar, suddenly sick.

The sound stopped, and the room was quiet, and there was the acrid smell of powder smoke. Three Tollivers were down and dead, and Ed Lowe was dying. Ches Lane crossed to him.

"We got 'em," Ed said, "we sure did. But they got me."

Suddenly his face changed. "Oh, Lord in heaven, what'll Angie do?" And then he crumpled over on the floor and lay still, the blood staining his shirt and mingling with the sawdust.

Stiff-faced, Ches looked up. "Who was Angie?" he asked.

"His wife," the bartender told him. "She's up north-east somewhere, in Apache country. He was tellin' me about her. Two kids, too."

Ches Lane stared down at the crumpled, used-up body of Ed Lowe. The man had saved his life.

One he could have beaten, two he might have beaten; three would have killed him. Ed Lowe, stepping in when he did, had saved the life of Ches Lane.

"He didn't say where?"

"No."

Ches Lane shoved his hat back on his head. "What's north-east of here?"

The bartender rested his hands on the bar. "Cochise," he said . . .

For more than three months, whenever he could rustle the grub, Ches Lane quartered the country over and back.

The trouble was, he had no lead to the location of Ed Lowe's homestead. An examination of Ed's horse revealed nothing. Lowe had bought seed and ammunition, and the seed indicated a good water supply, and the ammunition implied trouble. But in that country there was always trouble.

A man had died to save his life, and Ches Lane had a deep sense of obligation. Somewhere that wife waited, if she was still alive, and it was up to him to find her and look out for her. He rode north-east, cutting for sign, but found none. Sandstorms had wiped out any hope of back-trailing Lowe. Actually, West Dog Canyon was more east than north, but this he had no way of knowing.

North he went, skirting the rugged San Andreas Mountains. Heat baked him hot, dry winds parched his skin. His hair grew dry and stiff and alkali-whitened. He rode north, and soon the Apaches knew of him. He fought them at a lonely waterhole, and he fought them on the run. They killed his horse, and he switched his saddle to the spare and rode on. They cornered him in the rocks, and he killed two of them and escaped by night.

* * *

They trailed him through the White Sands, and he left two more for dead. He fought fiercely and bitterly, and would not be turned from his quest. He turned east through the lava beds and still more east to the Pecos. He saw only two white men, and neither knew of a white woman.

The bearded man laughed harshly. "A woman alone? She wouldn't last a month! By now the Apaches got her, or she's dead. Don't be a fool! Leave this country before you die here."

Lean, wind-whipped and savage, Ches Lane pushed on. The Mescaleros cornered him in Rawhide Draw and he fought them to a standstill. Grimly, the Apaches clung to his trail.

The sheer determination of the man fascinated them. Bred and born in a rugged and lonely land, the Apaches knew the difficulties of survival; they knew how a man could live, how he must live. Even as they tried to kill this man, they loved him, for he was one of their own.

Lane's jeans grew ragged. Two bullet holes were added to the old black hat. The slicker was torn; the saddle, so carefully kept until now, was scratched by gravel and brush. At night he cleaned his guns and by day he scouted the trails. Three times he found lonely ranch-houses burned to the ground, the buzzard- and coyote-stripped bones of their owners lying nearby.

Once he found a covered wagon, its canvas flopping in the wind, a man lying sprawled on the seat with a pistol near his hand. He was dead and his wife was dead, and their canteens rattled like empty skulls.

Leaner every day, Ches Lane pushed on. He camped one night in a canyon near some white oaks. He heard a hoof click on stone and he backed away from his tiny fire, gun in hand.

The riders were white men, and there were two of them. Joe Tompkins and Wiley Lynn were headed west, and Ches Lane could have guessed why. They were men he had known before, and he told them what he was doing.

Lynn chuckled. He was a thin-faced man with lank yellow hair and dirty fingers. "Seems a mighty strange way to get a woman. There's some as comes easier."

"This ain't for fun," Ches replied shortly. "I got to find her."

Tompkins stared at him. "Ches, you're crazy! That gent declared himself in of his own wish and desire. Far's that goes, the gal's dead. No woman could last this long in Apache country."

At daylight, the two men headed west, and Ches Lane turned south.

Antelope and deer are curious creatures, often led to their death by curiosity. The longhorn, soon going wild on the plains, acquires the same characteristic. He is essentially curious. Any new thing or strange action will bring his head up and his ears alert. Often a longhorn, like a deer, can be lured within a stone's throw by some queer antic, by a handkerchief waving, by a man under a hide, by a man on foot.

This character of the wild things holds true of the Indian. The lonely rider who fought so desperately and knew the desert so well soon became a subject of gossip among the Apaches. Over the fires of many a rancheria they discussed this strange rider who seemed to be going nowhere, but always riding, like a lean wolf dog on a trail. He rode across the mesas and down the canyons; he studied sign at every waterhole; he looked long from every ridge. It was obvious to the Indians that he searched for something – but what?

* * *

Cochise had come again to the cabin in West Dog Canyon. "Little warrior too small," he said, "too small for hunt. You join my people. Take Apache for man."

"No." Angie shook her head. "Apache ways are good for the Apache, and the white man's ways are good for white men – and women."

They rode away and said no more, but that night, as she had on many other nights after the children were asleep, Angie cried. She wept silently, her head pillowed on her arms. She was as pretty as ever, but her face was thin, showing the worry and struggle of the months gone by, the weeks and months without hope.

The crops were small but good. Little Jimmy worked beside her. At night, Angie sat alone on the steps and watched the shadows gather down the long canyon, listening to the coyotes yapping from the rim of the Guadalupes, hearing the horses blowing in the corral. She watched, still hopeful, but now she knew that Cochise was right: Ed would not return.

But even if she had been ready to give up this, the first home she had known, there could be no escape. Here she was protected by Cochise. Other Apaches from other tribes would not so willingly grant her peace.

At daylight she was up. The morning air was bright and balmy, but soon it would be hot again. Jimmy went to the spring for water, and when breakfast was over, the children played while Angie sat in the shade of a huge old cottonwood and sewed. It was a Sunday, warm and lovely. From time to time, she lifted her eyes to look down the canyon, half-smiling at her own foolishness.

The hard-packed earth of the yard was swept clean of dust; the pans hanging on the kitchen wall were neat and shining. The children's hair had been clipped, and there was a small bouquet on the kitchen table.

After a while, Angie put aside her sewing and changed her dress. She did her hair carefully, and then, looking in her mirror, she reflected with sudden pain that she *was* pretty, and that she was only a girl.

Resolutely, she turned from the mirror and, taking up her Bible, went back to the seat under the cottonwood. The children left their playing and came to her, for this was a Sunday ritual, their only one. Opening the Bible, she read slowly,

". . . though I walk through the valley of the shadow of death, I will fear no evil; for thou art with me; thy rod and thy staff, they comfort me. Thou preparest a table before me in the presence of mine enemies: thou . . ."

"Mommy." Jimmy tugged at her sleeve. "Look!"

* * *

Ches Lane had reached a narrow canyon by mid-afternoon and decided to make camp. There was small possibility he would find another such spot, and he was dead tired, his muscles sodden with fatigue. The canyon was one of those unexpected gashes in the cap rock that gave no indications of its presence until you came right on it. After some searching, Ches found a route to the bottom and made camp under a wind-hollowed overhang. There was water, and there was a small patch of grass.

After his horse had a drink and a roll on the ground, it began cropping eagerly at the rich, green grass, and Ches built a smokeless fire of ancient driftwood in the canyon bottom. It was his first hot meal in days, and when he had finished he put out his fire, rolled a smoke and leaned back contentedly.

Before darkness settled, he climbed to the rim and looked over the country. The sun had gone down, and the shadows were growing long. After a half hour of study, he decided there was no living thing within miles, except for the usual desert life. Returning to the bottom, he moved his horse to fresh grass, then rolled in his blanket. For the first time in a month, he slept without fear.

He woke up suddenly in the broad daylight. The horse was listening to something, his head up. Swiftly, Ches went to the horse and led it back under the overhang. Then he drew on his boots, rolled his blankets and saddled the horse. Still he heard no sound.

Climbing the rim again, he studied the desert and found nothing. Returning to his horse, he mounted up and rode down the canyon toward the flatland beyond. Coming out of the canyon mouth, he rode right into the middle of a war party of more than twenty Apaches – invisible until suddenly they stood up behind rocks, their rifles leveled. And he didn't have a chance.

Swiftly, they bound his wrists to the saddle horn and tied his feet. Only then did he see the man who led the party. It was Cochise.

He was a lean, wiry Indian of past fifty, his black hair streaked with grey, his features strong and clean-cut. He stared at Lane, and there was nothing in his face to reveal what he might be thinking.

Several of the young warriors pushed forward, talking excitedly and waving their arms. Ches Lane understood none of it, but he sat straight in the saddle, his head up, waiting. Then Cochise spoke and the party turned, and, leading his horse, they rode away.

The miles grew long and the sun was hot. He was offered no water and he asked for none. The Indians ignored him. Once a young brave rode near and struck him viciously. Lane made no sound, gave no indication of pain. When they finally stopped, it was beside a huge anthill swarming with big red desert ants.

Roughly, they untied him and jerked him from his horse. He dug in his heels and shouted at them in Spanish: "The Apaches are women! They tie me to the ants because they are afraid to fight me!"

An Indian struck him, and Ches glared at the man. If he must die, he would show them how it should be done. Yet he knew the unpredictable nature of the Indian, of his great respect for courage.

"Give me a knife, and I'll kill any of your warriors!"

They stared at him, and one powerfully built Apache angrily ordered them to get on with it. Cochise spoke, and the big warrior replied angrily.

Ches Lane nodded at the anthill. "Is this the death for a fighting man? I have fought your strong men and beaten them. I have left no trail for them to follow, and for months I have lived among you, and now only by accident have you captured me. Give me a knife," he added grimly, "and I will fight *him*!" He indicated the big, black-faced Apache.

The warrior's cruel mouth hardened, and he struck Ches across the face.

The white man tasted blood and fury. "Woman!" Ches said. "Coyote! You are afraid!" Ches turned on Cochise, as the Indians stood irresolute. "Free my hands and let me fight!" he demanded. "If I win, let me go free."

Cochise said something to the big Indian. Instantly, there was stillness. Then an Apache sprang forward and, with a slash of his knife, freed Lane's hands. Shaking loose the thongs, Ches Lane chafed his wrists to bring back the circulation. An Indian threw a knife at his feet. It was his own bowie knife.

Ches took off his riding boots. In sock feet, his knife gripped low in his hand, its cutting edge up, he looked at the big warrior.

"I promise you nothing," Cochise said in Spanish, "but an honourable death."

The big warrior came at him on cat feet. Warily, Ches circled. He had not only to defeat this Apache but to escape. He permitted himself a side glance toward his horse. It stood alone. No Indian held it.

The Apache closed swiftly, thrusting wickedly with the knife. Ches, who had learned knife-fighting in the bayou country of Louisiana, turned his hip sharply, and the blade slid past him. He struck swiftly, but the Apache's forward movement deflected the blade, and it failed to penetrate. However, as it swept up between the Indian's body and arm, it cut a deep gash in the warrior's left armpit.

The Indian sprang again, like a clawing cat, streaming blood. Ches moved aside, but a backhand sweep nicked him, and he felt the sharp bite of the blade. Turning, he paused on the balls of his feet.

He had had no water in hours. His lips were cracked. Yet he sweated now, and the salt of it stung his eyes. He stared into the malevolent black eyes of of the Apache, then moved to meet him. The Indian lunged, and Ches sidestepped like a boxer and spun on the ball of his foot.

The sudden sidestep threw the Indian past him, but Ches failed to drive the knife into the Apache's kidney when his foot rolled on a stone. The point left a thin red line across the Indian's back. The Indian was quick. Before Ches could recover his balance, he grasped the white man's knife wrist.

Desperately, Ches grabbed for the Indian's knife hand and got the wrist, and they stood there straining, chest to chest.

Seeing his chance, Ches suddenly let his knees buckle, then brought up his knee and fell back, throwing the Apache over his head to the sand. Instantly, he whirled and was on his feet, standing over the Apache. The warrior had lost his knife, and he lay there, staring up, his eyes black with hatred.

Coolly, Ches stepped back, picked up the Indian's knife, and tossed it to him contemptuously. There was a grunt from the watching Indians, and then his antagonist rushed. But loss of blood had weakened the warrior, and Ches stepped in swiftly, struck the blade aside, then thrust the point of his blade hard against the Indian's belly.

Black eyes glared into his without yielding. A thrust, and the man would be disembowelled, but Ches stepped back. "He is a strong man," Ches said in Spanish. "It is enough that I have won."

Deliberately, he walked to his horse and swung into the saddle. He looked around, and every rifle covered him.

So he had gained nothing. He had hoped that mercy might lead to mercy, that the Apache's respect for a fighting man would win his freedom. He had failed. Again they bound him to his horse, but they did not take his knife from him.

When they camped at last, he was given food and drink. He was bound again, and a blanket was thrown over him. At daylight they were again in the saddle. In Spanish he asked where they were taking him, but they gave no indication of hearing. When they stopped again, it was beside a pole corral, near a stone cabin.

When Jimmy spoke, Angie got quickly to her feet. She recognised Cochise with a start of relief, but she saw instantly that this was a war party. And then she saw the prisoner.

Their eyes met and she felt a distinct shock. He was a white man, a big, unshaven man who badly needed both a bath and a haircut, his clothes ragged and bloody. Cochise gestured at the prisoner.

"No take Apache man, you take white man. This man good for hunt, good for fight. He strong warrior. You take 'im."

Flushed and startled, Angie stared at the prisoner and caught a faint glint of humour in his dark eyes.

"Is this here the fate worse than death I hear tell of?" he enquired gently.

"Who are you?" she asked, and was immediately conscious that it was an extremely silly question.

The Apaches had drawn back and were watching curiously. She could do nothing for the present but accept the situation. Obviously they intended to do her a kindness, and it would not do to offend them. If they had not brought this man to her, he might have been killed.

"Name's Ches Lane, ma'am," he said. "Will you untie me? I'd feel a lot safer."

"Of course." Still flustered, she went to him and untied his hands. One Indian said something, and the others chuckled; then, with a whoop, they swung their horses and galloped off down the canyon.

Their departure left her suddenly helpless, the shadowy globe of her loneliness shattered by this utterly strange man standing before her, this big, bearded man brought to her out of the desert.

She smoothed her apron, suddenly pale as she realised what his delivery to her implied. What must he think of her? She turned away quickly. "There's hot water," she said hastily, to prevent his speaking. "Dinner is almost ready."

She walked quickly into the house and stopped before the stove, her mind a blank. She looked around her as if she had suddenly waked up in a strange place. She heard water being poured into the basin by the door, and heard him take Ed's razor. She had never moved the box. To have moved it would —

"Sight of work done here, ma'am."

She hesitated, then turned with determination and stepped into the doorway. "Yes, Ed — "

"You're Angie Lowe."

Surprised, she turned toward him, and recognised his own startled awareness of her. As he shaved, he told her about Ed, and what had happened that day in the saloon.

"He – Ed was like that. He never considered consequences until it was too late."

"Lucky for me he didn't."

He was younger-looking with his beard gone. There was a certain quiet dignity in his face. She went back inside and began putting plates on the table. She was conscious that he had moved to the door and was watching her.

"You don't have to stay," she said. "You owe me nothing. Whatever Ed did, he did because he was that kind of person. You aren't responsible."

He did not answer, and when she turned again to the stove, she glanced swiftly at him. He was looking across the valley.

There was a studied deference about him when he moved to a place at the table. The children stared, wide-eyed and silent; it had been so long since a man sat at this table.

Angie could not remember when she had felt like this. She was awkwardly conscious of her hands, which never seemed to be in the right place or doing the right things. She scarcely tasted her food, nor did the children.

Ches Lane had no such inhibitions. For the first time, he realised how hungry he was. After the half-cooked meat of lonely, trailside fires, this was tender and flavoured. Hot biscuits, desert honey . . . Suddenly he looked up, embarrassed at his appetite.

"You were really hungry," she said.

"Man can't fix much, out on the trail."

Later, after he'd got his bedroll from his saddle and unrolled it on the hay in the barn, he walked back to the house and sat on the lowest step. The sun was gone, and they watched the cliffs stretch their red shadows across the valley. A quail called plaintively, a mellow sound of twilight.

"You needn't worry about Cochise," she said. "He'll soon be crossing into Mexico."

"I wasn't thinking about Cochise."

That left her with nothing to say, and she listened again to the quail and watched a lone bright star.

"A man could get to like it here," he said quietly.

# THE MISFITS

(20th Century Fox, 1961)
Starring: Clark Gable, Marilyn Monroe
& Montgomery Clift
Directed by John Huston
Story 'The Misfits' by Arthur Miller

**This modern-day Western about a group of cowboys on a savage round-up of wild mustangs is today as famous for what went on *off*-screen as on it. The screenplay had been specially written by the playwright Arthur Miller from his own story as a starring vehicle for his wife, Marilyn Monroe. And with Clark Gable as co-star and John Huston as director it was hyped during the filming in Reno, Nevada as 'the ultimate motion picture'. In fact, it became a nightmare, with Marilyn continually ill or late on the set, John Huston losing thousands of dollars a night in the Reno casinos and Arthur Miller worried about the state of his marriage and the ending of the picture. *The Misfits* was finally completed forty days late and hugely over budget. Almost before the movie had time to reach the screen, Marilyn had divorced her husband, and Clark Gable – who had insisted on doing his own stunts during filming – was dead of a heart attack. Yet despite all these problems, the picture received good reviews and there was special mention for the 'slam-bang wild-horse round-up' and the scene at the end where Gable and Monroe drove off together into the Nevada night. Critic George Perry called it 'a poignant moment in cinema history'.**

# Arthur Miller

**Arthur Miller (1915– ) is widely acknowledged as one of America's leading dramatists, and has won many awards including the Pulitzer Prize for his classic productions including *Death of a Salesman*, *All My Sons* and *The Crucible*. Born in New York, he was educated at the University of Michigan where he first began to display his talent for the theatre. Most of his major plays have been filmed after their stage runs, and he has also revealed a considerable ability as a short-story writer with tales such as 'The Misfits', which was originally published in 1957. The story evidences a great sadness at the passing of a way of life in its portrayal of a group of drifting cowboys – all with unhappy backgrounds – who make their living rounding up noble wild animals probably destined to be turned into dog food. Whatever problems there were off-camera, *The Misfits* remains as moving an experience on the screen as it does on the printed page.**

Wind blew down from the mountains all night. A wild river of air swept and swirled across the dark sky and struck down against the blue desert and hissed back into the hills. The three cowboys slept under their blankets, their backs against the first upward curve of the circling mountains, their faces towards the desert of sage. The wind and its tidal washing seethed through their dreams, and when it stopped there was a lunar silence that caused Gay Langland to open his eyes. For the first time in three nights he could hear his own breathing, and in the new hush he looked up at the stars and saw how clear and bright they were. He felt happy and slid himself out of his blankets and stood up fully dressed.

On the silent plateau between the two mountain ranges Gay Langland was the only moving thing. He turned his head and then his body in a full circle, looking into the deep blue sky for sign of storm. He saw it that it would be a good day and a quiet one.

He walked a few yards from the two other sleepers and wet the sandy ground. The excitement of the stillness was awakening his body. He returned and lit the bundle of dry sage he had gathered last night, dropped some heavier wood on the quick flames, perched the blackened coffee-pot on the stones surrounding the fire bed and sat on one heel, staring at the fresh orange embers.

Gay Langland was forty-five years old but as limber as he had ever been in his life. The light of his face brightened when there were things to do, a nail to straighten, an animal to size up, and it dimmed when there was nothing in his hands, and his eyes then went sleepy. When there was something to be done in a place he stayed there, and when there was nothing to be done he went from it.

He had a wife and two children less than a hundred miles from here whom he had not seen in more than three years. She had betrayed him and did not want him, but the children were naturally better off with their mother. When he felt lonely for them all he thought of them longingly, and when the feeling passed he was left without any question as to what he might do to bring them all back together again. He had been born and raised on rangeland, and he did not know that anything could be undone that was done, any more than falling rain could be stopped in mid-air. And he had a smile and a look on his face that was in accordance.

His forehead was evenly tracked with deep ridges, as though his brows were always raised a little expectantly, slightly surprised, a little amused, and his mouth friendly. His ears stuck out, as they often do with little boys or young calves, and he had a boy's turned-up snub nose. But his skin was browned by the wind, and his small eyes looked and saw and, above all, were trained against showing fear.

Gay Langland looked up from the fire at the sky and saw that first delicate stain of pink. He went over to the sleepers and shook Guido Racanelli's arm. A grunt of salutation sounded in Guido's head, but he remained on his side with his eyes shut.

"The sumbitch died off," Gay said to him.

Guido listened, motionless, his eyes shut against the firelight, his bones warm in his fat.

Gay wanted to shake him again and wake him, but in the last two days he had come to wonder whether Guido was not secretly considering not flying at all. The plane's engine was rattling its valves and one shock absorber was weak. Gay had known the pilot for years and he knew and respected his moods. Flying up and down these mountain gorges within feet of the rock walls was nothing you could pressure a man to do. But now the wind had died Gay hoped very much that Guido would take off this morning and let them begin their work.

He got to his feet and again glanced skyward. Then he stood there thinking of Roslyn. And he had a strong desire to have money in his pocket that he had earned himself when he came to her tonight. The feeling had been returning again and again that he had somehow passed the kidding point and that he had to work again and earn his way as he always had before he met her. Not that he didn't work for her, but it wasn't the same. Driving her car, repairing her house, running errands – all that stuff wasn't what you would call work. Still, he thought, it was too. Yet, it wasn't either.

He stepped over to the other sleeper and shook him. Perce Howland opened his eyes.

"The sumbitch died, Perce," Gay said.

Perce's eyes looked toward the heavens and he nodded. Then he slid out of his blankets and walked past Gay and stood wetting the sand, breathing deeply as in sleep. Gay always found him humorous to watch when he woke up. Perce walked into things and sometimes stood wetting his own boots. He was a little like a child waking up, and his eyes now were still dreamy and soft.

Gay Langland called over to him, "Better'n wages, huh, Perce?"

"Dam right," Perce muttered and returned to the fire, rubbing his skin against his clothes.

Gay kneeled by the fire again, scraping hot coals into a pile and setting the frying pan over them on stones. He could pick up hot things without feeling pain. Now he moved an ember with his finger.

"You make me nervous doing that," Perce said, looking down over his shoulder.

"Nothin' but fire," Gay said, pleased.

They were in silence for a moment, both of them enjoying the brightening air.

"Guido goin' up —?" Perce asked.

"Didn't say. I guess he's thinkin' about it."

"Be light pretty soon," Perce warned.

He glanced off to the closest range and saw the purple rocks rising in their mystery towards the faintly glowing stars. Perce Howland was twenty-two, hipless and tall, and he stood there as effortlessly as the mountains he was looking at, as though he had been created there in his dungarees, with the tight plaid shirt and the three-button cuffs, the broad-rimmed beige hat set back on his blond head, and his thumbs tucked into his belt so his fingers could touch the engraved belt buckle with his name spelled out under the raised figure of the bucking horse. It was his first bucking-horse prize, and he loved to touch it when he stood waiting, and he liked to wait.

Perce had known Gay Langland for only five weeks, and Guido for three days. He had met Gay in a Bowie bar, and Gay had asked him where he was from and what he was doing, and he had told Gay his story, which was the usual for most of the rodeo riders. He had come on down from Nevada, as he had done since he was sixteen, to follow the local rodeos and win some money riding bucking horses, but this trip had been different, because he had lost the desire to go back home again.

They had become good friends that night when Gay took him to Roslyn's house to sleep, and when he woke in the morning he had been surprised that an educated Eastern woman should have been so regular and humorous and interested in his opinions.

So he had been floating around with Roslyn and Gay Langland, and they were comfortable to be with; Gay mostly, because Gay never thought to say he ought to be making something of his life. Gay made him feel it was all right to go from day to day and week to week. Perce Howland did not trust anybody too far, and it was not necessary to trust Gay because Gay did not want anything of him or try to manipulate him. He just wanted a partner to go mustanging, and Perce had never done anything like that and he wanted to see how it was.

And now he was here, sixty miles from the nearest town, seven thousand feet up in the air, and for two days waiting for the wind to die so the pilot could take off into the mountains where the wild horses lived.

Perce looked out towards the desert, which was beginning to show its silent horizon. "Bet the moon looks like this," he said.

Gay Langland did not answer. In his mind he could feel the wild horses grazing and moving about in the nearby mountains and he wanted to get to them. Indicating Guido Racanelli he said, "Give him a shake, Perce. The sun's about up."

Perce started over to Guido, who moved before Perce reached him.

"Gettin' light, Guido," Perce said.

Guido Racanelli rolled upright on his great behind, his belly slung over his belt, and he inspected the brightening sky in the distance as though some personal message were out there for him. The pink reflected light brightened his face. The flesh around his eyes was white where the goggles protected his face, and the rest of his skin was burned brown by wind. His silences were more profound than the silences of others because his cheeks were so deep, like the melon-half cheeks of a baboon that curve forward from the mouth. Yet they were hard cheeks, as hard as his great belly. He looked like a jungle bird now, slowly turning his head to inspect the faraway sky, a serious bird with a brown face and white eyes. His head was entirely bald. He took off his khaki army cap and rubbed his fingers slowly into his scalp.

Gay Langland stood up and walked to him and gave him his eggs and thick bacon on a tin plate.

"Wind died, Guido," Gay said, standing there and looking down at the pilot.

"It doesn't mean much what it did down here." Guido pointed skyward with his thumb. "Up there's where it counts."

"Ain't no sign of wind up there," Gay said. Gay's eyes seemed amused. He did not want to seem committed to a real argument. "We got no more eggs, Guido," he warned.

Guido ate.

Now the sky flared with true dawn, like damp paper suddenly catching fire. Perce and Gay sat down on the ground facing Guido, and they all ate their eggs.

The shroud of darkness quickly slipped off the red truck which stood a few yards away. Then, behind it, the little plane showed itself. Guido Racanelli ate and sipped his coffee, and Gay Langland watched him with a weak smile and without speaking. Perce blinked contentedly at the brightening sky, slightly detached from the other two. He finished his coffee and slipped a chew of tobacco into his mouth and sucked on it.

It was a pink day now all around the sky.

Gay Langland made a line in the sand between his thighs and said, "You goin' up, Guido?" He looked at Guido directly and he was still smiling.

Guido thought for a moment. He was older, about fifty. His pronunciation was unaccountably Eastern, with sharp r's. He sounded educated sometimes. He stared off toward the squat little plane. "Every once in a while I wonder what the hell it's all about," he said.

"What is?" Gay asked.

Perce watched Guido's face, thoroughly listening.

Guido felt their attention and spoke with pleasurable ease. He still stared past them at the plane. "I got a lousy valve. I know it, Gay."

"Been that way a long time, Guido," Gay said with sympathy.

"I know," Guido said. They were not arguing but searching now. "And we won't hardly get twenty dollars apiece out of it – there's only four or five horses back in there."

"We knew that, Guido," Gay said. They were in sympathy with each other.

"I might just get myself killed, for twenty dollars."

"Hell, you know them mountains," Gay said.

"You can't see wind, Gay," the pilot said.

Gay knew now that Guido was going up right away. He saw that Guido had just wanted to get all the dangers straight in his mind so he could see them and count them; then he would go out against them.

"You're flying along in and out of those passes and then you dive for the sons of bitches, and just when you're pulling up, some goddam gust presses you down and there you are."

"I know," Gay said.

There was silence. Guido sipped his coffee, staring off at the plane. "I just wonder about it every once in a while," the pilot said.

"Well, hell," Perce Howland said, "it's better than wages."

"You damn right it is, Perce," the pilot said thoughtfully.

"I seen guys get killed who never left the ground," Perce said.

The two older men knew that his father had been killed by a bull long ago and that he had seen his father die. He had had his own arms broken in rodeos and a Brahma bull had stepped on his chest.

"One rodeo near Salinas I see a feller get his head snapped right clear off his chest by a cable busted. They had this cable drawin' horses up on to a truck. I seen his head rollin' away like a bowlin' ball. Must've roll twenty-five yards before it hit a fence post and stopped." He spat tobacco juice and turned back to look at Guido. "It had a mustache. Funny thing, I never knowed that guy had a mustache. Never noticed it. Till I see it stop rolling and there it was, dust all over the mustache."

"That was a dusty mustache," Gay said, grinning against their deepening morbidity.

They all smiled. Then time hung for a moment as they waited. And at last Guido shifted on to one buttock and said, "Well, let's get gassed up."

Guido leaned himself to one side with his palm on the ground, then got to his feet by moving in a circle around this palm, and stood up. Gay and Perce Howland were already moving off towards the truck, Perce hoisting up his dungarees over his breakfast-full stomach, and the older Gay more sprightly and intent. Guido stood holding one hand open over the fire, watching them loading the six enormous truck tyres on the bed of the truck. Each tyre had a twenty-foot length of rope wired to it, and at the end of each rope was a loop. Before they swung the tyres on to the truck Gay inspected the ropes to be sure they were securely knotted to the tyres, and the loops open and ready for throwing.

Guido blinked against the warming sun, watching the other two, then he looked off to his right where the passes were, and the fingers of his mind felt around beyond those passes into the bowls and hollows of the mountains where last week he had spotted the small herd of wild horses grazing. Now he felt the lightness he had been hoping to feel for three days, the bodiless urge to fly. For three days he had kept away from the plane because a certain carelessness had been itching at him, a feeling that he always thought would lead him to his death.

About five weeks ago he had come up to this desert with Gay Langland and he had chased seven mustangs out of the mountains. But this time he had dived to within a foot of the mountainside, and afterwards as they sat around the fire eating dinner, Guido had had the feeling that he had made that deep dive so he could die. And the thought of his dead wife had come to him again, and the other thought that always came into his mind with her dead face. It was the wonderment, the quiet pressing-in of the awareness that he had never wanted a woman, after she had been buried with the stillborn baby beside her in the graveyard outside Bowie.

Seven years now he had waited for some real yearning for a woman, and nothing at all had come to him. It pleasured him to know that he was free of that, and it sometimes made him careless in the plane, as though some great bang and a wreckage would make him again what he had been. By now he could go around in Bowie for a week and only in an odd moment recall that he hadn't even looked at a girl walking by, and the feeling of carelessness would come on him, a kind of loose gaiety, as though everything was comical.

Until he had made that dive and pulled out with his nose almost scraping the grass, and he had climbed upward with his mouth hanging open and his body in a sweat. So that through these past three days up here he had refused to let himself take off until the wind had utterly died, and he had clung to moroseness. He wanted to take off in the absolute grip of his own wits, leaving nothing to chance. Now there was no wind at all, and he felt he had pressed the sinister gaiety out of his mind. He left the dying fire and walked past Gay and Perce and down the gentle slope to the plane, looking like a stout, serious football coach before the kick-off.

He glanced over the fuselage and at the bald doughnut tyres and he loved the plane. Again, as always, he looked at the weakened starboard shock absorber, which no longer held its spread so that the plane stood tilted a little to one side, and told himself that it was not serious. He heard the truck motor starting and he unfastened the knots of the ropes holding the plane to the spikes driven into the desert floor. Then the truck pulled up, and young Perce Howland dropped off and went over to the tail handle, gripped it, lifted the tail off the ground, and swung the plane around so she faced out across the endless desert and away from the mountains. Then they unwound the rubber hose from the gas drum on the truck and stuck the nozzle into the gas tank behind the engine, and Perce turned the pump crank.

Guido then walked around the wing and over to the cockpit, whose right door was folded down, leaving the inside open to the air. He reached in and took out his ripped leather flight jacket and got into it.

Perce stood leaning against the truck fender now, grinning. "That sure is a ventilated-type jacket, Guido," he said.

Then Guido said, "I can't get my size any more." The jacket had one sleeve off at the elbow, and the dried leather was split open down the back, showing the lamb's-wool lining. He had bombed Germany in this jacket long ago. He reached in behind the seat and took out a goggle case, slipped his goggles out, replaced the case, set his goggles securely on his face and reached in again and took out a shotgun pistol and four shells from a little wooden box beside his seat. He loaded the pistol and laid it carefully under his seat. Then he got into the cockpit, sat in his seat, drew the strap over his belly and buckled it. Meantime Gay had taken his position before the propeller.

Guido called through the open doorway of the cockpit, "Turn her over, Gay-boy."

Gay stepped up to the propeller, glanced down behind his heels to be sure no stone waited to trip him when he stepped back, pulled down on the blade and hopped back watchfully.

"Give her another!" Guido called in the silence.

Gay stepped up again, again glancing around his heels, and pulled the blade down. The engine inhaled and exhaled, and they could all hear the oily clank of her inner shafts turning loosely.

"Ignition on, Gay-boy!" Guido called and threw the switch.

This time Gay inspected the ground around him even more carefully and pulled his hat brim down tighter on his head. Perce stood leaning on the truck's front fender, spitting and chewing, his eyes softly squinted against the brazen sun. Gay reached up and pulled the propeller down and jumped back. A puff of smoke floated up from the engine ports.

"Goddam car gas," Guido said. "Ignition on. Go again, Gay-boy!" They were buying low octane to save money.

Gay again stepped up to the propeller, swung the blade down, and the engine said its "Chaaahh!" and the ports breathed white smoke into the morning air. Gay walked over to Perce and stood beside him, watching. The fuselage shuddered and the propeller turned into a wheel, and the dust blew pleasantly from behind the plane and towards the mountains.

Guido gunned her, and she tumbled towards the open desert, bumping along over the sage clumps and crunching whitened skeletons of cattle killed by the winter. The stiff-backed plan grew smaller, shouldering its way over the broken ground, and then its nose turned upward and there was space between the doughnut tyres and the desert, and lazily it climbed, turning back the way it had come. It flew over the heads of Perce and Gay, and Guido waved down, a stranger now, fiercely goggled and wrapped in leather, and they could see him exposed to the waist, turning from them to look through the windshield at the mountains ahead of him. The plane flew away, climbing smoothly, losing itself against the orange and purple walls that vaulted up from the desert to hide from the cowboys' eyes the wild animals they wanted for themselves.

They would have at least two hours before the plane flew out of the mountains driving the horses before it, so they washed the three tin plates and the cups and stored them in the aluminium grub box. If Guido did find horses they would break camp and return to Bowie tonight, so they packed up their bedrolls with sailors' tidiness and laid them neatly side by side on the ground. The six great truck tyres, each with its looped rope coiled within, lay in two piles on the bed of the truck. Gay Langland looked them over and touched them with his hand and stood for a moment trying to think if there was anything they were leaving behind.

He jumped up on the truck to see that the cap was screwed tight on the gas drum, which was lashed to the back of the cab up front, and it was. Then he hopped down to the ground and got into the cab and started the engine.

Perce was already sitting there with his hat tipped forward against the yellow sunlight pouring through the windshield. A thin and concerned Border collie came trotting up as Gay started to close his door, and he invited her into the cab. She leaped up, and he snugged her into the space between the clutch and the left wall of the cab. "Damn near forgot Belle" he said, and they started off.

Gay owned the truck and he wanted to preserve the front end, which he knew could be twisted out of line on broken ground. So he started off slowly. They could hear the gas sloshing in the drum behind them outside.

It was getting warm now. They rode in silence, staring ahead at the two-track trail they were following across the bone-cluttered sagebrush. Thirty miles ahead stood the lava mountains that were the northern border of this desert, the bed of a bowl seven thousand feet up, a place no one ever saw except the few cowboys searching for stray cattle every few months. People in Bowie, sixty miles away, did not know of this place. There were the two of them and the truck and the dog, and now that they were on the move they felt between them the comfort of purpose and their isolation, and Perce slumped in his seat, blinking as though he would go to sleep again, and Gay smoked a cigarette and let his body flow from side to side with the pitching of the truck.

There was a moving cloud of dust in the distance toward the left, and Gay said, "Antelope," and Perce tipped his hat back and looked.

"Must be doin' sixty," he said, and Gay said, "More. I chased one once and I was doin' more than sixty and he lost me." Perce shook his head in wonder, and they turned to look ahead again.

After he had thought awhile Perce said, "We better get over to Largo by tomorrow if we're gonna get into that rodeo. They's gonna be a crowd trying to sign up for that one."

"We'll drive down in the morning," Gay said.

"I'll have to see about gettin' me some stock."

"We'll get there early tomorrow; you'll get stock if you come in early."

"Like to win some money," Perce said. "I just wish I get me a good horse down there."

"They be glad to fix you up, Perce. You're known pretty good around there now. They'll fix you up with some good stock," Gay said.

Perce was one of the best bronc riders, and the rodeos liked to have it known he would appear.

Then there was silence. Gay had to hold the gear-shift lever in high or it would slip out into neutral when they hit bumps. The transmission fork was worn out, he knew, and the front tyres were going too. He dropped one hand to his pants pocket and felt the four silver dollars he had from the ten Roslyn had given him when they had left her days ago.

As though he had read Gay's mind, Perce said, "Roslyn would've liked it up here. She'd liked to have seen that antelope, I bet." Perce grinned as both of them usually did at Roslyn's Eastern surprise at everything they did and saw and said.

"Yeah," Gay said, "she likes to see things." Through the corners of his eyes he watched the younger man, who was looking ahead with a little grin on his face. "She's a damned good sport, old Roslyn," Gay said.

"Sure is," Perce Howland said. And Gay watched him for any sign of guile, but there was only a look of glad appreciation. "First woman like that I ever met," the younger man said.

"They's more," Gay said. "Some of them Eastern women fool you sometimes. They got education but they're good sports. And damn good *women* too, some of them."

There was a silence. Then the younger man asked, "You get to know a lot of them? Eastern women?"

"Ah, I get one once in a while," Gay said.

"Only educated women I ever know, they was back home near Teachers College. Students. Y'know," he said, warming to the memory, "I used to think, hell, education's everything. But when I saw the husbands some of them got married to – schoolteachers and everything, why I don't give them much credit. And they just as soon climb on a man as tell him good morning. I was teachin' them to ride for a while near home."

"Just because a woman's educated don't mean much. Woman's a woman," Gay said. The image of his wife came into his mind. For a moment he wondered if she was still living with the same man he had beaten up when he discovered them together in a parked car six years ago.

"You divorced?" Perce asked.

"No. I never bothered with it," Gay said. It always surprised him how Perce said just what was on his mind sometimes. "How'd you know I was thinkin' of that?" he asked, grinning with embarrassment. But he was too curious to keep silent.

"Hell, I didn't know," Perce said.

"You're always doin' that. I think of somethin' and you go ahead and say it."

"That's funny," Perce said.

They rode on in silence. They were nearing the middle of the desert, where they would turn east. Gay was driving faster now because he wanted to get to the rendezvous and sit quietly waiting for the plane to appear. He held on to the gear-shift lever and felt it trying to spring out of high into neutral. It would have to be fixed. The time was coming fast when he would need about fifty dollars or have to sell the truck, because it would be useless without repairs. Without a truck and without a horse he would be down to what was in his pocket.

Perce spoke out of the silence. "If I don't win Saturday I'm gonna have to do somethin' for money."

"Goddam, you always say what's in my mind." Gay turned his head.

Perce laughed. His face looked very young and pink. "Why?"

"I was just now thinkin'," Gay said, "what I'm gonna do for money."

"Well, Roslyn give you some," Perce said.

He said it innocently, and Gay knew it was innocent, and yet he felt angry blood moving into his neck. Something had happened in these five weeks, and Gay did not know for sure what it was. Roslyn had taken to calling Perce cute, and now and again she would bend over and kiss him on the back of the neck when he was sitting in the living room chair, drinking with them.

Not that that meant anything in itself, because he'd known Eastern women before who'd do something like that and it was just their way. Especially college graduate divorced women. What he wondered at was Perce's way of hardly ever noticing what she did to him. Sometimes it was like he'd already had her and could ignore her, the way a man will who know's he's boss. But then Gay thought it might just be that he really wasn't interested, or maybe that he was keeping cool in deference to Gay.

Again Gay felt a terrible longing to earn money working. He sensed the bottom of his life falling if it turned out Roslyn had really been loving this boy beside him. It had happened to him once before with his wife, but this frightened him more and he did not know exactly why.

Not that he couldn't do without Roslyn. There wasn't anybody or anything he couldn't do without. She was about his age and full of laughter that was not laughter and gaiety that was not gaiety and adventurousness that was laboured, and he knew all this perfectly well even as he laughed with her and was high with her in the bars and rodeos.

He had only lived once, and that was when he had had his house and his wife and his children. He knew the difference, but you never kept anything, and he had never particularly thought about keeping anything or losing anything. He had been all his life like Perce Howland, sitting beside him now, a man moving on or ready to. It was only when he discovered his wife with a stranger that he knew he had had a stake to which he had been pleasurably tethered. He had not seen her or his children for years and only rarely thought about any of them. Any more than his father had thought of him very much after the day he had gotten on his pony, when he was fourteen, to go to town from the ranch, and had kept going into Montana and stayed there for three years.

He lived in this country as his father did, and it was the same endless range wherever he went, and it connected him sufficiently with his father and his wife and his children. All might turn up sometime in some town or at some rodeo, where he might happen to look over his shoulder and see his daughter or one of his sons, or they might never turn up. He had neither left anyone nor not left as long as they were all alive on these ranges, for everything here was always beyond the farthest shot of vision and far away, and mostly he had worked alone or with one or two men, between distant mountains anyway.

In the distance now he could see the shimmering wall of the heat waves rising from the clay flatland they wanted to get to. Now they were approaching closer, and it opened to them beyond the heat waves, and they could see once again how vast it was, a prehistoric lake bed thirty miles long by seventeen miles wide, couched between the two mountain ranges. It was a flat, beige waste without grass or bush or stone, where a man might drive a car at a hundred miles an hour with his hands off the wheel and never hit anything at all.

They drove in silence. The truck stopped bouncing as the tyres rolled over harder ground where there were fewer sage clumps. The waves of heat were dense before them, nearly touchable. Now the truck rolled smoothly and they were on the clay lake bed, and when they had gone a few hundred yards onto it Gay pulled up and shut off the engine.

The air was still in a dead, sunlit silence. When he opened his door he could hear a squeak in the hinge he had never noticed before. When they walked around they could hear their shirts rasping against their backs and the brush of a sleeve against their trousers.

They stood on the clay ground, which was as hard as concrete, and turned to look the way they had come. They looked back toward the mountains at whose feet they had camped and slept, and scanned their ridges for Guido's plane. It was too early for him, and they made themselves busy, taking the gas drum off the truck and setting it a few yards away on the ground, because they would want the truck bed clear when the time came to run the horses down. Then they climbed up and sat inside the tyres with their necks against the tyre beads and their legs hanging over.

Perce said, "I sure hope they's five up there."

"Guido saw five, he said."

"He said he wasn't sure if one wasn't only a colt," Perce said.

Gay let himself keep silent. He felt he was going to argue with Perce. He watched Perce through the corners of his eyes, saw the flat, blond cheeks and the strong, lean neck, and there was something tricky about Perce now. "How long you think you'll be stayin' around here, Perce?" he asked.

They were both watching the distant ridges for a sign of the plane.

"Don't know," Perce said and spat over the side of the truck. "I'm gettin' a little tired of this, though."

"Well, it's better than wages, Perce."

"Hell, yes. Anything's better than wages."

Gay's eyes crinkled. "You're a real misfit, boy."

"That suits me fine," Perce said. They often had this conversation and savoured it. "Better than workin' for some goddam cow outfit buckarooin' so somebody else can buy gas for his Cadillac."

"Damn right," Gay said.

"Hell, Gay, you are the most misfitted man I ever saw and you done all right."

"I got no complaints," Gay said.

"I don't want nothin' and I don't want to want nothin'."

"That's the way, boy."

Gay felt closer to him again and he was glad for it. He kept his eyes on the ridges far away. The sun felt good on his shoulders. "I think he's havin' trouble with them sumbitches up there."

Perce stared out at the ridges. "Ain't two hours yet." Then he turned to Gay. "These mountains must be cleaned out by now, ain't they?"

"Just about," Gay said. "Just a couple small herds left. Can't do much more around here."

"What you goin' to do when you got these cleaned out?"

"Might go north, I think. Supposed to be some big herds in around Thighbone Mountain and that range up in there."

"How far's that?"

"North about a hundred miles. If I can get Guido interested."

Perce smiled. "He don't like movin' around much, does he?"

"He's just misfitted like the rest of us," Gay said. "He don't want nothin'." Then he added, "They wanted him for an airline pilot flyin' up into Montana and back. Good pay too."

"Wouldn't do it, huh?"

"Not Guido," Gay said, grinning. "Might not like some of the passengers, he told them."

Both men laughed, and Perce shook his head in admiration of Guido. Then he said, "They wanted me take over the ridin' academy up home. I thought about that. Two hundred a month and board. Easy work too. You don't hardly have to ride at all. Just stand around and see the customers get satisfied and put them girls off and on."

He fell silent. Gay knew the rest. It was the same story always. It brought him closer to Perce, and it was what he had liked about Perce in the first place. Perce didn't like wages either. He had come on Perce in a bar where the boy was buying drinks for everybody with his rodeo winnings, and his hair still clotted with blood from a bucking horse's kick an hour earlier.

Roslyn had offered to get a doctor for him and he had said, "Thank you kindly. But I ain't bad hurt. If you're bad hurt you gonna die and the doctor can't do nothin', and if you ain't bad hurt you get better anyway without no doctor."

Now it suddenly came upon Gay that Perce had known Roslyn before they had met in the bar. He stared at the boy's profile. "Want to come up north with me if I go?" he asked him.

Perce thought a moment. "Think I'll stay around here. Not much rodeoin' up north."

"I might find a pilot up there, maybe. And Roslyn drive us up in her car."

Perce turned to him, a little surprised. "Would she go up there?"

"Sure. She's a damn good sport," Gay said. He watched Perce's eyes, which had turned interested and warm.

Perce said, "Well, maybe; except to tell you the truth, Gay, I never feel comfortable takin' these horses for chicken feed."

"Somebody's goin' to take them if we don't."

"I know," Perce said. He turned to watch the far ridges again. "Just seems to me they belong up there."

"They ain't doin' nothin' up there but eatin' out good cattle range. The cow outfits shoot them down if they see them."

"I know," Perce said.

"They don't even bother takin' them to slaughter. They just rot up there if the cow outfits get to them."

"I know," Perce said.

There was silence. Neither bug nor lizard nor rabbit moved on the great basin around them, and the sun warmed their necks and their thighs. Gay said, "I'd as soon sell them for riding horses but they ain't big enough, except for a kid. And the freight on them's more than they're worth. You saw them – they ain't nothin' but skinny horses."

"I just don't know if I'd want to see like a hundred of them goin' for chicken feed, though. I don't mind like five or six, but a hundred's a lot of horses. I don't know."

Gay thought. "Well, if it ain't this it's wages. Around here anyway." He was speaking of himself and explaining himself.

"I'd just as soon ride buckin' horses and make out that way, Gay," Perce turned to him. "Although I might go up north with you. I don't know."

"Roslyn wouldn't come out here at first," Gay said, "but soon as she saw what they looked like she stopped complainin' about it. You didn't hear her complainin' about it."

"I ain't complainin', Gay, I just don't know. Seems to me God put them up there and they belong up there. But I'm doin' it and I guess I'd go on doin' it. I don't know."

"Sounds to me like the newspapers. They want their steaks, them people in town, but they don't want castration or branding or cleanin' wild horses off the ranges."

"Hell, man, I castrated more bulls than I got hairs on my head," Perce said.

"I better get the glasses," Gay said and slid out of the tyre in which he had been lounging and off the truck. He went to the cab and reached in and brought out a pair of binoculars, blew on the lenses, mounted the truck and sat on a tyre with his elbows resting on his knees. He put the glasses to his eyes and focused them.

The mountains came up close with their pocked blue hides. He found the pass through which he believed the plane would come and studied its slopes and scanned the air above it. Anger was still warming him. "God put them up there!" Why, Christ, God put everything everywhere. Did that mean you couldn't eat chickens, for instance, or beef? His dislike for Perce was flowing into him again.

They heard the shotgun off in the sky somewhere and they stopped moving. Gay narrowed his eyes and held the binoculars perfectly still.

"See anything?" Perce asked.

"He's still in the pass, I guess," Gay said.

They sat still, watching the sky over the pass. The moments went by. The sun was making them perspire now, and Gay wiped his wet eyebrows with the back of one hand. They heard the shotgun again from the general sky. Gay spoke without lowering the glasses. "He's probably blasting them out of some corner."

Perce quickly arched out of his tyre. "I see him," he said quickly. "I see him glintin', I see the plane."

It angered Gay that Perce had seen the plane first without glasses. In the glasses Gay could see it clearly now. It was flying out of the pass, circling back and disappearing into the pass again. "He's got them in the pass now. Just goin' back in for them."

"Can you see them?" Perce asked.

"He ain't got them in the clear yet. He just went back in for them."

Now through his glasses he could see moving specks on the ground where the pass opened onto the desert table. "I see them," he said. He counted, moving his lips. "One, two, three, four. Four and a colt."

"We gonna take the colt?" Perce asked.

"Hell, can't take the mare without the colt."

Perce said nothing. Then Gay handed him the glasses. "Take a look."

Gay slid off the truck bed and went forward to the cab and opened its door. His dog lay shivering on the floor under the pedals. He snapped his fingers, and she warily got up, leaped down to the ground and stood there quivering, as she always did when the wild horses were coming. He watched her sit and wet the ground, and how she moved with such care and concern and fear, sniffing the ground and moving her head in slow motion and setting her paws down as though the ground had hidden explosives everywhere. He left her there and climbed onto the truck and sat on a tyre beside Perce, who was still looking through the glasses.

"He's divin' down on them. God, they sure can run!"

"Let's have a look," Gay said and reached out, and Perce handed him the glasses, saying, "They're comin' on fast."

Gay watched the horses in the glasses. The plane was starting down toward them from the arc of its climb. They swerved as the roaring motor came down over them, lifted their heads, and galloped faster. They had been running now for over an hour and would slow down when the plane had to climb after a dive and the motor's noise grew quieter.

As Guido climbed again Gay and Perce heard a shot, distant and harmless, and the shot sped the horses on again as the plane took time to bank and turn. Then, as they slowed, the plane returned over them, diving down over their backs, and their heads shot up again and they galloped until the engine's roar receded over them. The sky was clear and lightly blue, and only the little plane swung back and forth across the desert like the glinting tip of a magic wand, and the horses came on towards the vast stripped clay bed where the truck was parked.

The two men on the truck exchanged the glasses from time to time. Now they sat upright on the tyres, waiting for the horses to reach the edge of the lake bed, when Guido would land the plane and they would take off with the truck. And now the horses stopped.

"They see the heat waves," Gay said, looking through the glasses. He could see the horses trotting with raised, alarmed heads along the edge of the barren lake bed, which they feared because the heat waves rose from it like liquid in the air and yet their nostrils did not smell water, and they dared not move ahead onto unknowable territory.

The plane dived down on them, and they scattered but would not go forward onto the lake bed from the cooler, sage-dotted desert behind them. Now the plane banked high in the air and circled out behind them over the desert and banked again and came down within yards of the ground and roared in behind them almost at the height of their heads, and as it passed over them, rising, the men on the truck could hear the shotgun. Now the horses leaped forward onto the lake bed, all scattered and heading in different directions, and they were only trotting, exploring the ground under their feet and the strange, superheated air in their nostrils.

Gradually, as the plane wound around the sky to dive again, they closed ranks and slowly galloped shoulder to shoulder out onto the borderless lake bed. The colt galloped a length behind with its nose nearly touching the mare's long silky tail.

"That's a big mare," Perce said. His eyes were still dreamy and his face was calm, but his skin had reddened.

"She's a bigger mare than usual up here, ya," Gay said.

Both men watched the little herd now, even as they got to their feet on the truck. There was the big mare, as large as any full-grown horse, and both of them downed their surprise at the sight of her. They knew the mustang herds lived in total isolation and that inbreeding had reduced them to the size of large ponies. The herd swerved now and they saw the stallion. He was smaller than the mare but still larger than any Gay had brought down before. The other two horses were small, the way mustangs ought to be.

The plane was coming down for a landing now. Gay and Perce Howland moved to the forward edge of the truck's bed where a strap of white webbing was strung at hip height between two stanchions stuck into sockets at the corners of the truck. They drew another web strap from one stanchion to the other and stood inside the two. Perce tied the back strap to his stanchion. Then they turned around inside their harness and each reached into a tyre behind him and drew out a coil of rope whose end hung in a loop.

They glanced out on the lake bed and saw Guido taxiing towards them, and they stood waiting for him. He cut the engine twenty yards from the truck and leaped out of the open cockpit before the plane had halted. He lashed the tail of the plane to a rope that was attached to a spike driven into the clay and trotted over to the truck, lifting his goggles off and stuffing them into his torn jacket pocket. Perce and Gay called out laughingly to him, but he seemed hardly to have seen them. His face was puffed with preoccupation. He jumped into the cab of the truck, and the collie dog jumped in after him and sat on the floor, quivering. He started the truck and roared ahead across the flat clay into the watery waves of heat.

They could see the herd standing still in a small clot of dots more than two miles off. The truck rolled smoothly, and in the cab Guido glanced at the speedometer and saw it was past sixty. He had to be careful not to turn over and he dropped back to fifty-five. Gay, on the right front corner of the truck bed, and Perce Howland on the left, pulled their hats down to their eyebrows and hefted the looped ropes, which the wind was threatening to coil and foul in their palms.

Guido knew that Gay Langland was a good roper and that Perce was unsure, so he headed for the herd's left in order to come up to them on Gay's side of the truck if he could. This whole method – the truck, the tyres, the ropes, and the plane – was Guido's invention, and once again he felt the joy of having thought of it all. He drove with both heavy hands on the wheel and his left foot ready over the brake pedal. He reached for the shift lever to feel if it was going to spring out of gear and into neutral, but it felt tight, and if they did not hit a bump he could rely on it. The herd had started to walk but stopped again now, and the horses were looking at the truck, ears raised, necks stretched up and forward. Guido smiled a little. They looked silly to him standing there, but he knew and pitied them their ignorance.

The wind smashed against the faces of Perce and Gay standing on the truck bed. The brims of their hats flowed up and back from a low point in front, and their faces were dark red. They saw the horses watching their approach at a standstill. And as they roared closer and closer they saw that this herd was beautiful.

Perce Howland turned his head to Gay, who glanced at him at the same time. There had been much rain this spring, and this herd must have found good pasture. They were well rounded and shining. The mare was almost black, and the stallion and the two others were deep brown. The colt was curly-coated and had a grey sheen. The stallion dipped his head suddenly and turned his back on the truck and galloped. The others turned and clattered after him, with the colt running alongside the mare.

Guido pressed down on the gas and the truck surged forward, whining. They were a few yards behind the animals now and they could see the bottoms of their hooves, fresh hooves that had never been shod. They could see the full manes flying and the thick and long black tails that would hang down to their fetlocks when they were still.

The truck was coming abreast of the mare now, and beside her the others galloped with only a loud ticking noise on the clay. It was a gently tacking clatter, for they were light-footed and unshod. They were slim-legged and wet after running almost two hours in this alarm, but as the truck drew alongside the mare and Gay began twirling his loop above his head the whole herd wheeled away to the right, and Guido jammed the gas pedal down and swung with them, but they kept galloping in a circle, and he did not have the speed to keep abreast of them; so he slowed down and fell behind them a few yards until they would straighten out and move ahead again. And they wheeled like circus horses, slower now, for they were at the edge of their strength, and suddenly Guido saw a breadth between the stallion and the two browns and he sped in between, cutting the mare off at the left with her colt.

Now the horses stretched, the clatter quickened. Their hind legs flew straight back and their necks stretched low and forward. Gay whirled his loop over his head, and the truck came up alongside the stallion, whose lungs were hoarsely screaming with exhaustion, and Gay flung the noose.

It fell on the stallion's head, and with a whipping of the lead Gay made it fall over his neck. The horse swerved away to the right and stretched the rope until the tyre was pulled off the truck bed and dragged along the hard clay. The three men watched from the slowing truck as the stallion, with startled eyes, pulled the giant tyre for a few yards, then leaped up with his forelegs in the air and came down facing the tyre and trying to back away from it. Then he stood still, heaving, his hind legs dancing in an arc from right to left and back again as he shook his head in the remorseless noose.

As soon as he was sure the stallion was secure Guido scanned the lake bed and without stopping turned sharply left toward the mare and the colt, which were trotting idly together by themselves. The two browns were already disappearing toward the north, but Guido knew they would halt soon because they were tired, while the mare might continue to the edge of the lake bed and back into her familiar hills where the truck could not follow.

He straightened the truck and jammed down the gas pedal. In a minute he was straight on behind her, and he drew up on her left side because the colt was running on her right. She was very heavy, he saw, and he wondered now if she was a mustang at all. As he drove alongside her his eyes ran across her flanks, seeking out a brand, but she seemed unmarked. Then through his right window he saw the loop flying out and down over her head, and he saw her head fly up, and then she fell back. He turned to the right, braking with his left boot, and he saw her dragging a tyre and coming to a halt, with the free colt watching her and trotting very close beside her.

Then he headed straight ahead across the flat toward two specks, which rapidly enlarged until they became the two browns, which were at a standstill and watching the oncoming truck. He came in between them, and as they galloped Perce on the left roped one, and Gay roped the other almost at the same time. And Guido leaned his head out of his window and yelled up at Perce, who was on the truck bed on his side.

"Good boy!" he hollered, and Perce let himself return an excited grin, although there seemed to be some trouble in his eyes.

Guido made an easy half circle and headed back to the mare and the colt, and in a few minutes he slowed to a halt some twenty yards away and got out of the cab. The dog remained sitting on the floor of the cab, her body shaking all over.

The three men approached the mare. She had never seen a man, and her eyes were wide in fear. Her ribcage stretched and collapsed very rapidly, and there was a trickle of blood coming out of her nostrils. She had a heavy, dark brown mane, and her tail nearly touched the ground. The colt, with dumb eyes, shifted about on its silly bent legs, trying to keep the mare between itself and the men, and the mare kept shifting her rump to shield the colt from them.

They wanted now to move the noose higher up on the mare's neck because it had fallen on her from the rear and was tight around the middle of her neck, where it could choke her if she kept pulling against the weight of the tyre. They had learned from previous forays that they could not leave a horse tied that way without the danger of suffocation, and they wanted them alive until they could bring a larger truck from Bowie and load them on it.

Gay was the best roper, so Perce and Guido stood by as he twirled a noose over his head, and then let it fall open softly just behind the forefeet of the mare. They waited for a moment, then approached her, and she backed a step. Then Gay pulled sharply on the rope, and her forefeet were tied together. Then with another rope Gay lass'd her hind feet, and she swayed and fell to the ground on her side. Her body swelled and contracted, but she seemed resigned. The colt stretched its nose to her tail and stood there as the men came to the mare and spoke quietly to her, and Guido bent down and opened the noose and slipped it up under her jaw. They inspected her for a brand, but she was clean.

"Never see a horse that size up here," Gay said to Guido.

Guido stood there looking down at the great mare.

Perce said, "Maybe wild horses was all big once," and he looked to Guido for confirmation.

Guido bent and sat on his heels and opened the mare's mouth, and the other two looked in with him. "She's fifteen if she's a day," Gay said, and to Perce he said, "She wouldn't be around much longer anyway."

"Ya, she's old," Perce agreed, and his eyes were filled with thought.

Guido stood up, and the three went back to the truck. Perce hopped up and sat on the truck bed with his legs dangling, and Gay sat in the cab with Guido. They drove across the lake bed to the stallion and stopped, and the three of them walked towards him.

"Ain't a bad-lookin' horse," Perce said.

They stood inspecting the horse for a moment. He was standing still now, heaving for breath and bleeding from the nostrils. His head was down, holding the rope taut, and he was looking at them with his deep brown eyes that were like the lenses of enormous binoculars.

Gay got his rope ready in his hand. "He ain't nothin' but a misfit," he said, "except for some kid. You couldn't run cattle with him, and he's too small for a riding horse."

"He is small," Perce conceded. "Got a nice neck, though."

"Oh, they're nice-*lookin*' horses, some of them," Guido said. "What the hell you goin' to do with them, though? Cost more to ship them anywhere than they'd bring."

Gay twirled the loop over his head, and they spread out around the stallion. "They're just old misfit horses, that's all," he said, and he flung the rope behind the stallion's forelegs, and the horse backed a step, and he drew the rope and the noose bit into the horse's lower legs, drawing them together, and the horse swayed but would not fall.

"Take hold," Gay called to Perce, who ran around the horse and grabbed on to the rope and held it taut. Then Gay went back to the truck, got another rope, returned to the rear of the horse, and looped the hind legs. But the stallion would not fall.

Guido stepped closer to push him over, but the horse swung his head and showed his teeth, and Guido stepped back. "Pull on it!" Guido yelled to Gay and Perce, and they pulled on their ropes to trip the stallion, but he righted himself and stood there bound by the head to the tyre and his feet by the two ropes the men held.

Then Guido hurried over to Perce and took the rope from him and walked with it toward the rear of the horse and pulled hard. The stallion's forefeet slipped back, and he came down on his knees and his nose struck the clay ground and he snorted as he struck, but he would not topple over and stayed there on his knees as though he were bowing to something, with his nose propping up his head against the ground and his sharp bursts of breath blowing up dust in little clouds under his nostrils.

Now Guido gave the rope back to young Perce Howland, who held it taut, and he came up alongside the stallion's neck and laid his hands on the side of the neck and pushed, and the horse fell over onto his flank and lay there; and, like the mare, when he felt the ground against his body he seemed to let himself out, and for the first time his eyes blinked and his breath came now in sighs and no longer fiercely. Guido shifted the noose up under the jaw, and they opened the ropes around the hooves, and when the horse felt his legs free he first raised his head curiously and then clattered up and stood there looking at them, from one to the other, blood dripping from his nostrils and a stain of deep red on both dusty knees.

For a moment the three men stood watching him to be sure he was tightly noosed around the neck. Only the clacking of the truck's engine sounded on the enormous floor between the mountains, and the wheezing inhale of the horse and his blowing out of air. Then the men moved without hurrying to the truck, and Gay stored his two extra ropes behind the seat of the cab and got behind the wheel with Guido beside him, and Perce climbed onto the back of the truck and lay down facing the sky, his palms under his head.

Gay headed the truck south toward where they knew the plane was, although it was still beyond their vision. Guido was slowly catching his breath, and now he lighted a cigarette, puffed it, and rubbed his left hand into his bare scalp. He sat gazing out the windshield and the side window. "I'm sleepy," he said.

"What you reckon?" Gay asked.

"What you?" Guido said. He had dust in his throat, and his voice sounded high and almost girlish.

"That mare might be six hundred pounds."

"I'd say about that, Gay," Guido agreed.

"About four hundred apiece for the browns and a little more for the stallion."

"That's about the way I figured."

"What's that come to?"

Guido thought. "Nineteen hundred, maybe two thousand," he said.

They fell silent, figuring the money. Two thousand pounds at six cents a pound came to a hundred and twenty dollars. The colt might make it a few dollars more, but not much. Figuring the gas for the plane and the truck, and twelve dollars for their groceries, they came to the figure of a hundred dollars for the three of them. Guido would get forty-five dollars, since he had used his plane, and Gay would get thirty-five including the use of his truck, and Perce Howland, if he agreed, as he undoubtedly would, would have the remaining twenty.

They fell silent after they had said the figures, and Gay drove in thought. Then he said, "We should've watered them the last time. They can pick up a lot of weight if you let them water."

"Yeah, let's be sure to do that," Guido said.

They knew they would as likely as not forget to water the horses before they unloaded them at the dealer's lot in Bowie. They would be in a hurry to unload and to be free of the horses, and only later, as they were doing now, would they remind themselves that by letting the horses drink their fill they could pick up another fifteen or twenty dollars in added weight. They were not thinking of the money any more, once they had figured it, and if Perce were to object to his smaller share they would both hand him a five or ten dollar bill or more if he wanted it.

Gay stopped the truck beside the plane at the edge of the lake bed. The tethered horses were far away now, except for the mare and her colt, which stood in view less than half a mile off. Guido opened his door and said to Gay, "See you in town. Let's get the other truck in the morning."

"Perce wants to go over to Largo and sign up for the rodeo tomorrow," Gay said. "Tell ya – we'll go in and get the truck and come back here this afternoon maybe. Maybe we bring them in tonight."

"All right, if you want to. I'll see you boys tomorrow," Guido said, and he got out and stopped for a moment to talk to Perce.

"Perce?" he said. Perce propped himself up on one elbow and looked down at him. He looked very sleepy. Guido smiled. "You sleeping?"

Perce's eyelids almost seemed swollen, and his face was indrawn and troubled. "I was about to," he said.

Guido let the reprimand pass. "We figure about a hundred dollars clear. Twenty all right for you?"

"Ya, twenty's all right," Perce said, blinking heavily. He hardly seemed to be listening.

"See you in town," Guido said and turned and waddled off to the plane, where Gay was already standing with his hands on the propeller blade. Guido got in, and Gay swung the blade down and the engine started immediately. Guido waved to Gay and Perce, who raised one hand slightly from the truck bed. Guido gunned the plane, and it trundled off and into the sky, and the two men on the ground watched as it flew towards the mountains and away.

Gay returned to the truck, and as he started to climb in behind the wheel he looked at Perce, who was still propped up on one elbow, and he said, "Twenty all right?" And he said this because he thought Perce looked hurt.

"Heh? Ya, twenty's all right," Perce answered. Then he let himself down from the truck bed, and Gay got behind the wheel. Perce stood beside the truck and wet the ground while Gay waited for him. Then Perce got into the cab, and they drove off.

The mare and her colt stood between them and the sage desert towards which they were heading. Perce stared out the window at the mare, and he saw that she was watching them apprehensively but not in real alarm, and the colt was lying upright on the clay, its head nodding slightly as though it would soon fall asleep. Perce looked long at the colt as they approached, and he thought about how it waited there beside the mare, unbound and free to go off, and he said to Gay, "Ever hear of a colt leave a mare?"

"Not that young a colt," Gay said. "He ain't goin' nowhere." And he glanced to look at Perce.

They passed the mare and colt and left them behind, and Perce laid his head back and closed his eyes. His tobacco swelled out his left cheek, and he let it soak there.

Now the truck left the clay bed, and it pitched and rolled on the sage desert. They would return to their camp and pick up their bedrolls and cooking implements and then drive to the road, which was almost fifteen miles beyond the camp across the desert.

"Think I'll go back to Roslyn's tonight," Gay said.

"OK" Perce said and did not open his eyes.

"We can pick them up in the morning and then take you down to Largo."

"OK," Perce said.

Gay thought about Roslyn. She would probably nag them about all the work they had done for a few dollars, saying they were too dumb to figure in their labour time and other hidden expenses. To hear her, sometimes they hadn't made any profit at all. "Roslyn's goin' to feel sorry for the colt," Gay said, "so might as well not mention it."

Perce opened his eyes, and with his head resting on the back of the seat he looked out of the window at the mountains. "Hell, don't she feed that dog of hers canned dogfood?"

Gay felt closer to Perce again and he smiled. "Sure does."

"Well, what's she think is in the can?"

"She knows what's in the can."

"There's wild horses in the can," Perce said, almost to himself.

They drove in silence for a while. Then Perce said, "That's what beats me."

After a few moments Gay said, "You comin' back to Roslyn's with me or you gonna stay in town?"

"I'd just as soon go back with you."

"OK," Gay said. He felt good about going into her cabin now. There would be her books on the shelves he had built for her, and they would have some drinks, and Perce would fall asleep on the couch, and they would go into the bedroom together. He liked to come back to her after he had worked, more than when he had only driven her here and there or just stayed around her place. He liked his own money in his pocket. And he tried harder to visualise how it would be with her, and he thought of himself being forty-six soon, and then nearing fifty. She would go back East one day, he knew, maybe this year, maybe next. He wondered again when he would begin turning grey and how he would look with grey hair, and he set his jaw against the picture of himself grey and an old man.

Perce spoke, sitting up in his seat. "I want to phone my mother. Damn, I haven't called her all year." He stared out of the window at the mountains. He had the memory of how the colt looked, and he wished it would be gone when they returned in the morning. Then he said, "I got to get to Largo tomorrow and register."

"We'll go," Gay said.

"I could use a good win," he said. He thought of five hundred dollars now, and of the many times he had won five hundred dollars. "You know something, Gay?" he said.

"Huh?"

"I'm never goin' to amount to a damn thing." Then he laughed. He was hungry, and he laughed without restraint for a moment and then laid his head back and closed his eyes.

"I told you that first time I met you, didn't I?" Gay grinned. He felt the mood coming on for some drinks at Roslyn's.

Then Perce spoke. "That colt won't bring two dollars, anyway. What you say we just left him there?"

"Why, you know what he'd do?" Gay said. "He'd just follow the truck right into town."

"I guess he would at that," Perce said. He spat a stream of juice out the window.

They reached the camp in twenty minutes and loaded the gasoline drum, the three bedrolls and the aluminium grub box in the truck and drove on towards Bowie. After they had driven for fifteen minutes without speaking, Gay said he wanted to go north very soon for the hundreds of horses that were supposed to be in the mountains there. But Perce Howland had fallen fast asleep beside him. Gay wanted to talk about that expedition because as they neared Bowie he began to visualise Roslyn nagging them again, and it was clear to him that he had somehow failed to settle anything for himself; he had put in three days for thirty-five dollars, and there would be no way to explain it so it made sense, and it would be embarrassing. And yet he knew that it had all been the way it ought to be even if he could never explain it to her or anyone else. He reached out and nudged Perce, who opened his eyes and lolled his head over to face him. "You comin' up to Thighbone with me, ain't you?"

"OK," Perce said and went back to sleep.

Gay felt more peaceful now that the younger man would not be leaving him. He drove in contentment . . .

The sun shone hot on the beige plain all day. Neither fly nor bug nor snake ventured out on the waste to molest the four horses tethered there, or the colt. They had run nearly two hours at a gallop, and as the afternoon settled upon them they pawed the hard ground for water, but there was none. Towards evening the wind came up, and they backed into it and faced the mountains from which they had come. From time to time the stallion caught the smell of the pastures up there, and he started to walk towards the vaulted fields in which he had grazed; but the tyre bent his neck around, and after a few steps he would turn to face it and leap into the air with his forelegs striking at the sky, and then he would come down and be still again.

With the deep blue darkness the wind blew faster, tossing their manes and flinging their long tails in between their legs. The cold of night raised the colt onto its legs, and it stood close to the mare for warmth. Facing the southern range, five horses blinked under the green glow of the risen moon, and they closed their eyes and slept. The colt settled again on the hard ground and lay under the mare.

In the high hollows of the mountains the grass they had cropped this morning straightened in the darkness. On the lusher swards, which were still damp with the rains of spring, their hoofprints had begun to disappear. When the first pink glow of another morning lit the sky the colt stood up, and as it had always done at dawn it walked waywardly for water. The mare shifted and her bone hooves ticked the clay. The colt turned its head and returned to her and stood at her side with vacant eye, its nostrils sniffing the warming air.

# A MAN CALLED HORSE

(United Artists, 1970)
Starring: Richard Harris, Gale Sondergaard
& Geoffrey Lewis
Directed by Elliot Silverstein
Story 'A Man Called Horse' by Dorothy M. Johnson

**A number of Western movies have tried to portray the Indian and his way of life sympathetically – D. W. Griffiths's *The Massacre* (1912), Delmer Daves's *Broken Arrow* (1950) and *Cheyenne Autumn* (1964) directed by John Ford are three good examples – but according to film historian Walter C. Clapham, *A Man Called Horse* 'gets nearer to the heart of Indian culture than most'. This comment is all the more remarkable because the star, Richard Harris, was British, and in the film played a British lord captured by the Sioux who becomes a man like his captors through a long series of trials and suffering. In fact, the producer Irvin Kershner and his director, Elliot Silverstein, had gone to great lengths to delve into Indian customs before shooting began, and its uncompromising stand coupled with some fine acting by the principals resulted in a landmark Western film. Six years later it inspired a sequel, *The Return of a Man Called Horse*, again starring Richard Harris and directed by Terry Kershner.**

**A vital element in making *A Man Called Horse* the classic it became was the wholly authentic short story by Dorothy Marie Johnson (1905–1984) on which it was based. She was a writer whose sympathetic and understanding stories about the Native**

**American Indians had earned her several awards as well as the distinction of being made an honorary member of the Blackfeet tribe in Montana. Dorothy was born in Iowa, but educated at the University of Montana, where she formed her lifelong interest in Western history. For a time she was a journalist and editor, later becoming Professor of Journalism at the University of Montana and writing novels, receiving widespread critical acclaim for her first, *Buffalo Woman*, published in 1977. She also produced a number of superb short stories which displayed her affinity with the Indians and won her the Western Literature Association Distinguished Achievement Award in 1981. 'A Man Called Horse' is certainly among the very best of her works and, as the reader who has seen the movie will now discover, was very faithfully brought to the screen in the United Artists' adaptation.**

He was a young man of good family, as the phrase went in the New England of a hundred-odd years ago, and the reasons for his bitter discontent were unclear, even to himself. He grew up in the gracious old Boston home under his grandmother's care, for his mother had died in giving him birth; and all his life he had known every comfort and privilege his father's wealth could provide.

But still there was the discontent, which puzzled him because he could not even define it. He wanted to live among his equals – people who were no better than he and no worse either. That was as close as he could come to describing the source of his unhappiness in Boston and his restless desire to go somewhere else.

In the year 1845, he left home and went out West, far beyond the country's creeping frontier, where he hoped to find his equals. He had the idea that in Indian country, where there was danger, all white men were kings, and he wanted to be one of them. But he found, in the West as in Boston, that the men he respected were still his superiors, even if they could not read, and those he did not respect weren't worth talking to.

He did have money, however, and he could hire the men he respected. He hired four of them, to cook and hunt and guide and be his companions, but he found them not friendly.

They were apart from him and he was still alone. He still brooded about his status in the world, longing for his equals.

On a day in June, he learned what it was to have no status at all. He became a captive of a small raiding party of Crow Indians.

He heard gunfire and the brief shouts of his companions around the bend of the creek just before they died, but he never saw their bodies. He had no chance to fight, because he was naked and unarmed, bathing in the creek, when a Crow warrior seized and held him.

His captor let him go at last, let him run. Then the lot of them rode him down for sport, striking him with their coup sticks. They carried the dripping scalps of his companions, and one had skinned off Baptiste's black beard as well, for a trophy.

They took him along in a matter-of-fact way, as they took the captured horses. He was unshod and naked as the horses were, and like them he had a rawhide thong around his neck. So long as he didn't fall down, the Crows ignored him.

On the second day they gave him his breeches. His feet were too swollen for his boots, but one of the Indians threw him a pair of moccasins that had belonged to the halfbreed, Henri, who was dead back at the creek. The captive wore the moccasins gratefully. The third day they let him ride one of the spare horses so the party could move faster, and on that day they came in sight of their camp.

He thought of trying to escape, hoping he might be killed in flight rather than by slow torture in the camp, but he never had a chance to try. They were more familiar with escape than he was and, knowing what to expect, they forestalled it. The only other time he had tried to escape from anyone, he had succeeded. When he had left his home in Boston, his father had raged and his grandmother had cried, but they could not talk him out of his intention.

The men of the Crow raiding party didn't bother with talk.

Before riding into camp they stopped and dressed in their regalia, and in parts of their victims' clothing; they painted their faces black. Then, leading the white man by the rawhide around his neck as though he were a horse, they rode down toward the tepee circle, shouting and singing, brandishing their weapons. He was unconscious when they got there; he fell and was dragged.

He lay dazed and battered near a tepee while the noisy, busy life of the camp swarmed around him and Indians came to stare. Thirst consumed him, and when it rained he lapped rain water from the ground like a dog. A scrawny, shrieking, eternally busy old woman with ragged greying hair threw a chunk of meat on the grass, and he fought the dogs for it.

When his head cleared, he was angry, although anger was an emotion he knew he could not afford.

It was better when I was a horse, he thought – when they led me by the rawhide around my neck. I won't be a dog, no matter what!

The hag gave him stinking, rancid grease and let him figure out what it was for. He applied it gingerly to his bruised and sun-seared body.

Now, he thought, I smell like the rest of them.

While he was healing, he considered coldly the advantages of being a horse. A man would be humiliated, and sooner or later he would strike back and that would be the end of him. But a horse had only to be docile. Very well, he would learn to do without pride.

He understood that he was the property of the screaming old woman, a fine gift from her son, one that she liked to show off. She did more yelling at him than at anyone else, probably to impress the neighbours so they would not forget what a great and generous man her son was. She was bossy and proud, a dreadful bag of skin and bones, and she was a devilish hard worker.

The white man, who now thought of himself as a horse, forgot sometimes to worry about his danger. He kept making mental notes of things to tell his own people in Boston about this hideous adventure. He would go back a hero, and he would say, "Grandmother, let me fetch your shawl. I've been accustomed to doing little errands for another lady about your age."

Two girls lived in the tepee with the old hag and her warrior son. One of them, the white man concluded, was his captor's wife and the other was his little sister. The daughter-in-law was smug and spoiled. Being beloved, she did not have to be useful. The younger girl had bright, wandering eyes. Often enough they wandered to the white man who was pretending to be a horse.

The two girls worked when the old woman put them at it, but they were always running off to do something they enjoyed more. There were games and noisy contests, and there was much laughter. But not for the white man. He was finding out what loneliness could be.

That was a rich summer on the plains, with plenty of buffalo for meat and clothing and the making of tepees. The Crows were wealthy in horses, prosperous and contented. If their men had not been so avid for glory, the white man thought, there would have been a lot more of them. But they went out of their way to court death, and when one of them met it, the whole camp mourned extravagantly and cried to their God for vengeance.

The captive was a horse all summer, a docile bearer of burdens, careful and patient. He kept reminding himself that he had to be better-natured than other horses, because he could not lash out with hooves or teeth. Helping the old woman load up the horses for travel, he yanked at a pack and said, "Whoa, brother. It goes easier when you don't fight."

The horse gave him a big-eyed stare as if it understood his language – a comforting thought, because nobody else did. But even among the horses he felt unequal. They were able to look out for themselves if they escaped. He would simply starve. He was envious still, even among the horses.

Humbly he fetched and carried. Sometimes he even offered to help, but he had not the skill for the endless work of the women, and he was not trusted to hunt with the men, the providers.

When the camp moved, he carried a pack trudging with the women. Even the dogs worked then, pulling small burdens on travois of sticks.

The Indian who had captured him lived like a lord, as he had a right to do. He hunted with his peers, attended long ceremonial meetings with much chanting and dancing and lounged in the shade with his smug bride. He had only two responsibilities: to kill buffalo and to gain glory. The white man was so far beneath him in status that the Indian did not even think of envy.

One day several things happened that made the captive think he might sometime become a man again. That was the day when he began to understand their language. For four months he had heard it, day and night, the joy and the mourning, the ritual chanting and sung prayers, the squabbles and the deliberations. None of it meant anything to him at all.

But on that important day in early fall the two young women set out for the river, and one of them called over her shoulder to the old woman. The white man was startled. She had said she was going to bathe. His understanding was so sudden that he felt as if his ears had come unstopped.

Listening to the racket of the camp, he heard fragments of meaning instead of gabble.

On that same important day the old woman brought a pair of new moccasins out of the tepee and tossed them on the ground before him. He could not believe she would do anything for him because of kindness, but giving him moccasins was one way of looking after her property.

In thanking her, he dared greatly. He picked a little handful of fading fall flowers and took them to her as she squatted in front of her tepee, scraping a buffalo hide with a tool made from a piece of iron tied to a bone. Her hands were hideous – most of the fingers had the first joint missing. He bowed solemnly and offered the flowers.

She glared at him from beneath the short, ragged tangle of her hair. She stared at the flowers, knocked them out of his hand and went running to the next tepee, squalling the story. He heard her and the other women screaming with laughter.

The white man squared his shoulders and walked boldly over to watch three small boys shooting arrows at a target. He said in English, "Show me how to do that, will you?"

They frowned, but he held out his hand as if there could be no doubt. One of them gave him a bow and one arrow, and they snickered when he missed.

The people were easily amused, except when they were angry. They were amused, at him, playing with the little boys. A few days later he asked the hag, with gestures, for a bow that her son had just discarded, a man-size bow of horn. He scavenged for old arrows. The old woman cackled at his marksmanship and called her neighbours to enjoy the fun.

When he could understand words, he could identify his people by their names. The old woman was Greasy Hand, and her daughter was Pretty Calf. The other young woman's name was not clear to him, for the words were not in his vocabulary. The man who had captured him was Yellow Robe.

Once he could understand, he could begin to talk a little, and then he was less lonely. Nobody had been able to see any reason for talking to him, since he would not understand anyway. He asked the old woman, "What is my name?" Until he knew it, he was incomplete. She shrugged to let him know he had none.

He told her in the Crow language, "My name is Horse." He repeated it, and she nodded. After that they called him Horse when they called him anything. Nobody cared except the white man himself.

They trusted him enough to let him stray out of camp, so that he might have got away and, by unimaginable good luck, might have reached a trading post or a fort, but winter was too close. He did not dare leave without a horse; he needed clothing and a better hunting weapon than he had, and more certain skill in using it. He did not dare steal, for then they would surely have pursued him, and just as certainly they would have caught him. Remembering the warmth of the home that was waiting in Boston, he settled down for the winter.

On a cold night he crept into the tepee after the others had gone to bed. Even a horse might try to find shelter from the wind. The old woman grumbled, but without conviction. She did not put him out.

They tolerated him, back in the shadows, so long as he did not get in the way.

He began to understand how the family that owned him differed from the others. Fate had been cruel to them. In a short, sharp argument among the old women, one of them derided Greasy Hand by sneering, "You have no relatives!" and Greasy Hand raved for minutes of the deeds of her father and uncles and brothers. And she had had four sons, she reminded her detractor – who answered with scorn, "Where are they?"

Later the white man found her moaning and whimpering to herself, rocking back and forth on her haunches, staring at her mutilated hands. By that time he understood. A mourner often chopped off a finger joint. Old Greasy Hand had mourned often. For the first time he felt a twinge of pity, but he put it aside as another emotion, like anger, that he could not afford. He thought: What tales I will tell when I get home!

He wrinkled his nose in disdain. The camp stank of animals and meat and rancid grease. He looked down at his naked, shivering legs and was startled, remembering that he was still only a horse.

He could not trust the old woman. She fed him only because a starved slave would die and not be worth boasting about. Just how fitful her temper was he saw on the day when she got tired of stumbling over one of the hundred dogs that infested the camp. This was one of her own dogs, a large, strong one that pulled a baggage travois when the tribe moved camp.

Countless times he had seen her kick at the beast as it lay sleeping in front of the tepee, in her way. The dog always moved, with a yelp, but it always got in the way again. One day she gave the dog its usual kick and then stood scolding at it while the animal rolled its eyes sleepily. The old woman suddenly picked up her axe and cut the dog's head off with one blow. Looking well satisfied with herself, she beckoned her slave to remove the body.

It could have been me, he thought, if I were a dog. But I'm a horse.

His hope of life lay with the girl, Pretty Calf. He set about courting her, realising how desperately poor he was both in property and honour. He owned no horse, no weapon but the old bow and the battered arrows. He had nothing to give away, and he needed gifts, because he did not dare seduce the girl.

One of the customs of courtship involved sending a gift of horses to a girl's older brother and bestowing much buffalo meat upon her mother. The white man could not wait for some far-off time when he might have either horses or meat to give away. And his courtship had to be secret. It was not for him to stroll past the groups of watchful girls, blowing a flute made of an eagle's wing bone, as the flirtatious young bucks did.

He could not ride past Pretty Calf's tepee, painted and bedizened; he had no horse, no finery.

Back home, he remembered, I could marry just about any girl I'd want to. But he wasted little time thinking about that. A future was something to be earned.

The most he dared do was wink at Pretty Calf now and then, or state his admiration while she giggled and hid her face. The least he dared do to win his bride was to elope with her, but he had to give her a horse to put the seal of tribal approval on that. And he had no horse until he killed a man to get one . . .

* * *

His opportunity came in early spring. He was casually accepted by that time. He did not belong, but he was amusing to the Crows, like a strange pet, or they would not have fed him through the winter.

His chance came when he was hunting small game with three young boys who were his guards as well as his scornful companions. Rabbits and birds were of no account in a camp well fed on buffalo meat; but they made good targets.

His party walked far that day. All of them at once saw the two horses in a sheltered coulee. The boys and the man crawled forward on their bellies, and then they saw an Indian who lay on the ground, moaning, a lone traveller. From the way the boys inched forward, Horse knew the man was fair prey – a member of some enemy tribe.

This is the way the captive white man acquired wealth and honour to win a bride and save his life: he shot an arrow into the sick man, a split second ahead of one of his small companions, and dashed forward to strike the still-groaning man with his bow, to count first coup. Then he seized the hobbled horses.

By the time he had the horses secure, and with them his hope for freedom, the boys had followed, counting coup with gestures and shrieks they had practiced since boyhood, and one of them had the scalp. The white man was grimly amused to see the boy double up with sudden nausea when he had the thing in his hand . . .

There was a hubbub in the camp when they rode in that evening, two of them on each horse. The captive was noticed. Indians who had ignored him as a slave stared at the brave man who had struck first coup and had stolen horses.

The hubbub lasted all night, as fathers boasted loudly of their young sons' exploits. The white man was called upon to settle an argument between two fierce boys as to which of them had struck second coup and which must be satisfied with third. After much talk that went over his head, he solemnly pointed at the nearest boy. He didn't know which boy it was and didn't care, but the boy did.

The white man had watched warriors in their triumph. He knew what to do. Modesty about achievements had no place among the Crow people. When a man did something big, he told about it.

The white man smeared his face with grease and charcoal. He walked inside the tepee circle, chanting and singing. He used his own language.

"You heathens, you savages" he shouted. "I'm going to get out of here someday! I am going to get away!" The Crow people listened respectfully. In the Crow tongue he shouted, "Horse! I am Horse!" and they nodded.

He had a right to boast, and he had two horses. Before dawn, the white man and his bride were sheltered beyond a far hill, and he was telling her, "I love you, little lady. I love you."

She looked at him with her great dark eyes, and he thought she understood his English words – or as much as she needed to understand.

"You are my treasure," he said, "more precious than jewels, better than fine gold. I am going to call you Freedom."

When they returned to camp two days later, he was bold but worried. His ace, he suspected, might not be high enough in the game he was playing without being sure of the rules. But it served.

Old Greasy Hand raged – but not at him. She complained loudly that her daughter had let herself go too cheap. But the marriage was as good as any Crow marriage. He had paid a horse.

He learned the language faster after that, from Pretty Calf, whom he sometimes called Freedom. He learned that his attentive, adoring bride was fourteen years old.

One thing he had not guessed was the difference that being Pretty Calf's husband would make in his relationship to her mother and brother. He had hoped only to make his position a little safer, but he had not expected to be treated with dignity. Greasy Hand no longer spoke to him at all. When the white man spoke to her, his bride murmured in dismay, explaining at great length that he must never do that. There could be no conversation between a man and his mother-in-law. He could not even mention a word that was part of her name.

Having improved his status so magnificently, he felt no need for hurry in getting away. Now that he had a woman, he had as good a chance to be rich as any man. Pretty Calf waited on him; she seldom ran off to play games with other young girls, but took pride in learning from her mother the many women's skills of tanning hides and making clothing and preparing food.

He was no more a horse but a kind of man, a half-Indian, still poor and unskilled but laden with honors, clinging to the buckskin fringes of Crow society.

Escape could wait until he could manage it in comfort, with fit clothing and a good horse, with hunting weapons. Escape could wait until the camp moved near some trading post. He did not plan how he would get home. He dreamed of being there all at once, and of telling stories nobody would believe. There was no hurry.

Pretty Calf delighted in educating him. He began to understand tribal arrangements, customs and why things were as they were. They were that way because they had always been so. His young wife giggled when she told him, in his ignorance, things she had always known. But she did not laugh when her brother's wife was taken by another warrior. She explained that solemnly with words and signs.

Yellow Robe belonged to a society called the Big Dogs. The wife stealer, Cut Neck, belonged to the Foxes. They were fellow tribesmen; they hunted together and fought side by side, but men of one society could take away wives from the other society if they wished, subject to certain limitations.

When Cut Neck rode up to the tepee, laughing and singing, and called to Yellow Robe's wife, "Come out! Come out!" she did as ordered, looking smug as usual, meek and entirely willing. Thereafter she rode beside him in ceremonial processions and carried his coup stick, while his other wife pretended not to care.

"But why?" the white man demanded of his wife, his Freedom. "Why did our brother let his woman go? He sits and smokes and does not speak."

Pretty Calf was shocked at the suggestion. Her brother could not possibly reclaim his woman, she explained. He could not even let her come back if she wanted to – and she probably would want to when Cut Neck tired of her. Yellow Robe could not even admit that his heart was sick. That was the way things were. Deviation meant dishonour.

The woman could have hidden from Cut Neck, she said. She could even have refused to go with him if she had been *ba-wurokee* – a really virtuous woman. But she had been his woman before, for a little while on a berrying expedition, and he had a right to claim her.

There was no sense in it, the white man insisted. He glared at his young wife. "If you go, I will bring you back!" he promised.

She laughed and buried her head against his shoulder. "I will not have to go," she said. "Horse is my first man. There is no hole in my moccasin."

He stroked her hair and said, "*Ba-wurokee*."

With great daring, she murmured, "*Hayha*," and when he did not answer, because he did not know what she meant, she drew away, hurt.

"A woman calls her man that if she thinks he will not leave her. Am I wrong?"

The white man held her closer and lied, "Pretty Calf is not wrong. Horse will not leave her. Horse will not take another woman, either." No, he certainly would not. Parting from this one was going to be harder than getting her had been. "*Hayha*," he murmured. "Freedom."

His conscience irked him, but not very much. Pretty Calf could get another man easily enough when he was gone, and a better provider. His hunting skill was improving, but he was still awkward.

There was no hurry about leaving. He was used to most of the Crow ways and could stand the rest. He was becoming prosperous. He owned five horses. His place in the life of the tribe was secure, such as it was. Three or four young women, including the one who had belonged to Yellow Robe, made advances to him. Pretty Calf took pride in the fact that her man was so attractive.

By the time he had what he needed for a secret journey, the grass grew yellow on the plains and the long cold was close. He was enslaved by the girl he called Freedom and, before the winter ended, by the knowledge that she was carrying his child . . .

The Big Dog society held a long ceremony in the spring. The white man strolled with his woman along the creek bank, thinking: When I get home I will tell them about the chants and the drumming. Sometime. Sometime.

Pretty Calf would not go to bed when they went back to the tepee.

"Wait and find out about my brother," she urged. "Something may happen."

So far as Horse could figure out, the Big Dogs were having some kind of election. He pampered his wife by staying up with her by the fire. Even the old woman, who was a great one for getting sleep when she was not working, prowled around restlessly.

The white man was yawning by the time the noise of the ceremony died down. When Yellow Robe strode in, garish and heathen in his paint and feathers and furs, the women cried out. There was conversation, too fast for Horse to follow, and the old woman wailed once, but her son silenced her with a gruff command.

When the white man went to sleep, he thought his wife was weeping beside him.

The next morning she explained.

"He wears the bearskin belt. Now he can never retreat in battle. He will always be in danger. He will die."

Maybe he wouldn't, the white man tried to convince her. Pretty Calf recalled that some few men had been honoured by the bearskin belt, vowed to the highest daring, and had not died. If they lived through the summer, then they were free of it.

"My brother wants to die," she mourned. "His heart is bitter."

Yellow Robe lived through half a dozen clashes with small parties of raiders from hostile tribes. His honours were many. He captured horses in an enemy camp, led two successful raids, counted first coup and snatched a gun from the hand of an enemy tribesman. He wore wolf tails on his moccasins and ermine skins on his shirt, and he fringed his leggings with scalps in token of his glory.

When his mother ventured to suggest, as she did many times, "My son should take a new wife, I need another woman to help me," he ignored her. He spent much time in prayer, alone in the hills or in conference with a medicine-man. He fasted and made vows and kept them. And before he could be free of the heavy honour of the bearskin belt, he went on his last raid.

The warriors were returning from the north just as the white man and two other hunters approached from the south, with buffalo and elk meat dripping from the bloody hides tied on their restive ponies. One of the hunters grunted, and they stopped to watch a rider on the hill north of the tepee circle.

The rider dismounted, held up a blanket and dropped it. He repeated the gesture.

The hunters murmured dismay. "Two! Two men dead!" They rode fast into the camp, where there was already wailing.

A messenger came down from the war party on the hill. The rest of the party delayed to paint their faces for mourning and for victory. One of the two dead men was Yellow Robe. They had put his body in a cave and walled it in with rocks. The other man died later, and his body was in a tree.

There was blood on the ground before the tepee to which Yellow Robe would return no more. His mother, with her hair chopped short, sat in the doorway, rocking back and forth on her haunches, wailing her heartbreak. She cradled one mutilated hand in the other. She had cut off another finger joint.

Pretty Calf had cut off chunks of her long hair and was crying as she gashed her arms with a knife. The white man tried to take the knife away, but she protested so piteously that he let her do as she wished. He was sickened with the lot of them.

Savages! he thought. Now I will go back! I'll go hunting alone, and I'll keep on going.

But he did not go just yet, because he was the only hunter in the lodge of the two grieving women, one of them old and the other pregnant with his child.

In their mourning, they made him a pauper again. Everything that meant comfort, wealth and safety they sacrificed to the spirits because of the death of Yellow Robe. The tepee, made of seventeen fine buffalo hides, the furs that should have kept them warm, the white deerskin dress, trimmed with elk teeth, that Pretty Calf loved so well, even their tools and Yellow Robe's weapons – everything but his sacred medicine objects – they left there on the prairie, and the whole camp moved away. Two of his best horses were killed as a sacrifice, and the women gave away the rest.

They had no shelter. They would have no tepee of their own for two months at least of mourning, and then the women would have to tan hides to make it. Meanwhile they could live in temporary huts made of willows, covered with skins given them in pity by their friends. They could have lived with relatives, but Yellow Robe's women had no relatives.

The white man had not realised until then how terrible a thing it was for a Crow to have no kinfolk. No wonder old Greasy Hand had only stumps for fingers. She had mourned, from one year to the next, for everyone she had ever loved. She had no one left but her daughter, Pretty Calf.

Horse was furious at their foolishness. It had been bad enough for him, a captive, to be naked as a horse and poor as a slave, but that was because his captors had stripped him. These women had voluntarily given up everything they needed.

He was too angry at them to sleep in the willow hut. He lay under a sheltering tree. And on the third night of the mourning he made his plans. He had a knife and a bow. He would go after meat, taking two horses. And he would not come back. There were, he realised, many things he was not going to tell when he got back home.

In the willow hut, Pretty Calf cried out. He heard rustling there, and the old woman's querulous voice.

Some twenty hours later his son was born, two months early, in the tepee of a skilled medicine-woman. The child was born without breath, and the mother died before the sun went down.

The white man was too shocked to think whether he should mourn, or how he should mourn. The old woman screamed until she was voiceless. Piteously she approached him, bent and trembling, blind with grief. She held out her knife and he took it.

She spread out her hands and shook her head. If she cut off any more finger joints, she could no more work. She could not afford any more lasting signs of grief.

The white man said, "All right! All right!" between his teeth. He hacked his arms with the knife and stood watching the blood run down. It was little enough to do for Pretty Calf, for little Freedom.

Now there is nothing to keep me, he realised. When I get home, I must not let them see the scars.

He looked at Greasy Hand, hideous in her grief-burdened age, and thought: I really am free now! When a wife dies, her husband has no more duty toward her family. Pretty Calf had told him so, long ago, when he wondered why a certain man moved out of one tepee and into another.

The old woman, of course, would be a scavenger. There was one other with the tribe, an ancient crone who had no relatives, toward whom no one felt any responsibility. She lived on food thrown away by the more fortunate. She slept in shelters that she built with her own knotted hands. She plodded wearily at the end of the procession when the camp moved. When she stumbled, nobody cared. When she died, nobody would miss her.

Tomorrow morning, the white man decided, I will go.

His mother-in-law's sunken mouth quivered. She said one word, questioningly. She said, "*Eero-oshay?*" She said, "Son?"

Blinking, he remembered. When a wife died, her husband was free. But her mother, who had ignored him with dignity, might if she wished ask him to stay. She invited him by calling him Son, and he accepted by answering Mother.

Greasy Hand stood before him, bowed with years, withered with unceasing labour, loveless and childless, scarred with grief. But with all her burdens, she still loved life enough to beg it from him, the only person she had any right to ask. She was stripping herself of all she had left, her pride.

He looked eastward across the prairie. Two thousand miles away was home. The old woman would not live for ever. He could afford to wait, for he was young. He could afford to be magnanimous, for he knew he was a man. He gave her the answer. "*Eegya*," he said. "Mother."

He went home three years later. He explained no more than to say, "I lived with Crows for a while. It was some time before I could leave. They called me Horse."

He did not find it necessary either to apologise or to boast, because he was the equal of any man on earth.

# LONESOME DOVE

(ABC TV, 1989)
Starring: Robert Duvall, Tommy Lee Jones
& Danny Glover
Directed by Yves Simoneau
Story 'The Legend of Billy' by Larry McMurtry

**In the late Eighties and Nineties, one Western writer above all has dominated the screen with adaptions of his work. He is Larry McMurtry, whose Pulitzer Prize-winning novel, *Lonesome Dove*, about two Texas ranchers, Gus McCrae and Woodrow Call, and their hunt for some unclaimed land in Montana was made into a hugely popular eight-hour special in 1989, winning nine TV awards in the process. It has since been followed by *Return to Lonesome Dove* (1993), and *Dead Man's Walk* (1996) in which McCrae and Call – now played by Jonny Lee Miller and David Arquette – are seen at the start of their friendship as young Texas Rangers. In the interim, another McMurty novel, *Buffalo Girls* (1991), a table of Calamity Jane and her apparent affair with Wild Bill Hickcock which resulted in her bearing a child, has also been made into a four-hour mini-series starring Anjelica Huston and Sam Elliot (1995). Melanie Griffith co-starred as Calamity's friend, the brothel owner Dora DuFran. At the time of writing several more of McMurty's novels are under option for filming, which would seem to ensure that he will remain the Western Movies' number one author for the foreseeable future!**

**Larry Jeff McMurtry (1936– ) was born in the heart of the West at Wichita Falls in Texas and attended North Texas**

**State College, where he obtained a BA. Later he took an MA at Rice University in Houston, where he lectured for some years while developing his literary career. From the start, Larry's intention in his work has been clear: 'to break down the myths of the old West', in his own words. His first novel, *Horseman Pass By* (1961), about a callous young drifter, won the Texas Institute of Letters' Jesse H. Jones Award and was superbly filmed two years later with Paul Newman. Larry followed this with the equally successful *Leaving Cheyenne* (1963) and *The Last Picture Show* (1966), for which he wrote the screenplay with Peter Bogdanovich. Since then he has divided his time between writing on the family ranch in Texas where he grew up and Washington, where he is the part owner of a rare-book shop. This final story in the collection, 'The Legend of Billy', in which Larry debunks the myth of Billy the Kid, is a fine example of his approach to frontier history and an excellent example of why he is seen by many critics and readers as the trailblazer of the Western novel and movie in the future . . .**

There's a popular book called *The Wind's Four Quarters*, written by a newspaperman who spends all his holidays researching Billy's life. He's made it his hobby to ride all the trails that led to Greasy Corners. Of course there's nothing left of the place now – even the last adobe wall has been broken up and the chunks sold for souvenirs, no different except in colour from what they try to sell you in Greece or Rome, if you try to have a picnic on the Acropolis or in the Colosseum.

This newspaperman has written the longest book yet about what happened the next morning: he's taken Isinglass and Tully Roebuck, Katie and Bloody Feathers and the killer Long Dog Hawkins, and followed them practically from birth to their arrival at that clump of hovels on the Rio Pecos. He's mapped each arrival, marked where each one stood, developed very reasonable theories about how each meant to kill Billy that morning.

Of course, like all the rest, the historians and outlaw collectors, he came up against the awkward fact that I was sitting there in Lord Snow's camp chair, not thirty feet from where Billy fell. He was polite, though – he came to see me and told me what happened that day, and when I demurred and explained how it really happened, he smiled and did his best to overlook my bad manners.

I don't guess I blame those people much – the scholars and the believers. Billy's death was simple, and yet even the simplest events grow mossy with the passage of years. If the students accepted the simple view of events in past times, how would their stiff brains ever get any exercise?

After Billy went in at midnight, I relaxed a little. His calm had an effect on me. Perhaps I was just doing too much speculating. Isinglass sometimes went as far afield as New Orleans – he might not return for weeks. Tully Roebuck hated to leave his blind daughter – perhaps he wasn't coming at all. The talk of Long Dog Hawkins could have been pure rumour – and no one knew for sure that the Indian boy Billy killed had even been one of Bloody Feathers's people.

Katie Garza I gave no thought to – of all of us, Katie loved Billy best; I assumed she was merely nursing her bruised heart in San Isidro.

Perhaps it was all worry for nothing; perhaps no one was coming. Billy and Cecily might have a slow trip to Galveston and sail away to live happily ever after in some great Cavendish pile in the grey North. Billy might dispense with his shabby saddle and learn to canter and jump in the English style – though I admit *that* was hard to imagine.

I suppose I dozed, as the night waned, but it was not a deep sleep, and the sound of a racing horse brought me wide awake. Billy Bone must have heard it too, for he hobbled out of the tent, grimacing at the soreness of his leg. He was using the stock of his shotgun as a crutch.

It was full dawn; I saw it all quite clearly. Billy's old shirt hung open, as it had during the night. We had not cleared the table after dinner – I was not as well trained a servant as Mahmood. The plates were still on the table, and Cecily had forgotten one of her fine ivory combs. Billy picked up a scrap – a bite of cheese, I think – and awaited the approaching rider with half-awake curiosity; he seemed anything but scared.

Then I saw the white mare come racing out of the long shadow to the south – Katie Garza almost ran past me before she checked her horse. The mare was flecked with sweat. I remember clearly how anxious Katie looked, as if fearful of having arrived too late. She had her gun in her hand.

"Oh, dern!" Billy said, with a horrified glance at Katie. "This is gonna give me a headache."

Katie swung off the mare, dropped the rein and shot Billy before he could move. He didn't fall flat; he gripped the shotgun and slid into a seated position. Katie walked closer to him, her gun cocked; I saw her glance at the ivory comb on the camp table.

There was a spot of blood on Billy's breast – not much.

"I guess it's one cure for a headache," he said, still clinging to the shotgun.

Then, from the wind's four quarters, the losers in the race to kill him moved out of their hiding places. Isinglass stepped in view from behind the tent, Winchester in the crook of his arm. Tully Roebuck emerged from the China Pond, a pistol in each hand. Bloody Feathers stood atop the old, rotting pile of buffalo hides where Jim Saul and his crew had made their last stand. And a small weasel in a dark coat – it was Long Dog Hawkins – appeared practically at my elbow, carrying a huge Colt: he had been hiding behind my own hut.

"Now here, goddammit, it ain't fair!" Long Dog complained, addressing himself to Old Whiskey. "I've rode all the way from the Wind River and this Mexican whore has cheated me of my bounty."

Katie raised her gun and shot him, as coolly as she had broken the beer bottles that morning on the plain nearby. Long Dog fell backward, almost beside me, slumped down, and didn't move. The spot of blood, in his case, was in the middle of his forehead.

"Well, Long Dog's a dead dog, like I predicted," Billy said, and he too slumped flat. Tully Roebuck came walking over, his guns still cocked. Bloody Feathers jumped off the hides and joined his father.

Katie knelt down by Billy and shielded his eyes with her hat, for the sun had broken the horizon and was shooting its strong rays into his face.

I joined the group around the fallen boy.

"Hi, Tully," Billy said in a weaker tone.

He looked at Katie with a crook of a smile.

"You ought to let on that Tully got me," he said. "Tully's got politics to think of."

"Hurry up and die, *chapito*," Katie said softly. "I've ridden a long way and I need to water this horse."

The remark scored big with Billy Bone.

"That's spunk, ain't it, Sippy?" he said.

"That's spunk," I agreed, but before my words were out Billy Bone had obeyed her request.

Katie Garza laid her hat over Billy's face. Then she stood up, broke into sobs, and flung herself into her father's arms. Tully Roebuck – he really liked Billy – was crying too, and my own eyes were not dry.

Bloody Feathers had a long knife in his hand. While Katie sobbed on Isinglass's breast, he stepped over to the corpse of Long Dog Hawkins and took his scalp – the last scalp taken on the Southern plains, some say.

"I promised old Grandmother a scalp for that boy she lost," he said. "I guess this dirty hank of hair will do as good as any."

"Brash boys always come to bad ends," Isinglass said, looking down at Billy.

Cecily Snow stepped out of the tent then, wearing a long white gown. She noticed her comb, picked it up and fixed it in her tumbled tresses. Then she smiled at Isinglass. Though her scheme had failed – if it *was* her scheme – she showed no trace of disappointment.

"Well, Willie, you took your good time coming," she said. "I suppose it's no longer of much moment to you what sort of brute kidnaps me."

Then Cecily walked over and knelt by Billy. The harmonica she had given him was still in his shirt pocket; she lifted it out. Then she raised Katie's hat briefly, and placed it back over his eyes.

"Why, my little beast is dead," Cecily remarked, looking at me. "Things do catch up with one, don't they, Ben?"

I didn't answer – I was too shocked by the realisation that the enmity she had always claimed she felt for Will Isinglass was clearly very much less than absolute.

Cecily raised the harmonica and began to play 'Barbara Allen' – the air she had tried to teach Billy. Then a low voice began to sing to the tune – it was La Tulipe, standing by her donkey. Somewhere the old yellow woman had learned the English air. I broke down completely, as I had the first time Cecily played the song. It was such a sad thing to hear, on the cusp of the great American plain, with Billy Bone dead in the dust.

Katie Garza jerked away from her father, flinging Cecily a look of disgust. I expected Katie to shoot her, but instead she caught her tired mare and led her down to the Rio Pecos to water. Bloody Feathers wiped off his knife and followed her to the river.

Isinglass whistled up some cowboys, who soon dismantled Lord Snow's tent and packed it back on the mule. Then he and Cecily rode away, with no more said.

Bloody Feathers comforted Katie as best he could, while Tully Roebuck and I dug Billy's grave on the plain behind the China Pond. Since the earth that covered Des Montaignes was still loose, we decided to economise, which meant uncovering him briefly so we could tuck the small body of Long Dog Hawkins in with him.

Billy, though, had his own private grave.

"Ever notice how all these famous gunmen are no bigger than a pint?" Tully remarked as we worked. "Hill Coe was small, too."

"I suppose presenting a small target helps one last, in that profession," I said.

Katie cried and cried over Billy before she would let us throw the dirt in.

"I didn't want nobody who didn't love him to kill him," she said. "That's why I hurried. Billy was like me – he never had no place."

I thought, even allowing for her grief, that the remark was rather off. "Katie, this whole land is your place," I said.

She didn't answer. Her eyes were swollen. She cut one of the silver nuggets off her vest and laid it on Billy's breast.

"Heaven be your bed, *chapito*," she said. "*Soy el tuyo.*"

Then she got up and started back for Mexico, a woman with a sadly torn heart. Bloody Feathers rode with her out of town; when they left, La Tulipe left too, hobbling off with Bonaparte across the plain toward Colorado.

Tully Roebuck rode back to Lincoln that afternoon, to his sheriffing and his blind daughter. I thought of going up to Winds' Hill and attempting to rid the earth of Cecily Snow, but of course I did no such thing. Instead, benumbed by life and death, I plodded over to the good hotel in Las Cruces and immediately penned the dime novel that I assumed would assure my glory and my income as well.

I called it *Billy the Kid; or, The Wandering Boy's Doom.* I expected high fame, but I suppose I was too quick off the mark, for the book sold poorly. The only thing that caught on was the nickname: now that Billy's risen in legend, the white star of the West, talk of Billy the Kid is all you hear – it's the one phrase I contributed to the language, of all the millions I wrote, though the book it introduced is forgotten, and was never believed.

The irony is that Tully Roebuck's silly memoir, written two years after my novel, caught the public fancy. It had been a terrible winter, Tully lost all his cattle and no doubt needed money, so he sat down with one of the Buntline secretaries and wrote *The True Authentic Adventures of the Notorious Billy the Kid*. It had the kind of lurid cover they used to put on my Orson Oxx tales, and it sold a million. Tully got so rich he began to buy racehorses, but he had only a year in which to enjoy his riches before Brushy Bob Wade ambushed him near the Bitter Lake and sent him where Billy is, and Hill Coe and all the rest.

Tully borrowed the nickname I had invented, but I bore him no grudge for that. What's puzzling to me still is how an earnest fellow such as Tully Roebuck could fool himself so easily and in the process confuse the story so completely.

It's true that Billy, as he was dying, asked Katie to let on that Tully had killed him – I suspect now that Billy didn't want it thought that he was killed by a woman, even one who loved him. But the puzzling thing is that Tully somehow convinced himself that he *did* kill Billy Bone. He claims in his booklet that he fired a second before Katie, which is nonsense – he was still inside the China Pond when Katie fired.

I was there and I know; and yet Tully is believed and I'm not. What makes it all the harder to fathom is that Tully was generally an honest man; still, he not only convinced himself of a wild lie, he convinced the public too.

Of course 'eyewitnesses' kept popping up for years – cowboys who happened to be passing Greasy Corners at just the right moment and saw it all happen from behind one of the huts, unobserved by any of the people who were actually there that morning, though all of us had perfectly adequate vision and might have been primed to notice lurking strangers.

Because of the conflicting accounts of all these 'eyewitnesses' – and also because newspapermen and historians, jealous of the fact that novelists get to make things up and they don't, encroach into fiction whenever they think they can get away with it – the brief, clear events of that morning in Greasy Corners have spawned at least a dozen theories already, and no doubt will spawn more. Every person in the town that morning has been championed by some 'authority' as being the one who shot Billy down.

Some hold that Bloody Feathers shot him from atop the buffalo hides, and merely jumped down with the knife to take his scalp. Some hold that Isinglass shot him from behind the tent, or Cecily Snow through a slit in the tent, or Long Dog Hawkins from behind the hut. One man claims La Tulipe poisoned him; and the radical fellow from Roswell thinks *I* shot him because I was jealous of his advantage with Cecily. The fact that I had fifty opportunities to shoot him before we arrived in Greasy Corners has not occurred to the man.

But most of the 'eyewitnesses' seem to favour Tully's account – you'd have to say it's the accepted account now – and maybe for the same reason that Billy himself favoured making Tully his official killer: no one wants to admit that a Mexican girl killed the greatest outlaw of the era. The *Liebestod* business is hardly favoured in our Old West.

They'd rather have it a man – it's that simple – though Katie, wild in her heartbreak, went on to a distinguished career in massacre, joining Villa and then Zapata, shooting down *federales* whenever they got in her way, and finally plunging all the way south to Nicaragua to foment revolution and blow up Yankee banana boats.

Of course, the books give her that: they allow her any number of *federales* and banana boats; they just don't want to give her the white star of the West, Billy the Kid.

No more was heard of La Tulipe, and little more of Bloody Feathers, the great Jicarilla; he never became one of the parade Indians so popular in Washington a little later, though he was mentioned as being at his father's funeral, which occurred more than a dozen years after Billy's death.

Will Isinglass and Cecily Snow went back to Winds' Hill to resume their strenuous but I suppose not entirely unsweetened contest of wills. Cecily finished the drawings for her great book, but not before Isinglass got her with child a third time. This time, not to be thwarted, he found and took away the useful herbs recommended by the old Comanche woman; more than that, he nailed Cecily into her spacious third-floor rooms – for several months her food was sent up to her on a little elevator that Lord Snow had devised some twenty years before.

In the end, though, Cecily beat even Old Whiskey. She had had the forethought to hide the rope that Lord Snow had used in his great days as an alpinist. Just before the child was due she slid down the rope during a blizzard and escaped on her thoroughbred, making her way over a route cowboys call the Dim Trail into the Blue Mounds of Kansas. Of course, an expedition was raised at once; half the cowboys on the plains were sent after her, but only her sidesaddle was ever found. Most people now believe she died in the blizzard, but Tully – it was the last time I spoke to him, just before his own death – did claim that he had talked with a Whiskey Glass cowboy, a member of the posse, who claimed to have come across a coyote dragging a human afterbirth through the snow.

A few of the more radical fellows argue that Cecily Snow survived the blizzard and made it back to England – terribly disfigured and heavily veiled, some claim, though that sounds like Monk Lewis to me – and lived to direct the long legal battle mounted by Lord Snow's nephews, which eventually destroyed the Whiskey Glass ranch.

As to Cecily, I can't say – I've not bothered to tour the Cavendish or the Montstuart demesnes in search of her – but it's certain that Will Isinglass, the scourge of Kiowas and Comanches, suffered a long dismemberment at the torture stake of the law – until, in the end, the three million acres he once ruled had shrunk to fifty thousand. In his heyday fifty thousand acres would not have pastured his *remuda*.

I read of his death in a rooming house in Trenton, New Jersey, where I was conducting a pallid romance with a quarrelsome and affected parlourmaid not half so appealing as Kate Molloy.

It seemed Will Isinglass, nearly one hundred at the time, had bought a motor car – the first to be shipped to the Eastern New Mexican plains – where he was living out his days with a scattering of cattle and a few pet buffalo he had acquired from Quanah Parker. The old man knew how to start the vehicle, but was vague about how to stop it; the car – they're the new buffalo, I guess; someday they'll cover the prairies in vast herds – ran away with him and sailed off into one of the canyons of the Canadian, crushing the great plainsman underneath it when it hit. They say he was emptying his pistol into the motor, in a vain effort to kill the thing, when the car went off the cutbank.

The ex-parlourmaid only grew more quarrelsome as I sat in silence, holding the newspaper, with tears in my eyes – the story only ran six lines – and thinking about that great, violent old man.

* * *

I went home, of course – rode Rosy to Denver and caught the train. Philadelphia was no different, nor was family life. Dora discovered me back in my study one morning, took a quick look, said, "You ought to trim that ugly beard," and went on with her life. The girls squealed "Papa!" a few times, and went on with theirs. Cook was the only person who asked where I had been out West, she assumed I meant Cincinnati and talked for an hour about a sister of hers who had emigrated to Ohio. "Thank the Lord, she hasn't been scalped yet," Cook said, stirring her pudding.

Well, home life must have its little vexations everywhere. The worst I had to put up with was the insufferable Waddy Peacock, Dora's beau, who had been required to buy a mansion a block away so he would always be on hand when Dora needed an escort, which was often – she had not lost her taste for balls and socialising.

After some thought, I declined to trim my beard. Dora took this refusal as an act of raw defiance and stopped speaking to me. She adopted Cook's view of my travels and let it out that I had contracted brain fever in Cincinnati and could no longer summon the coherence to fulfill my duties as a husband – at least that's what was reported by cronies at my club.

I soon gave up the club and the cronies, family life, parlourmaids and all the rest, to devote myself to art. It seemed to me I had real experience to draw on at last, and I set about to turn the rough scribblings I had done on the llano into books which I felt sure would far eclipse the popularity of Sandycraw, Orson Oxx or even *The Butler's Sorrow*. How could material so colourful and so rich possibly miss? True, *Billy the Kid* had failed, but I dismissed that as a fluke.

So I all but nailed myself into my study and raced through a dozen books, confident that at last I had graduated from mere tales into literary works to be proud of. I wrote *Skunkwater Flats; or, The Desperate Battle*. I polished up *Mutes of the Mesa*, and *Sister of the Sangre* as well. I rewrote the ending of *Black Beans* to give it more human depth.

Then I applied myself to all of those vivid characters I had met on the plains. I wrote *The Missed Bottle; or, Hill*

*Coe's Disgrace.* I wrote *Emperor of the Llano* about Will Isinglass; *The Ophelia of the Prairies* about Cecily, even generously excusing her behaviour on grounds of madness.

*The Girl Who Robbed the Governor; or, Jornado del Muerto* was the first of my books about Katie; later I penned *The Flame of the Cantinas; or, The Pecos Beauty.* Mesty-Woolah lived again in *The Negro of the Nile; or, Son of the Mahd*; and I wept my way through *Joe Lovelady; or, The Cowboy's Lament.* To this day I only have to remember that kind, lonely man to feel decidedly weepy.

The brute fact is, all the books failed. I had once stood at the head of the Beadle and Adams list; I wrote *The Butler's Sorrow*, the most popular dime novel of all time; but publishers are not long on sentiment, and after eight or nine failures it became clear they had ceased to look with enthusiasm on the parcels I mailed them so regularly.

Finally they sent one back – it was *The Trapper's Mistress; or, The Yellow Witch* – with a chilly note from some young editor I had never heard of. 'Dear Mr Sippy' – it read – 'This Wild West stuff won't do. Our readers won't tolerate cowboys now; what we want are detectives, Pinkertons especially. If you care to send us a few Pinkerton yarns we'll give them prompt consideration. We all hope to see you return to the form you had when you wrote the great Sandycraw stories.'

I don't think of myself as having a particularly frail spirit, but the fact is I never recovered from that letter: the sting was too sharp. No one wanted my new knowledge, my human depth – they only wanted my old, silly heroes – or, failing that, Pinkertons.

I never wrote again. As abruptly as it started, it stopped.

As it happened, Dora was looking particularly well just then: she seemed alight again after some rather shaded years – and a woman can flash as brilliantly as any firefly.

I decided – after all, I *was* married to her – to try my human depth on Dora, so I put out a hand, only to have it slapped away quite briskly; no more than the publishers did Dora want the new, the finer, me.

"If that's your attitude I wouldn't care if you moved back to Cincinnati," she said.

I did her one better, catching the train the very next day for New Mexico. Unwanted as a writer, or as a husband, there seemed little reason for me to make do with the small, smudged Pennsylvania skies and second-rate parlourmaids, all of them a far cry from the glimmering ideal of the lost Kate Molloy.

In Las Cruces I built a fine house and did a good deal of reading. I acquired a mule with a better disposition than Rosy's. Often I would ride to the top of the pass and look down on the ocean of plain, shimmering to the east. Now and again I would travel home, to marry a daughter and to marvel, only a little wistfully, at the lovely late light which Dora never again lost.

Though I never wrote another dimer or half-dimer – I never got over the fact that living had had such a disastrous effect on my powers of creation – the cheques continued to flow in, from Sandycraw, from Orson Oxx and from *The Butler's Sorrow*.

It seems, now I think about it, that I had embarked without knowing it on a kind of endless goodbye, starting that morning when J. M. Chittim dropped dead on the sidewalk. Goodbye to Chittim, and Cook, to Dora and my girls, to the winsome Kate Molloy – how I wish I'd kissed her.

From that time it had been goodbye to everyone: to the buffalo hunters and the buffalo; to Hill Coe and Happy Jack and all the sweethearts of Greasy Corners; to La Tulipe and Des Montaignes; to Viv Maldonado and Barbecue Campbell; to Sister Blandina; to Esteván and the mutes of the Mesa; to *los Guajolotes* and their flying leader, Katerina Garza; to Bertram and Mahmood and Mesty-Woolah; to Bloody Feathers and Isinglass and my lovely

Cecily Snow, whose tongue was as exacting as her draftsmanship; to Joe Lovelady and our rough friend, Billy Bone.

Now I guess it's even goodbye to words, for I can't see to read them any more, and don't care to write them. Of course I was never one of the great heroes of the language, such as Mr Dickens or the poet Longfellow or W.D. Howells – *there's* a man who understood Yankees if anyone ever did – but, in my way, from the moment I picked up *Hurricane Nell, Queen of Saddle and Lasso*, I loved words and did my best by them.

I don't know what's to become of the old language now, thanks to a curious thing I myself had a small hand in popularising. Once I was in Trenton – it was probably the time I heard of Isinglass's death – and happened to be drinking in a tavern with an acquaintance named Eddie Porter. I got to telling Eddie about my comical failures as a train robber, which caused him nearly to split his sides laughing. The more I elaborated on how hard it actually was to get a train to stop so one could rob it, the harder he laughed. And I suppose it *was* ludicrous, the thought of me robbing something; but then, cowboys and Indians used to chase those trains just for the sport, and that's all I was doing, really. I don't know what I would have done if one had stopped: bought a ticket home, most likely.

Eddie Porter worked as a camera mechanic for old man Edison. Next thing I knew he'd rented a train and a few horses and cowboy costumes – this was up in East Rutherford, New Jersey – and persuaded the company to do a moving picture of my adventures. They called it *The Great Train Robbery*. The thing caught on and probably earned more money than *The Butler's Sorrow*.

Eddie invited me to see it, and of course I did. The action moved so fast it made my eyes water a little, trying to watch, but I could tell it was my yarn that gave him the idea. Of course, his bandits got the train stopped, which is more than

I ever did – the crowd whooped when they got caught as if it was all real.

I figured right then it was goodbye to the dime novel: for who wouldn't rather sit in a vaudeville house, munch a sandwich and watch the whole story flow by like a pure dream, with perhaps a snatch of burlesque afterward, than squint at print in a book?

Not long after that, I happened to be in Denver, and who should I run into but the old Whiskey Glass cowboy Dewey Sharp – one of the ones who had had the forethought to leave Greasy Corners just a few hours before Billy Bone got killed.

But Dewey was as foolish as Tully Roebuck; he argued up and down that he *hadn't* left Greasy Corners at all; he had ducked out on Waco Charlie and the rest, got drunk in a wagon and woke up just in time to see the shooting. I didn't argue too strenuously; by then half the old-timers in the West had convinced themselves they had been in Greasy Corners the day Billy Bone got killed.

The point about Dewey is that he was just finally getting around to his long-awaited trip to California. He had bumped into a motion-picture man – they were as common then as buffalo hunters had once been – and filled him full of Greasy Corners stories, all of them featuring that young Galahad, Billy the Kid. The man got all fired up and wanted Dewey to come right away to Hollywood, California, so they could make a picture about it.

"Come with me, Sippy – you know more about it all than I do," Dewey said. It was an unusually generous admission, I thought.

Having little else to occupy me, I did go with Dewey and saw the first palm trees I had seen since Dora and I did the Nile. The motion-picture man was a fan of my Sandycraw tales and promptly hired me to do the scenario for Dewey's stories. All Dewey got to do was wrangle the horses – it annoyed him bitterly. We called the picture *Sweethearts of*

*Greasy Corners*, and it turned out to be the biggest hit of 1908.

I had better specs by then and could see fine. I don't know where they came up with the little actor who played Billy, but for my money he was not only good, he was too good. I cried all twenty-five times I saw the picture: it reminded me of all my hard goodbyes, and of my murdering friend, the wandering boy himself, Billy Bone, white star of the West, whose dust is now one with the billions and billions of particles that compose that ancient plain.